THE DO-OVER

PHOEBE MACLEOD

First published in Great Britain in 2024 by Boldwood Books Ltd.

Cover Design by Head Design Ltd.

Cover Images: Shutterstock

A CIP catalogue record for this book is available from the British Library.

Paperback ISBN 978-1-83533-350-1

Large Print ISBN 978-1-83533-351-8

Hardback ISBN 978-1-83533-349-5

Ebook ISBN 978-1-83533-352-5

Kindle ISBN 978-1-83533-353-2

Audio CD ISBN 978-1-83533-344-0

MP3 CD ISBN 978-1-83533-345-7

Digital audio download ISBN 978-1-83533-347-1

This book is printed on certified sustainable paper. Boldwood Books is dedicated to putting sustainability at the heart of our business. For more information please visit https://www.boldwoodbooks.com/about-us/sustainability/

Boldwood Books Ltd, 23 Bowerdean Street, London, SW6 3TN

www.boldwoodbooks.com

To Laura.

PROLOGUE

Do you ever stop to ponder what pivotal events in your life shaped you? I don't. For me, everything changed on the day Dad left. Although it's much less regular than it used to be when I was younger, it still haunts my dreams occasionally, playing out the same way every time. It opens on one of those crisp autumn days, where the sky is bright but the wind is cold. I'm eight years old, and I'm walking home from school. Mum is holding my right hand, and my sister Saffy is on the other side of Mum. She's three years older than me and resists holding hands with Mum because it's 'babyish'.

'Before we get home, there's something I need to tell you, girls,' Mum says in a quiet voice. 'It's about your father.'

I glance at Saffy, meeting her eye briefly. News about Dad is never good.

'What's he done now? Is it the money thing again?' Saffy asks with the world-weary tone of a pre-teen desperately trying to act older than her years.

'I'm afraid so,' Mum says gently.

Saffy rolls her eyes. 'What did they take?' None of us are

strangers to visits from the bailiffs. It's been a constant pattern of our childhood so far. Every time it happens, Dad promises to turn over a new leaf, showers us with tatty gifts and things improve for a while. Then, just when we think that he might finally mean it, the bailiffs turn up again to repossess the TV and anything else they can squeeze a bit of value out of, and we go back to square one.

'It's a bit more serious this time, love,' Mum tells her, sighing deeply. 'It seems that your father hasn't been paying the rent on our house, which he didn't tell me about until this morning when the man from the council turned up. I'm not sure how to tell you this, girls, so I'm just going to say it. They've thrown us out of our home.'

'But where are we going to live?' Saffy asks in horror.

'I've spoken to Nan, and she's agreed to let us stay with her until we get back on our feet. She's waiting for us at home. The important thing you need to hear is that none of this is your fault, and it's not your job to try to fix it.'

'Dad will fix it, though, won't he?' I ask.

'Not this time, Thea love. Your dad's gone.'

'Gone? Gone where?'

Another deep sigh. 'I don't know, and I don't particularly care. There comes a time when you just can't wait any longer for someone to make the right choice. He's had chance after chance and I can't do this any more. It's not fair on me and it's not fair on the pair of you. From now on, he's no longer part of our life. It's us three against the world.'

I can still remember the burning sense of humiliation as we loaded the bin bags containing our meagre possessions into the back of Nan's car, under the watchful gaze of our neighbours. People we'd counted as friends suddenly wanted nothing to do with us, as if we had some infectious disease they were frightened of catching. The only place I felt safe was school, where the teachers watched carefully to make sure we weren't bullied. We never saw Dad again; Mum got a letter a few years later to say that he'd died and did she want to organise a funeral for him. By then, our lives were already radically different. As soon as Saffy and I were safely ensconced in secondary school, Mum had swapped her part-time job at the shop for a full-time role as receptionist for a firm of accountants. There, she met Phil, who couldn't be more different from Dad if he tried. However, after wrestling with it for a while, she decided that closure would be good for all of us, so she paid the fees and we went to Dad's funeral. It was a perfunctory service and we were the only mourners. We didn't cry; I don't think any of us really knew what to feel. Afterwards, Phil bought us all ice creams to break the sombre mood, and I'm not sure we thought about Dad at all after that. We certainly didn't talk about him.

Given that our story has, generally speaking, a happy ending, I sometimes wonder why the dream still haunts me. I know the answer, of course: it's to remind me of the seed that was planted that day as I looked out of the back of Nan's car at our securely padlocked house. I'd always been a happy, slightly lackadaisical child, content to potter along in the middle ranks. That day changed my outlook completely; I studied harder than anyone else, achieving top grades across the board in every set of exams. Nobody was ever going to take my home from me again. I was never going to feel that humiliation again. I was going to defy the odds and be the best I possibly could be. At everything.

1

I sense Margaret's approach long before she comes into view. Every fibre of my being has been on high alert since this morning, and I subconsciously sit up a little straighter in my chair and focus my eyes firmly on the agreement I've been trying to work on. I need to come across as a totally dedicated professional, today of all days.

'They're ready for you now, Thea. Would you like to come with me?' she says softly. 'Bring your things.'

As we make our way through the open-plan area where the junior associates sit, I'm aware of their eyes following me. My heart is thudding so hard it feels like it might smash a rib and break free at any moment, and my hands are trembling with nerves. I've put everything I've got into this and, if I haven't been successful, I'll have to wait another whole year before the opportunity comes again, so the stakes couldn't be higher. Although nothing will be announced officially until the end of the day, when all the candidates have been seen, the office grapevine has been humming and, so far, only one of my fellow applicants seems to have made partner. Alana, who was widely considered to be one of the favourites, was spotted crossing the lobby in floods of tears earlier so it would seem she didn't make it.

Morton Lansdowne is one of the largest firms on the corporate law landscape; as well as the London office where I'm based, we have offices in pretty much every major capital city in the world. For most wannabe corporate lawyers, just getting a traineeship here is considered the dream ticket. Becoming a partner, albeit a junior one, is akin to winning the lottery. The difference between partnership and winning the lottery, however, is that only one of them has any element of luck. Put it this way: you don't join a company like Morton Lansdowne if you value personal time. There is a work/life balance inasmuch as you live to work. The harder you work, the better you will do. If you expect idiotic things like set office hours, uninterrupted weekends and holidays, then this life is not for you.

One of the highlights of the year, apart from partnership day, is trainee induction day. Like most big law firms, we take a set number of law graduates onto our trainee programme each year. They spend two years with us, moving between departments to get maximum exposure to the different types of work we do for our corporate clients. At the end of the traineeship, only a handful are selected to stay with us as junior associates. The rest, to use the office term, are 'released back into the wild'. As part of the induction day, the existing associates are invited to meet the new trainees over lunch in the office, and there's always a good deal of speculation afterwards about which of them are going to make it and which don't stand a chance.

The lift is taking forever to come. Next to me, Margaret is gently drumming her fingers against her thigh. As personal assistant to Martin Osborne, the managing partner of the London office, she will already know my fate, and it's hard not to try to read meaning into every little micro-gesture. Where I'm so tense I suspect even my eyelids are stretched tight, she appears to be totally relaxed. Is that good news, or is it because she's not taking me seriously?

'Stop it, Thea,' she murmurs discreetly.

'Stop what?' I whisper back.

'Trying to read me. This isn't my first rodeo. Do I know whether you've been successful or not? Yes. Am I going to somehow give it away between here and the boardroom? No.'

'I'm a lawyer, Margaret. I wouldn't be very good at my job if I wasn't trying to read you.'

'And I'm Martin's PA because of my absolute discretion, among other things. So I can assure you it's a fruitless exercise. Ah, here we are at last.'

The lift doors open and we step inside. I'm surprised to see my friend Alasdair among the other occupants. He and I joined in the same intake and we hit it off pretty much straight away. He works in Property now, rather than Mergers and Acquisitions where I am, so we rarely see each other. Conversation in the lift is severely frowned upon, so I meet his eyes, raise my eyebrows quizzically and mouth 'Singapore?' at him. In return he subtly draws his finger across his neck to indicate that something has obviously gone south with the transaction he was working on, hence his return to London. When the lift stops at the sixth floor, Alasdair steps out, mouthing 'Good luck' to me as he goes. On the seventh, the remaining occupants disembark, leaving just Margaret and me to climb to the top floor.

By the time the lift pings and the doors swing open on the eighth floor, where the senior partners have their offices and the boardroom is located, my legs are trembling and I've had to clamp my jaws together to stop my teeth chattering. Margaret is obviously aware of my increasing anxiety because she touches me lightly on the arm.

'Try not to have a coronary,' she says with a smile. 'I am first-aid trained, but I'd prefer not to have to demonstrate my skills today, if it's all the same to you.'

Although her tone is light, office folklore has many stories of associates having meltdowns of various kinds on this journey. One famously threw up in the lift two years ago. Incredibly, he's still with the firm but has never submitted another partnership application and had to move to another office to escape the fall-out. The most humiliating, though, the one we all dread, dates from the year after I joined. I would dismiss it as apocryphal if I hadn't been a trainee in the senior associate's team at the time. He was the absolute model of what we believed a partner should be. Fiercely intelligent and a real powerhouse, nothing escaped his notice. Rumour had it that he had a flat in the Barbican somewhere, but we used to joke that he probably didn't know exactly where it was and had definitely never been inside it because he was always in the office.

On the day of the partnership announcements, Margaret came to get him like she always has. Although we tried to focus on our work, very little got done while we waited to see whether he'd made it. An hour went by and none of us suspected anything unusual. For some people, the meetings are very quick because the senior partners are all in agreement. For others, the meetings can drag on, taking the form of a final viva interview, a last chance for the candidate to prove they meet the criteria and convince the sceptics. After two hours, we were getting fidgety, and nearly three hours had gone by before word trickled down that our man had left the firm and wouldn't be returning. By the end of the day, another senior associate had taken his place at the head of our team, but it wasn't until weeks later that we learned what had happened. As we had suspected at the time, the meeting had taken the form of an intense interview and the pressure, on top of the exhaustion from the hours he'd been putting in, had proved too much for our candidate. He'd fainted in the boardroom and, if that wasn't humiliating enough, he'd apparently wet himself while out cold.

The memory of that disaster serves as a prompt and, as we're making our way along the corridor, I turn to Margaret.

'Have I got time for a quick trip to the loo?' I ask.

'Yes,' she replies. 'But hurry. The senior partners don't like to be kept waiting.'

The toilets are in the same place on every floor so, although this is probably only the second time I've been up here since joining Morton Lansdowne, I know where to find them. Having squeezed out every last drop, I wash my hands and stare at myself in the mirror.

'Come on, Thea,' I tell my reflection fiercely. 'Knock them dead.'

'All set?' Margaret asks when I rejoin her in the corridor.

'Yes. Thank you.'

The offices of law firms in London tend to fall into two distinct camps. The first are those who have probably been around since the dawn of time; their offices are dark, with lots of polished wood and brass fittings. Although it's a well-established firm with a long history, Morton Lansdowne falls firmly into the second category; our offices are light and modern. The boardroom that we're now approaching could be straight off the set of a TV series like *Suits*. The glass wall has a carefully applied translucent pattern with the letters ML etched into it in a swirly font at regular intervals. It gives the appearance of transparency without you actually being able to see anything meaningful from the outside. Unlike the lower floors, which have light-coloured doors and desks with dark grey carpets, the carpet on this floor is light grey deep pile, with dark mahogany-coloured doors that reach all the way to the ceiling, no doubt to create an air of extra gravitas. My heart has given up trying to break out of my ribcage as Margaret knocks on the boardroom door; it's now taken up residence in my throat and, for a moment, I worry that I might join the folklore hall of fame by throwing up in front of the senior partners.

'Come in,' a deep voice that I recognise as belonging to Martin Osborne calls.

'I have Thea Rogers for you,' Margaret tells him before standing aside to let me pass. As soon as I'm over the threshold, the door closes behind me with a soft click.

'Thea. Thank you so much for sparing the time to see us,' Martin says warmly, as if I'm somehow doing him a favour. 'Please, take a seat.'

The sound of my name on the lips of the most powerful man in the London office sparks a familiar momentary feeling of resentment. The truth is that I fell out of love with my name when I reinvented myself; to me it sounds soft and a little doughy, the kind of name that might suit a librarian but not a top-flight lawyer. I should have been called something more warrior-like, such as Xena. When I was at secondary school, one of my classmates was called Xanthe and, although I ribbed her about it along with the rest of the class, I always secretly envied her. Having X as an initial makes you stand out. Thea Rogers is the precise opposite; it's an instantly forgettable name without a single hard consonant to give it some bite.

This brief distraction is thankfully enough to allow me to

make it from the doorway to the seat Martin has indicated without any disasters. Although there are a couple of other empty seats, most of the senior partners are here, I notice as I look around the room.

'I think you know everyone,' Martin continues, 'and we obviously all know you so, unless you feel it's necessary, I suggest we skip introductions and get straight down to it. Jeremy and Helen couldn't be with us in person today, but they have dialled in remotely.' He indicates a screen on the wall behind him with two faces staring out of it.

'Hello, Thea,' they say together.

'Right. Before we start, have you got any questions you'd like to ask us about the process?' Martin says to me.

'No, thank you.'

'Great.' He taps a button on the laptop open in front of him and a slide appears on the screen with my face and name underneath it. 'As you'll be aware, Thea, a partnership at Morton Lansdowne is only offered to truly exceptional candidates. In our business, reputation is everything and we cannot allow that reputation to be diluted by mediocrity. I'm sure I don't need to bore you with the precise figures, but the percentage of people who join us as trainees, like you did, and subsequently go on to make partner is witheringly small. Regardless of the outcome, you should therefore be immensely proud of the fact that you've made it as far as this meeting. Whatever happens, I want you to hold on to that.'

I'm listening intently to every word, trying to gauge which way this is going to go, and so far it's not sounding positive. My mood is plummeting fast.

'Let us look at the specifics of your application,' he continues, tapping the laptop again to bring up a graph. 'From this, we can see that you have consistently exceeded your billing targets every quarter since being promoted to senior associate. That's no mean feat; we deliberately set aggressive targets here, not just for the good of the company, but also as a means of identifying those with the kind of stamina we're looking for in our next leaders.' He taps again and a pie chart comes up. 'You are also held in high regard by your colleagues and your team members. It doesn't influence our decision, but when we asked them whether they felt you would be the right kind of leader for a firm like ours, their response was universally positive. More importantly, and I don't have a slide for this as it's not something we can quantify on a graph, the clients value you. You're seen as someone who is trustworthy, hard-working and with an exceptional eye for detail.'

OK, this is sounding more positive. I allow the flame of hope to re-ignite.

'However,' Martin continues, 'while these are all laudable qualities in a senior associate, they don't automatically translate into a good candidate for partnership. A partner has to take all of these superlative qualities and manage to add an extra layer to them. Do you understand?'

Shit. I allowed myself to hope too soon.

'Yes,' I say.

'As a partner, you are an ambassador for the firm. Our partners are the public face of who we are, and clients will hire or reject us based in no small part on whether they like the partners or not. We're therefore looking for someone who can earn the respect of a new client and bring them on board, making Morton Lansdowne their trusted guide for all aspects of commercial law. As senior partners, we have to decide whether we believe you have those qualities. There is also your age to take into account. At thirty-two, you are at the very bottom of the age range that we would even begin to consider for partnership. I'm not betraying any confidences if I tell you that some of the senior partners felt that it might be better for you to spend another couple of years as a senior associate and reapply after that.'

That's it then. They think I'm too young. It's all been for nothing, and I focus all my energy on maintaining a neutral expression. The howls of frustration will have to wait until I'm alone so nobody witnesses my moment of weakness.

'Deciding whether or not to offer a partnership is a responsibility we take very seriously,' Martin is saying, but I'm barely listening now that I know my fate, 'and I can assure you that we haven't taken your application lightly. After considerable thought and discussion, we have agreed that you do exhibit all the qualities we're looking for, and we'd therefore like to offer you the position of junior partner at Morton Lansdowne. Congratulations, Thea.'

For a moment, I stare at him, dumbfounded. Did I hear that correctly? The ripple of applause from the other senior partners would indicate that I did.

'Now,' Martin says when the applause has died down. 'You know the rules, I'm sure. Regardless of the outcome, we expect you to leave the office immediately. We will make a formal announcement at the end of the day, after which you are of course welcome to share the news with friends and family. You will also have the weekend to conduct any celebrations you deem appropriate, and then we expect you in the office ready to go at seven o'clock on Monday morning. Do you have any questions before I ask Margaret to escort you out?'

'No. Thank you. I won't let you down, I promise.'

Martin smiles. 'See that you don't.'

As I descend towards the ground floor with Margaret by my

side, I allow myself the tiniest of fist pumps. After all those years, and particularly the last four months without a single day off, I've actually bloody done it. Thea Rogers, youngest ever female partner at Morton Lansdowne at the tender age of thirty-two.

2

As I make my way back to my terraced house in Walthamstow, I look around at the other people on the Tube, half expecting them to pick up that something extraordinary has just happened to me, that I'm different somehow. There's a girl sitting opposite me with big headphones clamped over her ears and her head buried in a dog-eared book that she probably picked up in a charity shop, and I find myself willing her to raise her eyes and recognise me, as if I'm some sort of celebrity because I'm now a partner at a major law firm.

It's irrational nonsense, I know it is. Within the walls of Morton Lansdowne, I will definitely be a celebrity for the next week or so, but even there it won't be long until I'm just 'one of the partners'. Out here, there's no reason for anyone to give a damn, but it's hard not to feel a tinge of disappointment nonetheless. I'm burning to share the news with someone, but grabbing a random stranger and blurting it out is unlikely to end well, particularly in a city like London. Also, there's the moratorium to consider. I check my watch: four and a half hours before I can tell anyone.

The house is silent as I close the front door behind me and pick up the post from the floor, but I can almost hear its question in my head. 'It's lunchtime on a Friday. What are you doing here?' I'm inordinately proud of my house, even though I barely spend any time in it. When I first started as a trainee at Morton Lansdowne, I deliberately looked for the cheapest lodgings I reckoned I could put up with. I ended up in a shared flat in Peckham, with a box room so small even a standard single bed wouldn't fit in it. The enterprising landlord, evidently keen to squeeze every drop of income from his investment, had fashioned a bed using a sheet of plywood supported by batons fixed to the wall. The mattress was a foam affair that he'd shortened by simply chopping the end off. It was boiling in summer, freezing in winter and the whole place smelled permanently of weed, thanks to the thriving business of a guy on the floor above. I didn't care about any of that, though. It was cheap, and that enabled me to start saving.

When I made junior associate, the temptation to move out to somewhere better was nearly irresistible, but I stuck to my plan and watched my savings grow almost exponentially. My very limited downtime was spent researching property prices in different parts of London, always following the mantra to look for the shittiest house on the nicest street, as that was where the best potential growth lay. By the time I had enough to put down an acceptable deposit and secure a mortgage, I knew exactly what I was looking for and where. I also knew that I wasn't going to get the best bang for my buck by playing safe and going through an estate agent. To my mother and stepfather's horror, I snapped up my three-bedroom terraced house in Walthamstow at auction, without even visiting it to look round first. It was a probate sale, described in the listing as being 'in need of modernisation', which turned out to be something of an understatement. Luckily for me, it was at least structurally sound, but that was where the good news ended.

For the first three years, I essentially lived in a building site, renovating room by room as I could afford to. The bathroom was first; the original was at the back of the house on the ground floor, with horribly stained turquoise sanitaryware that made my skin crawl. With the help of Brian, a local builder who defied the stereotypes by charging surprisingly reasonable prices and working his socks off even during my frequent absences, the bathroom was soon relocated into one of the first-floor bedrooms, with gorgeous contemporary fixtures and fittings and a shower nearly powerful enough to take your skin off. Once that was done, I found I could live quite happily with the rest of the house in various states of chaos. It was only an occasional place to sleep, after all, and Brian kept me abreast of the renovations by email when I wasn't around.

The finished house is almost unrecognisable from the run-down property I bought. The front door still opens onto a narrow hallway with the original Victorian tiles on the floor, and there is a door on the left that leads into a small front room that I've set up as a study; useful for weekend working when I don't need to be in the office. That's where the similarities end though; the real magic happens when you step through the door at the end of the hallway. The middle reception room, original kitchen and bathroom have been combined into a large open-plan living area that spans the entire rear of the house. There's a high-tech kitchen on one side and a floating staircase tucked into the corner on the other. Between them sit two comfortable squishy sofas for 'entertaining' (not that I ever do), separated by a low coffee table. We've pushed the back wall as far as we dared with a conservatory extension that houses the dining area. Bifold doors open onto what remains of the garden, where a small patio is surrounded by hanging baskets and abundant flowerbeds that I pay a gardening firm handsomely to maintain.

The post yields nothing of interest; a couple of bills that I can ignore because they're paid by direct debit, and the usual collection of takeaway menus and other junk. I dump my laptop bag in the study and consign the post to the bin before kicking off my shoes in the hallway and wandering through to the kitchen to make a cup of tea. This plan quickly falls apart when I realise that the box of teabags in the cupboard is empty and the milk in the fridge has solidified. I shove it in the bin without either daring to open it or read the sell-by date; a vague memory of using the last teabag comes to mind and, as I explore the mental picture, I'm horrified to realise that there was snow on the ground at the time. I glance to the left, at the wall that Brian suggested he paint with blackboard paint so I could use it as an 'expression wall' and, sure enough, the word 'teabags' is scrawled on there in my handwriting.

With a free weekend stretching ahead of me and currently no idea as to how I'm going to fill it, I decide a shopping trip is in order. I'll head to the Sainsbury's on the high street and stock up with a few essentials and one of those mini bottles of champagne so I can celebrate when the news breaks on the company website. I could even get a full-sized one; seeing as Alasdair is in the country, he might be free to come and help me celebrate. With a smile on my face, I lock the front door behind me and set off down the pavement. All being well, I should be able to kill a couple of hours on this trip, which would take me almost to the magic moment at five o'clock when I can start ringing people to tell them my news.

* * *

As I dump my bag of groceries on the worktop in the kitchen, my eyes lift automatically to the oversized clock on the wall. Half past two. I doubt very much that Walthamstow high street boasts a time portal, which means the battery must be flat. A glance at my smart watch, however, isn't much more encouraging. Even though I tried to walk slowly and browse in the supermarket, my excursion has taken me less than an hour, and I still have an hour and a half to kill. A brief rummage through the drawers after I've put the shopping away reveals a packet of batteries that I probably bought when I moved in, so I put a new one in the clock and reset it while the kettle heats up for my second attempt at a cup of tea.

What on earth do people do on Friday afternoons, I wonder as I sit at my desk sipping my tea and staring out of the window. The parking space outside my house is empty but, while I'm watching, a black SUV swings into it, bumping up onto the kerb as it does. The driver makes no attempt to straighten it, leaping out almost before it's even stopped. It's a woman, probably around the same age as me, dressed in tight leggings and a crop top.

'Hurry up, Rollo,' I can hear her urging as she hauls open the rear door. 'You've barely got time to change before your piano lesson.'

I watch as a boy climbs slowly out of the back seat. He can't be more than seven years old, and his school uniform consists of black leather shoes with grey socks, grey flannel shorts and a green blazer with a logo on it over white shirt and green tie. You don't have to be a great detective to work out that he doesn't attend the local primary dressed like that. The woman practically drags him along the pavement and, for amusement because I'm ludicrously bored, I set a timer.

They reappear seven minutes and forty-three seconds later.

The woman is still dressed in the same clothes and looking even more harassed, but the boy appears oblivious as he saunters along behind her. He's now wearing a white T-shirt, dark blue shorts and white trainers and carrying a music book. She bundles him into the SUV and, with dexterity evidently born of much practice, swings back out of the space and hurtles up the road.

'If that's what people do on Friday afternoons, they can keep it,' I mutter to myself with a smile.

* * *

Five o'clock at last. My pulse quickens again as I log onto the Morton Lansdowne website and navigate to the relevant page. When I see my picture and bio among the other partners, I allow a bubble of pride to form in my gut. I study it for a while, letting my achievement sink in, before calling my mum and Phil. They've never really understood anything to do with my work, but surely even they will understand that this is a big thing.

'Thea! This is a nice surprise,' Phil answers. 'Is everything all right?'

'Everything's fine, Phil,' I reassure him. 'I'm just calling because I have some good news.'

'Oh. Hang on then. I'd better get your mother on the other handset. She'll only grill me otherwise and then get upset if I can't remember all the details.' There's a clunk as he puts the handset down, and then I hear him calling, 'Cath, *Cath!* Come quickly. It's Thea on the phone and she says she has news.'

'Hello, darling,' my mother's voice says after a short pause. 'Phil says you have news. Are you OK? You're not in any trouble, are you?'

Despite her best efforts, encouragement has never been one of my mother's strong points. If we were describing her style of parenting since Dad left, as far as I'm concerned anyway, the politest word would be 'detached'. To give her her dues, she did have a lot to cope with initially, and things only improved after she started dating Phil when I was thirteen. By that time, her somewhat patchy parenting style had become embedded. I suspect the fact that I was fiercely independent also played a part, as she's always been closer to Saffy than me.

'I'm not in trouble,' I explain once Phil has rejoined the conversation. 'As I said to Phil, this is good news. I've been made partner, can you believe it?'

There's a long pause. Too long.

'That's lovely, darling,' Mum says eventually. 'Congratulations. We're very proud.'

'You don't know what that is, do you.' I sigh.

'Not exactly,' she admits. 'But it's obviously important to you, so we're very pleased. Thinking of good news, did Phil tell you about Saffy's OFSTED report?'

I tune her out as she witters on happily about my sister and the pre-school she works at in the town where we grew up. I'm trying not to be annoyed by it; Mum finds it easier to understand what Saffy does, but there's no doubt that my bubble of pride has sprung a nasty leak. It wouldn't have killed her to be a little more enthusiastic, would it?

After ten minutes or so, she dries up and we end the call with our usual promises to speak soon. We probably won't; she never calls me and I only call them once a month or so. Hoping for a better result, I text Alasdair.

Guess you heard the news. I have champagne in the fridge if you fancy celebrating with me. Txx

The ticks go blue straight away and I can see he's typing.

Sounds lovely. Unfortunately I'm at the airport. Singapore deal is back on, surprise surprise. Congrats though – you totally deserve it. Maybe we can have a belated celebration when I'm back? Axx

What to do now? For a brief moment, I contemplate calling Mum and Phil back to tell them I'm coming home for the weekend. Maybe, after I've explained it properly, they'll be able to show a bit more excitement. Oh, who am I kidding? It'll just be a weekend of them droning on about how clever Saffy is while my expensive champagne goes warm and flat in their glasses. With a sigh, I fire up my laptop, log into the network and navigate to the agreement I was working on earlier. As soon as I double-click to open it, I get a message:

This document is locked for editing by Jessica Thorne.

Wow. They obviously haven't hung around reassigning my existing work. It's going to be a very long weekend.

3

Monday at last. The weekend felt like it was never going to end; I'll confess to having spent quite a bit of it in my study watching the comings and goings of Rollo and the woman with the SUV. I've been trying to work out whether she's his mother or a nanny. They don't share similar physical characteristics; she's blonde with a thin, slightly pinched face and he's dark haired with rounder features. He could get those from his father though, I suppose. By Saturday evening, I'd decided that she probably is the unfortunately named Rollo's mother, simply because of the way she speaks to him. If I were ever to have a child, which is highly unlikely, and a nanny spoke to it like she does, we'd be having a difficult conversation.

Being at home with nothing to do is obviously not good for me, because I did start to obsess a little bit about her, trying to imagine what her life is like. Poor Rollo, from what I've seen, is hot housed to within an inch of his life; she's been in and out with him all weekend and, looking at the accessories for each trip, none of them seem to have been for pleasure. He had a swimming lesson on Saturday morning followed by some kind of martial art. They then came home for lunch before he was bundled back into the SUV with a pile of books, I'm guessing for some sort of extra tutoring. Sunday didn't appear to be any more restful, as they were up and out early for football. Judging by the look on his face as he reluctantly clambered into the car in his strip, football is really not his thing. I think Sunday afternoon was some sort of social visit, as she finally swapped the gym gear for a summer dress, but Rollo didn't look any more enthusiastic about it than he had his other activities.

Watching Sarah (my made-up name for her) and Rollo has made me reconsider whether I should have taken the opportunity of a rare weekend off to visit my family after all. Although I think I am justified in being pissed off by Mum's lack of engagement on the phone, I've had time to reflect and I can see it's not all her fault. She sees Saffy several times a week and even helped with childcare when her son Louis was a baby, looking after him while Saffy was at work until he was old enough to join the pre-school. The last time I saw them, on the other hand, was Christmas, a snatched visit for a few hours nearly six months ago. I can still remember Saffy's puzzled face as Louis unwrapped the chemistry set I'd thought would be both fun and educational, but which I hadn't noticed was labelled as not suitable for children under ten. 'I'll put it to one side for now,' she'd said kindly as my cheeks burned with embarrassment. 'He'll love it when he's old enough to understand it.'

Given all of that, is it surprising that Mum and Phil find it easier to connect with Saffy than me? Maybe, my critical inner voice told me sternly as I watched Rollo departing for one of his many activities, they would take more of an interest in me if I had taken more time to engage with them and explain my life to them. I came very close to calling them again on Sunday afternoon, even picking up my phone a couple of times and bringing up their number, before realising it would probably be counter-productive. We're all creatures of habit to some extent, and breaking a pattern of monthly phone calls with two in the same weekend would probably make them worry that I was having some kind of secret breakdown. So I left it, and now the opportunity has passed.

I'm a creature of habit myself and, when I'm not travelling, my daily routine follows a set pattern. I wake with a jolt just before five, throw on the clothes that I've laid out the night before and leave the house just over ten minutes later, dragging my precisely packed cabin bag if I'm going away. It's not much fun in the winter when it's cold and dark, but I find the early mornings magical in the summer. The streets are quiet and the Tube on my half-hour ride to Farringdon, the closest station to the office, is empty apart from a few other early starters like me. On arriving at the office just before six, I greet the night security guard and make my way down to the gym in the basement for my workout. After showering and drying my hair, I'm usually at my desk by seven. If we're in the early stages of a transaction, I'm generally away by eight in the evening, but it can be ten, midnight, or even not at all if a deal is close to the wire. Like I said, you don't go into this line of work if you value your personal time. I love it, though; the constant problem solving, finding innovative ways around obstacles to deliver results for our clients. The adrenaline surge when you're under intense pressure and spot a way to break through a seemingly impossible barrier is better than the high you could get from any drug, I reckon.

In among the usual raft of emails that I dealt with over the weekend, including information about a three-week trip to New York for my new assignment, was one from our HR department, congratulating me on my new role and summoning me to a meeting with someone called Janice at seven o'clock in one of the meeting rooms on the seventh floor before I leave for the airport. When I get there, my hair still a little damp from the shower, I find her waiting for me. She's one of those people who looks vaguely familiar; I've probably seen her around but never had occasion to talk to her before. I'd estimate that she's in her early forties, and her generous figure is flattered by her beautifully cut trouser suit.

'Sorry I'm late,' I tell her, checking my watch.

'Oh, you're not. Don't worry,' she assures me in a no-nonsense tone. 'I had an issue to sort out for one of the other junior partners, so I came in a bit early. I'm Janice, by the way, your PA.'

'Oh.' I'm not sure what else to say. I know the partners have personal assistants, but it's not a part of the role I'd really connected to and, if I'm honest, I'm not sure what they do.

'It's funny,' she remarks. 'Every new partner reacts the same way. You're all so focused on the application process and whether you'll get through that you never consider what happens afterwards. I liken it to getting married.'

I'm intrigued. 'What do you mean?'

'Partnership applicants are like brides to be. All your energy is poured into creating the perfect wedding day, ensuring absolutely nothing can go wrong, because the smallest mishap will ruin everything. That's you during the application process, if you haven't guessed. Then the wedding-slash-partnership interview happens, nothing goes wrong, and you glide through it on a wave of euphoria before going off on honeymoon. But what happens when you get back? You have to learn to be married, and nobody ever seems to think about that part. How was your weekend off, by the way?'

'Honestly? I've never been so bored.'

She laughs. 'I think they do that deliberately. Bore you to tears to make sure you're champing at the bit when you come back in. Anyway, the wedding's over and I'm your new wife. Pleased to meet you.' She holds out her hand for me to shake.

'Let me see if I can guess what you're thinking now,' she continues as we take our seats at the table and she opens the folder in front of her. 'You're wondering what it is I do and whether you need me. After all, you've never needed a PA before.'

I smile. 'Guilty as charged.'

'OK, let's start with the basics. This is a polygamous marriage. Illegal in the real world but that's how it is in here. What I mean by that is that I don't work exclusively for you. I have another four junior partners that I look after, so please don't fool yourself into thinking that I spend every waking hour looking for ways to make you happy. If this marriage is going to thrive, it requires give and take. It may sound rude, but I often liken junior partners to puppies. You need a firm hand and a bit of house training before we settle down into a rhythm. So please don't be offended if I have to say "no" to you a few times while we're getting to know each other. You're busy; I'm busy; if we don't have clear boundaries we'll quickly end up in a mess. Does that make sense?'

There's something about her direct approach that gels with me, and I'm starting to suspect that Janice and I will get on very well. 'Yes, perfect,' I tell her.

'Good. Let's move on to what I do and what I don't do. Rule number one: I don't do legal stuff. I know a bit about it because you can't work in a place like this without some of it rubbing off on you, but I'm not legally trained and it's not my role. You want documents finding or stuff copying, that's what the trainees and associates are for. My job is to make sure everything else runs smoothly, so you have 100 per cent mental capacity for your work. I'm on call pretty much twenty-four seven every day except for Christmas Day. If your cat gets stuck up a tree while you're in Kuala Lumpur, you call me and I sort it. Do you have a cat?'

'No.' I smile again. 'But what if I did have a cat and it got stuck up a tree on Christmas Day?'

I'm pleased to see her mouth turn up at the corners. 'Then you either rescue it yourself or it waits. Cats are resilient creatures. A day in a tree won't kill it, and it'll have the opportunity to learn a valuable life lesson. Do you live alone?'

'I do.'

'I'd like a key to your house, please.'

'Why?'

'You're in New York and you suddenly wonder whether you've left the oven on.'

I laugh. 'Unlikely. I'm not sure I've ever used the oven in my house, actually. On the rare occasions I'm there, I tend to order in.'

'Fine. Your central heating explodes. I organise the plumber and let them in.'

'That makes sense. I haven't got a spare with me, though.'

'Not a problem. Give me the one you have; I'll get it copied and have the original back to you before you leave for the airport. You're booked on the 10.45 BA flight out of Heathrow so I've ordered a car to collect you at 8.45. Plenty of time to get a key copied.'

'Eight forty-five seems pretty tight,' I observe as I detach my front door key from the keyring and hand it to her. 'I wouldn't want to get stuck in traffic and miss the flight.'

'You won't. In fact, I've allowed extra time as I don't know you yet. Your boarding pass is printed and I assume you don't have any hold baggage to check in, so you should be through fast-track security over an hour before the flight goes. Even if you did have hold baggage, I've factored in enough time for the business class check-in. You might even have time for a quick cup of coffee in the lounge if you're lucky. Now, I need you to fill these in.' She hands over a couple of sheets of paper which I scan quickly.

'Janice. Why do you need to know what bra size I am and where I buy my underwear?'

'Disaster recovery,' she says simply. 'You're mid-negotiation in Singapore and your hotel burns down. By the time you finish your day, I have you a new hotel room and I've replaced all your clothes.'

'Surely just knowing the right size is enough?' I query again as I start to fill it in.

'Nope. As I'm sure you know, a size ten in one store is not the same as a size ten in another. You are a size ten, I'm guessing?'

'Is there anything you don't know?'

'By the time you've filled that lot in, I would sincerely hope not. Do you buy your suits off the shelf or do you have a tailor?'

'Off the shelf.'

'I thought so. I'll get you an appointment with my tailor. You'll thank me.'

'That's a lovely thought, Janice, but I hardly think I'm going to have time—'

'She comes to the office. I'll book her in for you. Don't worry about the cost; she's surprisingly reasonable and your clothing allowance will pretty much cover it.'

Having completed the forms, which were forensic down to which type of tampon I preferred, I slide them back to her. She glances over them and pronounces herself satisfied.

'Final thing,' she says, pushing a card across the table to me.

'That's your keycard to access the underground car park. We don't have allocated bays, so just park wherever's free.'

'I won't need that,' I tell her, pushing it back. 'I don't have a car.'

'You have a driving licence, don't you?'

'Yes, but I've never felt the need for a car, living in London.'

'Rookie error.' She tuts. 'Always have a backup. The representatives of the petrochemical company who have flown in from Doha to meet with you are unlikely to be impressed if you're late because the trains are on strike.'

This is a step too far. 'Janice,' I begin. 'I don't have time or mental capacity to put into buying a car. Even if I had one, I have no idea how to go about getting a parking permit or any of the other things it would need, and I doubt your friends from the petrochemical company will be happy if I'm late because I was looking for insurance or whatever.'

'Of course not!' she exclaims as if I'm a particularly dim toddler. 'That's what I'm for. I assume you're happy for me to source something suitable? What colour do you like – black, dark blue or silver?'

'Are those the only choices?'

'You could have grey, but the senior partners frown on what they call "party" colours.'

'Umm. Dark blue, I guess.'

'Leave it with me. Now, is there anything else before I go?'

'No. Thank you, Janice,' I tell her meekly. I've decided I like her, but this meeting has felt a little like being run over by one of the trains she no longer wants me to use.

4

As New York fades into the darkness behind me and the cabin crew begin circulating with our pre-dinner drinks, I stretch my legs and allow myself a sigh of satisfaction. There's a long way to go, but the initial discussions have been promising and I'm happy with the way I've acquitted myself. The deal itself is on the smaller side for Morton Lansdowne; I worked on much bigger ones as a senior associate, but the difference this time is that I'm leading the negotiations on behalf of our client, rather than playing a supportive role as I have in the past. The client in this instance is a small but well-known British publishing house, who have been approached by a leading, and much larger, US publisher in a takeover bid. Our initial discussions have focused on analysing the financial position of each company, their assets and liabilities and, so far, we haven't uncovered any red flags. I've got a week back in London now before we reconvene to start looking at the potential timelines for the merger.

Janice, unsurprisingly, has been a model of no-nonsense efficiency; although I haven't needed to call on her for any of the disaster scenarios she outlined, various forms have popped up in my inbox during my trip. My initial horror that the finance forms she sent me for the car had the Porsche logo all over them was dismissed in typical Janice style.

A Porsche is pretty much standard uniform for an unmarried partner and I had to pull some fairly big levers to bypass the waiting list. Don't worry about the cost; your car allowance will do most of the heavy lifting, so it won't actually cost you much more than something humdrum would have when you were an associate.

Completed forms also magically appeared for the insurance, and a parking permit application from Walthamstow borough council. When I queried how she knew which council to approach, her response bordered on the terse. 'I know where you live. It's not exactly rocket science. You can thank me later.'

Any lingering views about the sanctity of my private life were comprehensively exploded by the arrival of two further forms. The first wanted details of all my immediate family members, along with addresses and dates of birth. My inevitable query about why she needed this information was met with a one-line response.

When was the last time you remembered to send anyone in your family a birthday card?

I tend to text them on the day, if I remember.

I think we can do better. I'll send you some cards to sign, and I'll make sure they go out at the appropriate times.

Things went from bad to worse when I had to confess that, not only did I not know my nephew's birthday, but I wasn't entirely sure how old he was. I'd laughed when I read her reply the next day.

Louis will be six on 15 September. I'll send him a card, shall I?

How on earth did you find that out?

Register of Births, Marriages and Deaths. Again, hardly rocket science.

The final form concerned my relationship status, and was labelled optional. Although I've read through it, I haven't filled it in as I'm not entirely sure what to say. Janice did explain in her accompanying email that I didn't have to disclose any details to her, but it would be helpful to know if I had a significant other in case they became needy and demanding, requiring intervention from her to bring them back into line. The idea of Janice 'intervening' in a relationship is too terrifying even for me to contemplate.

As I sip my champagne and start to read through the most recent pack of documents the associates have prepared, I think back to my initial meeting with Janice and my doubts about whether I actually needed a PA at all. Three weeks into the job and, apart from the relationship questionnaire, I'm now starting to wonder how I ever managed without one.

* * *

Although it's Saturday morning when my flight lands, I've got a debrief meeting with one of the senior partners followed by a next steps meeting with the associates working on the merger, so the taxi takes me straight to the office, which is humming with life as usual. On the way, I get a text from Janice.

Sorry I won't be in the office today, but I've left a pack with documents, your car keys and birthday/Christmas cards for your family at reception. Tailor booked for Tuesday at 3 p.m. I've put it in your calendar as a smear test to scare off anyone else thinking of booking that slot. Any issues let me know, otherwise I'll see you on Monday. J.

I smile as I read it. Although I'm not completely comfortable using gynaecology as a cover, I can see the wisdom behind Janice's logic. If she'd put something as banal as an appointment with a tailor in my calendar, it would have been bumped almost immediately. However, Morton Lansdowne makes a big song and dance about its equal opportunity policies, so nobody's going to dare to interfere with a medical appointment, especially one relating to female biology. We just have to hope that nobody is tracking the frequency of my smear test appointments, otherwise alarm bells might start to ring if they think I'm having them more often than I should. To be honest, I'm not convinced that I need tailor-made suits, but I can see it matters to Janice, so I figure letting her tailor measure me is a small price to pay for the work she's doing for me. If I buy one suit, hopefully that will make her feel I've taken her advice and get me off the hook.

My debrief meeting with John Curbishley, one of the senior partners, is scheduled for 11 a.m. Being assigned to John is the one part of my partnership so far that has proved to be a struggle. Although he's enormously experienced and I do respect him, his overly brusque manner and tendency to tear into you for missing the slightest detail makes him difficult to work with, to put it tactfully. Meetings with him are very much things to endure rather than look forward to. It's very much not the done thing to be late for a meeting with a senior partner, but being too early is also frowned upon, as it suggests poor time management, so I make sure to arrive outside his office on the eighth floor exactly five minutes early. The courtesy is rarely repaid, of course, and it's nearly quarter past eleven by the time the door opens and Andrew, another newly anointed partner, appears, looking harassed.

'He definitely got out of bed the wrong side this morning,' he murmurs to me after double-checking that the door is properly closed. 'There was only one clause in the draft agreement that he didn't like the look of, but he still chewed me a new one.'

Before I have a chance to answer, the door opens again.

'Come in, Thea,' John says curtly. No apology for keeping me waiting, but then I didn't expect one. He's known for not giving a damn about other people's calendars, or anything else. Rumour has it that a junior partner asked to move a meeting once so he could visit his mother on her deathbed, and his response was so caustic that, not only did the junior partner not get to see his mother before she died, his visceral assessment of said partner's commitment to the firm left the partner in tears. He's an old-school bruiser, and I'm wary as I follow him into his office.

'Have a seat,' he tells me as he closes the door. His watery blue eyes are expressionless behind his wire-framed glasses as he unbuttons his suit jacket and eases his substantial frame into a chair on the other side of the small conference table.

'So,' he says, fixing his gaze unblinkingly on me. 'What the bloody hell are a company the size of Bookisti doing buggering around with a tiny publisher like MacOsterley? Surely they have bigger fish to fry?' This is a classic opener; he wants to see if I understand the business context.

'On the surface, that would seem to be the case,' I tell him smoothly. 'But MacOsterley is a disruptor. Their business model is radically different from most publishers, and Bookisti wants to be on the crest of that wave if MacOsterley proves to be on to something.'

'Buy the competition before they become a threat,' he observes.

'Exactly.'

'And what do MacOsterley get out of it? Is Bookisti actually planning to invest in the business, or just steal the name and move everything to China like everyone else?'

'They say they're going to expand production in the UK. Publishing has a bit of an image problem with the eco lobby, so MacOsterley's view that we need to be printing fewer books closer to the point of consumption is very topical at the moment.'

'What the hell do they mean by "fewer books closer to the point of consumption"? They're a fucking publishing house, not a sodding snack manufacturer.' He's trying to needle me now, I can tell. If he can pick away at my understanding to the point where I doubt myself, he'll consider it a victory. He really is a toad.

'Take your China model,' I say, keeping my voice level. 'Yes, you could print five thousand copies of a title pretty cheaply, but the environmental impact is problematic. You've got the trees that have to be chopped down to make the paper, the ink, fuel used in shipping and so on. Out of the five thousand originals, maybe only three thousand sell, so you end up pulping two thousand of them. MacOsterley has been investing heavily in PoD, and that's what Bookisti wants a slice of.'

'PoD?'

'Print on Demand.'

'What a waste of time. It'll never pay.'

'Amazon manages to make it pay, and where Amazon leads—'

'—the others always follow,' he grudgingly agrees. I might actually be winning this conversation, I realise.

'Exactly. I think Bookisti sees MacOsterley as a way to put a toe into the PoD market without contaminating their main brand if it doesn't work.'

'Is that what they've said?'

'No, of course not. They're spouting all the usual guff about wanting to partner with a well-respected British publishing house, but nobody's fooled.'

He stares at me for what feels like an age before speaking again.

'Good work, Thea,' he growls eventually. 'But don't get complacent, understand? Little deals like this that seem simple on the surface have a nasty habit of turning round and fucking you in the arse when you least expect it. If we get fucked in the arse by this, be in no doubt that I will fuck you in the arse twice as hard. Metaphorically speaking, obviously, before you run off to HR squealing about sexual harassment. Am I making myself very clear?'

'Yes, John.'

'Good. Get out.'

As I gather my things and open the door, he fires his final shot. 'Don't make the mistake of thinking you're beyond my reach in New York. I expect regular reports, and I can easily fuck you in the arse from here if you screw up. Got it?'

I smile sweetly as I close the door, before very carefully flicking a series of highly unprofessional V-signs at it.

* * *

By the time I've finished the next steps meeting and followed up on a few crucial emails, it's nearly four in the afternoon, but the jetlag means I still have plenty of energy as I ride the elevator down to the underground car park where my new car is allegedly waiting for me. It takes a little while to locate the bay, but the reassuring flash of the indicators when I press the unlock button on the key fob confirms that I'm in the right place. It's a while since I last drove, so I take time to familiarise myself with all the controls before easing my way up the ramp into the traffic for my journey home. Janice, naturally, has already fixed the parking permit to the windscreen, and I'm surprised to see the space outside my house is empty when I drive up. Taking great care not to scrape the expensive-looking alloy wheels on the kerb, I manoeuvre my way into the spot before grabbing my luggage out of the passenger seat and opening the front door of my house. There's no sign of the SUV, but then I remember that Saturday afternoons are Rollo's extra tuition times. Sure enough, I've barely started annotating the updated documents that came out of the next steps meeting when the SUV appears. I watch as it stops dead, completely blocking the road next to my car, and Rollo's mum hops out, looking furious. She peers closely at the parking permit on the Porsche and then, to my surprise, marches up my front path and rings the doorbell.

'Hi,' I say as I open the door to her.

'Yes, hello,' she replies distractedly. 'Sorry to bother you, but I wonder whether you saw which house the owner of that car went into?'

'That's my car,' I reply neutrally.

'Ah, right,' she says, adopting a faux-jovial tone that completely doesn't correspond with the fury in her eyes. 'You must be new because this house has been empty for as long as I can remember. The thing is, that's my space. You'll have to move.'

For a moment, I'm silenced by the bare-faced entitlement of the woman. I may not have owned a car since I've lived here, but I'm perfectly aware that none of the spaces are pre-allocated. It's strictly first come, first served.

'Oh, goodness. I'm so sorry,' I tell her. 'Let me just grab the keys.' I half shut the door and steal a look at her out of the study window as I retrieve my car keys. She's actually tapping her foot impatiently. Sorry, Sarah-or-whatever-your-name-is, but you're about to get a lesson in manners.

'Here they are,' I say as I join her outside, locking the door behind me. 'Now, would you mind just showing me how I tell which space is allocated to which house before I get out of your way? I'd hate to inconvenience anyone else.'

'It's, ah, more of an informal thing,' she replies, looking less full of herself all of a sudden. 'I always park here.'

I fix a puzzled expression on my face. 'Sorry, I must be missing something. I thought you said this space belonged to you officially.'

'Look,' she says, changing tack again, this time to naked aggression. 'I don't have time to stand here arguing the ins and outs of street parking etiquette with you. The fact is that this is where I always park, I'm on a tight schedule, and I'd appreciate you moving your car so I can get on with my day.'

'No.'

'What? What do you mean, no? Have you not listened to a word I've said?'

I have, Sarah-or-whoever-you-are, and your attitude frankly stinks. 'The fact is that I've lived here for several years,' I tell her. 'And, although the car is new, I'm well aware of the parking regulations on this street. This space is occupied. I suggest you do what everyone else would do in your circumstances and look for another, rather than trying to bully me out of a space I've parked in quite legitimately.'

For a moment, she stares at me, as if unable to comprehend what I've said. An insistent beeping from a delivery van that's pulled up behind her brings her back down to earth.

'This is unbe-fucking-lievable,' she yells as she storms back to her car and climbs in, slamming the door behind her. As she screeches off up the road, my eyes meet Rollo's for a fraction of a second, and I could swear I see him mouth the word 'sorry' at me.

5

I'm still reflecting on my surreal encounter with Rollo's mum when my phone pings with a message. It's Alasdair.

Whereabouts in the world are you ATM?

At home, would you believe… Got in from NY this morning. You?

The ticks go blue instantly and I can see he's typing so, rather than returning to my annotations, I wait for his reply to come in.

Also in London. Fancy celebrating your elevation?

I smile as I type my response.

Sounds good. I have wine in the fridge…

His reply is immediate.

Sod wine. I'll pick up some champagne on the way. See you in an hour.

I return my attention to the document, and it seems like no time at all has passed before the doorbell sounds to announce his arrival. I mark my place so I know where I've got to, and go to open the front door.

'*La Porsche obligatoire*?' he asks with a raised eyebrow and a mischievous grin, waving a bottle of Dom Pérignon in the direction of my car. 'Such a cliché, darling. I never had you down as following the corporate herd mentality.'

'Sod off,' I laugh as I stand back to let him in. 'I didn't choose it, if you must know.'

'How did it arrive then? Is it true that they're delivered by the secret partner Porsche fairy?'

'My PA organised it while I was in New York. Apparently, I'm too important and expensive to rely on trains now.'

'Of course you are, your majesty.' He bows deeply. 'What's the view like from the heady heights of Olympus?'

'Have you come to celebrate or take the piss?'

'Both, naturally. On a serious note, I couldn't be happier for you. If anyone deserved to make partner, it's you.'

'Thanks. Why didn't you apply?'

'I've still got a bit of a grey smudge against my name, I reckon.'

'Surely that's long forgotten, isn't it?'

One of the things I've always admired about Alasdair is the way his brain can switch from work to play mode in an instant. When we were trainees together, I was regularly in awe of his ability to grasp a concept and run with it, often while the rest of us were still getting our heads around it. But then, come the end of the day, he'd waltz out of the office as if he didn't have a care in the world. Unfortunately, although his competence was never in doubt, his ability to switch off so easily did cause questions to be asked about his commitment, and his first annual appraisal was, in his words, a bit of a car crash. He was much more careful after that, but the stigma followed him for quite a while.

'Well, now that you're the other side of the great divide, maybe you can put in a good word for me.' He grins to let me know that he's not serious and waves the bottle again. 'I think this might have got a bit shaken up on the way over, so shall I stick it in the fridge to calm down a bit before we open it? It's the good stuff, so it would be a shame to redecorate your hallway with it.'

I return his grin. 'That sounds like a good idea. How on earth do you plan to entertain me in the meantime though?'

* * *

Alasdair and I first had sex the night it was announced that we were the only two from our intake group that Morton Lansdowne wanted to keep on as junior associates. We hit the town to celebrate and, with clichéd inevitability, ended up drunkenly falling into bed together at his rather grotty bedsit. The next morning, I woke with a splitting headache, ready for the usual guilt-ridden recriminations and awkward conversations, but quickly realised to my relief that Alasdair doesn't work like that. He took me out for breakfast to cure my hangover, we had sex again, and then I went home. Since then, we've had a tacit understanding that, although we're more than friends sexually, we aren't a 'thing'. We're just mates who hook up when the feeling takes us, as it has today.

Sex with Alasdair is very much like the man himself. Honest, joyful and reassuringly straightforward. I've never timed it, but I think it would fit pretty neatly into one of the fifteen-minute billing slots that Morton Lansdowne lawyers live and die by. He's not one of those angsty lovers who spends hours faffing about down there, making you feel inadequate because whatever they're doing hasn't reduced you to instant shuddering orgasms. I don't think I've ever had an orgasm during a sexual encounter with a man, but that doesn't mean I don't enjoy it, and fifteen minutes is plenty long enough in my book. I read an article once about how tantric sex can last for hours and my immediate reaction was 'Who would want it to?'

Thankfully, Alasdair is as uninterested in tantric sex as I am, and sets to work with typical gusto. Although we don't see each other very often, our bodies instinctively know the moves and I'll admit there have been times when I've let the whole thing happen on autopilot while I've wrestled with a thorny work issue. Alasdair doesn't generally notice; in fact, I was once able to read and answer an email while he was mid-flow. We were in the missionary position and I'd heard my phone buzz on my bedside table. I'd very carefully lifted it and held it at arm's length behind him, tapping out my reply with my thumb while keeping up the necessary encouraging noises. I'd been pretty pleased with it as a piece of multitasking, but when I tried it again on another occasion and he caught me, we agreed that sex probably ought to be a phone- and work-free activity.

Although I can always find something work-related to worry about, we're early enough in the current transaction that I can mentally park it and be in the moment with Alasdair today. Afterwards, he wraps himself in my dressing gown and heads downstairs to fetch the champagne. I lie back in bed, listening to him moving about before I hear the telltale pop as he opens the bottle.

'Here we go,' he says when he reappears with two full champagne flutes, handing one to me before he clambers back into bed. 'Here's to you, Morton Lansdowne's newest, most beautiful and certainly most talented partner.' He raises his glass and chinks it against mine, before taking a big mouthful.

'Flatterer,' I chide him as I take a sip, enjoying the dry biscuity flavour and the sensation of the bubbles popping on my tongue. 'Actually, I could do with your opinion on something. Stay there.'

He's still wearing my dressing gown, so I slip out of bed and sprint down the stairs in the nude, checking the pavement outside is clear before retrieving my laptop from my study and beating an equally hasty retreat.

'What do you make of this?' I ask him as I bring up Janice's relationship questionnaire and hand him the laptop so he can read it.

'Is this an HR thing?' he asks when he's scanned it.

'No. Janice, my PA, wants me to fill it in so she knows who to put the frighteners on if my personal life threatens to interfere with my professional one.'

'You can't put me on this,' he says, suddenly looking deadly serious.

'Why not?' I ask. 'If you're worried that being in a relationship with a partner will be another black mark against you in some way, I can tell you categorically that it wouldn't. We don't even work in the same department, so it would be pretty difficult for me to give you preferential treatment, and the relationship started when we were both associates, so nobody could accuse me of coercing you in some kind of quid-pro-quo arrangement.'

'Oh, I'm not worried about any of that.' He laughs, obviously delighted to have wound me up. 'It's just there isn't a category for me. Look here where it says "Nature of relationship". The options are Spouse/Partner, Fiancé(e) or Boyfriend/Girlfriend. Friend and sometime fuck buddy evidently doesn't count. I'll give Janice this, though. She's bloody thorough.'

'Tell me about it. She's so into contingency planning that I'm surprised she hasn't asked for a comprehensive list of physical features and birthmarks in case I get caught in an earthquake somewhere and she has to identify my body. She's terrifyingly efficient. So, shall I forget about this form then?'

'I would. We don't see each other often enough for me to become needy and demanding, do we? Although...' He stops and looks at me seriously again. 'There is something I've been wanting to tell you. I didn't mention it before because, well, there are some things you don't bring up in the throes of passion, aren't there.'

Oh, shit. Is he going to break the rules of our relationship and drop the L bomb? I'm very fond of Alasdair, but I've never seen what we have as any more serious than the fuck buddies he's just described. One of the things that makes us work is that, being a lawyer himself, he understands the pressures on me and doesn't try to take more than I have to give him – and vice versa. If he's going to start declaring that he loves me, that changes the dynamic in a way that I'm not at all comfortable with.

'What is it?' I ask him nervously.

He fixes his gaze on mine and leans forward very slowly, brushing my lips with his a few times. Normally, I like the sensation, but he's making me anxious. Eventually he speaks, his voice no more than a murmur.

'I'm starving,' he says. 'Shall we order in from that Vietnamese place you like? My treat, of course.'

'You absolute bastard,' I scold him as I punch him on the shoulder. 'I thought you were going to say something deep and meaningful.'

'Oh.' He feigns surprise. 'I was saving that for later, but now that you've brought it up, I guess you've forced my hand. Will you marry me, Thea?'

'Of course not.'

'All righty. Vietnamese it is then.'

* * *

'Can I ask you a question?' he asks some time later. We've polished off the Vietnamese takeaway with the rest of the champagne, and we're now sitting on the sofa making good progress through a bottle of wine. My head is in Alasdair's lap and, for the first time in ages, I'm feeling relaxed and a little bit woozy.

'Go on,' I tell him without opening my eyes.

'Do you think you will get married, one day?'

'Is that a serious question, or another one of your wind-ups?'

'It's a serious question.'

'I think it's unlikely.'

'Because?'

I open my eyes and sit up. 'Because all sorts of things. When am I going to find time for the kind of relationship that might lead to marriage, for starters? Who'd want to be married to me, anyway? I'm married to my job. You, of all people, ought to understand that.'

'I do. Don't you ever think about it though?'

'What, a little cottage with roses over the door and a white picket fence? Adorable, rosy-cheeked children running wild in the fields while I bake wholesome goodies? A ruggedly handsome husband who chops down trees with his bare hands but is oh so gentle in the bedroom?'

He laughs. 'It sounds like you've given it quite a lot of thought.'

'Only because it's my waking-up-in-hell scenario. The reality is that I'd either have to marry another lawyer, because they're the only people who understand the pressures of the job, but I'd never see them, so what's the point? Or I marry someone from outside the profession and we spend two years rowing about why I'm never at home before divorcing messily and expensively.'

'When did you get so jaded?'

'I'm not jaded, I'm realistic. What about you? Do you think you'll get married? Do the whole 2.4 children and a Labrador thing?'

He thinks for a long time before answering and I take the opportunity to top up our glasses. I'm not going to admit it, but his question is one I've asked myself several times before, and I've never found a completely satisfactory answer. Would I like to meet someone to share my life with? Yes. Would I be prepared to give up the career I love in order to do it? No, I think that would destroy me after all the work I've put in to get here. Is Alasdair my person? Definitely not, but I hope we'll always be friends, whatever happens.

'Do you know,' he says eventually, startling me out of my uncomfortable train of thought, 'I reckon I'd happily give up the law for the right person. I think, deep down, I've always known that, and maybe that's why I'm not that fussed about whether I become a partner or not. Don't tell them at work, will you?'

'Don't worry,' I reply, trying to hide my surprise. 'Your secret's quite safe with me. I never had you pegged as such a romantic though.'

'How can you say that?' he demands, mock-affronted. 'I've bought you champagne and dinner today.'

'That you did,' I admit. 'Where are the roses though?'

'Aw, bollocks. I left them in the shop.'

I lean over and give him a kiss. 'You'll make someone a very good husband one day, I'm sure. Now, I hate to admit it, but I'm starting to fade. Do you want to stay the night? The only rule is you shut up about marriage.'

'Yeah, go on then.'

6

I can't believe it's Christmas already. It feels like my feet have hardly touched the ground in the last six months. Although the publishing deal has gone quiet due to some restructuring at Bookisti, I was immediately reassigned onto another deal which has had me flitting back and forth to Paris. The transaction is starting to accelerate, so I'm desperately hoping Bookisti doesn't resurface just yet, as two transactions running concurrently is every M&A lawyer's worst nightmare.

I'm in a good mood as I point the Porsche towards Mum and Phil's home in Maidstone. The traffic is almost non-existent at this time on Christmas morning, so the satnav is predicting I should easily make it in time for the all-important present-opening ceremony before lunch. I glance at the shopping bag full of neatly wrapped presents on the passenger seat next to me; to my amusement, not only did Janice buy all the gifts and wrap them, but she also provided me with a helpful crib sheet so I could talk knowledgeably enough about each one to complete the illusion that I'd bought them myself.

One thing I can be absolutely sure about, as I join the M25

heading for the Dartford crossing and Kent, is that Rollo's mum will already have moved her car into the now vacant space outside my house. She seems to be curiously obsessed about it and, although things have calmed down a little lately, she's made various attempts to stop me parking there over the months. I came home one Saturday to find it blocked off with those yellow cones that councils use to stop people parking when they want to do roadworks. I will admit to being taken in by that one for a moment, until I got suspicious about the fact that only one space was affected. A quick bit of investigation revealed that she'd whipped them from a site round the corner, so I moved them and stacked them neatly outside her front door before parking as usual. Her dirtiest trick, for which I grudgingly admire her ingenuity, was revealed when I came back from a three-week trip to New York to discover that she'd reported my car as abandoned. Obviously, the polite letter from the council informing me that there had been a complaint didn't mention who had contacted them, but it was pretty obvious.

It sounds petty, but I couldn't let that one go without a retaliatory strike. Not because I care particularly about the space; I just wanted to let her know that I knew what she'd done and I wouldn't be pushed around. So, the following weekend, I'd deliberately moved my car round the corner about five minutes before I knew she and Rollo would return from his extra tuition. Sure enough, she swooped eagerly into the space with a look of triumph on her face as she hopped out of the car. Unluckily for her, her typically cavalier parking played straight into my hands, and a quick call to the council to inform them of a car parked on the kerb resulted in a clamp and the highly satisfactory sight of her howling with rage when she came to leave the next morning. I'm not proud, but she hasn't tried anything since, so I reckon the end justifies the means.

'Darling! Merry Christmas.' My mother beams as she throws open the door of the house she and Phil have lived in since they married. She envelops me in a bosomy hug that takes me back to my childhood as I return the embrace.

'Let me look at you,' she continues after a moment, holding me by the shoulders and scrutinising me closely. 'You've lost weight again, haven't you? You look tired, are you eating properly?'

'I'm fine, Mum. Honestly.'

'Hm. You're very pale. Are you sure you can't stay the night? Your room is all made up and you look like you could do with a bit of spoiling. Your uncle Ted's coming over with Gina and the girls tomorrow. I'm sure they'd love to see you.'

'Sorry, Mum. Boxing Day is a work day in France, so I'm on the early-morning Eurostar.'

'Ah, well. If it can't be helped then we'll just have to make the most of you while we have you. Come on in. We've doled out the presents and it's been a full-time job persuading Louis to wait for you to arrive before opening them.'

I follow her down the hall to the sitting room, where the rest of my family are gathered. Phil is ensconced in his usual spot, a squishy leather armchair in front of the TV, and my sister Saffy is on the sofa with her husband Tim and a very wriggly Louis.

'Sorry to keep you waiting, everyone,' I tell them as Mum settles herself into the chair next to Phil's.

'No worries. Lovely to see you, Thea, and Merry Christmas. Would you like a glass of fizz?' Phil heaves himself out of his chair and wanders over to the sideboard that serves as his bar. It's one of those ones that opens up to reveal an illuminated mirror-lined interior, and is full of bottles of weird liqueurs he and Mum have picked up on various holidays over the years. If you wanted a template for someone solidly middle class, Phil is it. He likes his home, his creature comforts and he loves my mother to bits. He may not be exciting, but we love him like the father Dad never was.

'Just half a glass, please, Phil,' I tell him. 'I need to pace myself.'

'Is there a present in your bag for me?' Louis asks hopefully.

'There is indeed,' I tell him. 'Would you like me to give it to you?'

He nods excitedly, eyes wide as I fish out the box with his name on it and hand it to him, before handing round the rest of the presents to my family.

'Can I open it, Mum? Can I?'

I can see Saffy looking at me warily, evidently concerned about a repeat of chemistry-set-gate.

She sighs. 'Go on then.'

He tears eagerly into the paper and I find myself holding my breath.

'Oh, wow! Look, Mum. Look what Auntie Thea bought me.'

Her mouth drops open. 'A Spiderman hero figurine? Where the bloody hell did you get one of those? They've been sold out literally everywhere since forever.'

'I, umm, got lucky,' I tell her. 'There was one store in London that had some, and I guess I was in the right place at the right time.' I make a mental note to tell Janice that she's an absolute star.

'You are a *very* lucky boy, Louis. What do you say to Auntie Thea?'

'Thank you,' he says dutifully.

'It's my pleasure, Louis,' I tell him, breathing a sigh of relief.

The rest of 'my' presents are equally well received, and I don't do too badly as a recipient either. Saffy and Tim have given me a small bottle of the Dior perfume I like, and Mum and Phil have played it safe with M&S vouchers as they do every year.

'We'd love to get you something different,' Mum says apologetically as I thank them. 'But you're so difficult to buy for.'

'It's fine,' I reassure her. 'You can never go wrong with M&S vouchers.'

'So, how's it going at work?' Saffy asks in the lull between present opening and lunch. Mum has disappeared into the kitchen to check the turkey, Louis is engrossed in his presents, and Phil and Tim are 'checking the wine is OK', which seems to involve pouring large glasses for each other and muttering about giving it room to breathe as an excuse.

'Yeah, busier than ever. You?'

'Oh, same old, same old. Can I ask you something?'

'Of course.'

'How is it that you claim to be busier than ever, but you miraculously find time to source this year's must-have toy for your nephew? A toy so sought after that us mere mortals couldn't get within sniffing distance of it. What did you do? Bribe a government official? Buy the company?'

'Why does it have to be something suspicious? Maybe I just got lucky, like I said.'

'Come on, Thea. This is me you're talking to.'

I sigh. 'If I tell you, will you promise not to be cross?'

'You've made my son's Christmas. How could I be cross?'

I smile at her conspiratorially. 'My PA bought it. I have no idea where she got it from.'

She laughs. 'I might have known. Your presents this year have been suspiciously on point. When I saw the shape of the box, I'll admit I was worried it was going to be a Barbie doll for a moment.'

'Would that have been so wrong? Aren't we supposed to be moving away from gender-orientated toys?'

'Mm. I'm not sure Louis is that politically aware yet. Anyway, do thank your PA on my behalf.'

* * *

I'm actually a little sad that I couldn't stay the night in the end, as it was one of the nicest Christmas days I've spent with my family in ages. Mum, bless her, was determined to feed me up, and even sent me away with some leftovers as a food parcel. I didn't have the heart to tell her I'd have to put them straight in the bin as they'd go off before I came back from Paris. The biggest surprise of the day, however, came when I got home and found the space outside my house empty and no sign of Rollo's mum's SUV anywhere. Perhaps they've gone away for Christmas. For a moment, I wondered what sort of presents poor Rollo would have been unwrapping. Probably educational and nothing as frivolous as the action figure that Louis was so delighted with.

As the Eurostar streaks through northern France, I temporarily abandon the document I'm looking at and open my email program to send a note of thanks to Janice.

I'm just about to start typing when a notification pops up on my screen to say there is a new email from our managing partner, Martin Osborne. There's nothing unusual about this; he sends out emails periodically either to announce promotions, share results or congratulate teams on successful transactions. I think they're supposed to be motivational, but I generally skim read the subject line and delete them without reading the detail. The subject line of this mail is simply 'John Curbishley', which piques my interest sufficiently for me to open the mail and read the rest.

> To all Partners and Associates,
>
> It is with great sadness that I have to announce the death of our friend and senior partner, John Curbishley, after a short illness. He is survived by his wife, Alice, and his two sons, Richard and Stephen. I have offered sincere condolences to the family on behalf of everyone at Morton Lansdowne, and assured his wife that we will do everything in our power to support her during the difficult days ahead.
>
> The funeral directors will be organising an electronic book of condolence, and I have asked Margaret to share the link with you all as soon as it is available. Obviously, things will take a little longer during the holiday season.
>
> On a personal note, I'd just like to say how much I admired John, both as a friend and colleague, and I know many of you will feel the same. In light of that, we would ask all UK-based associates to make every effort to clear their diaries so they can attend his memorial service. Margaret will circulate the date as soon as we receive word from the family. It's expected that there will be a service in the Temple church, followed by a reception at Skinners' Hall, the home of the Worshipful Company of Skinners, of which John was an active member.

My first reaction is disbelief. Although I didn't like John at all, he's been a part of the furniture at Morton Lansdowne for the entire time I've been there, and I can't imagine the eighth floor without his brooding, malevolent presence. I'm also a little disorientated by the mention of his family. I've never imagined John, or any of the other senior partners, having a life outside work. I wonder what the illness was. He seemed to be in his usual acerbic form when I met with him just over a week ago for one of our regular debriefs. I bring up a mental image of his office to try to see if I can remember there being any pictures of his family. I think there was a frame on his desk, but I never got to see what it contained.

'Ladies and gentlemen,' the voice comes over the tannoy as the train begins to slow, 'we will shortly be arriving at Paris Gare du Nord. On behalf of the train manager and all the crew, I'd like to thank you for choosing Eurostar for your journey today, and we wish you a pleasant stay in Paris. If Paris is not your final destination, please contact one of our station staff, who will be pleased to assist you with your connection. Thank you, and good morning.'

I snap my laptop shut and start gathering my stuff together, pushing all thoughts of John aside as I focus my mind in preparation for the day ahead.

7

John was obviously well connected as, despite barely two weeks having passed since the email announcing his death, everything has been arranged and the memorial service is today. The Temple church is already packed by the time that Alasdair and I arrive and, to begin with, I worry that there won't be anywhere for us to sit. There's an empty block of pews in the middle, but I can spot the reserved signs even from here. I'm scanning the other pews despondently when I suddenly spot Janice waving and pointing to a seat next to her.

'I saved a seat for my favourite partner,' she tells me conspiratorially when I reach her. 'Although I didn't realise you'd be bringing a plus one.' She looks curiously at Alasdair for a moment before speaking again. 'I've seen you before somewhere. Property, am I right?'

'Very good,' Alasdair tells her.

'I expect we can squeeze you both in if I shuffle up a bit,' she tells him as she wriggles along to make room. When we sit, it's so tight that I can feel both Janice's and Alasdair's hips digging into mine.

'Although I'm grateful,' I murmur to Janice, 'I'm not sure you're supposed to have favourites.'

'Well, I do,' she retorts. 'You're the only one who ever says thank you, and that gets you preferential treatment.'

I'm just about to tell her how depressingly low that sets the bar when the organ music swells and the doors swing open to reveal a man in robes, holding an ornate cross on a long wooden pole. As the organ continues to get louder, he raises it high and advances into the church. Behind him, in solemn procession, walk Martin Osborne and the other senior partners, decked out in their academic regalia. The guy with the cross halts by the empty block and the partners file into the second row of pews.

'Wow,' I whisper to Alasdair. 'He's got the full complement. All the senior partners are here.'

After the partners come another set of men wearing fur robes. 'Representatives from the Skinners' company,' Janice informs me as they take up their places behind the partners. 'And here come the Freemasons,' she continues as another block of men in dark suits, wearing colourful sashes and chains around their necks, file into the pews behind the Skinners.

'I tell you what,' Janice murmurs. 'If you wanted to wipe out the legal heart of London, a bomb in here right now would do a pretty fine job.'

The final group to enter the church are, I'm guessing, John's family. There's an elegantly dressed woman I'd estimate to be in her late fifties, along with two young men who are very obviously his sons, from their facial features. I watch them closely as they take their place in the front row, admiring their poise under pressure. It's got to be an emotional moment for them, but all three are perfectly dry eyed and holding their heads up high.

'She's doing well, isn't she?' Alasdair whispers. 'It must have been a hell of a shock. I heard it was a heart attack. Not quite face down in the soup, but not far off.'

I nod my head as the final members of the family procession take their seats. My cursory glance turns into a full-on double-take as I realise that I recognise the two people sitting next to John's sons. What the bloody hell are Rollo and his mum doing here? Before I have a chance to say anything to Alasdair, however, the minister is asking us to stand for the choir introit.

* * *

'I think John would have been pleased with that,' I observe to Alasdair and Janice as we make our way through the city towards Skinners' Hall for the reception. The firm laid on buses, but it's a beautiful crisp winter's day so the three of us decided to walk.

'Don't you think it's odd that neither of his sons gave a tribute?' Alasdair remarks. 'I mean, it was nice what the other people said about him, but you didn't get any insight into what he was like at home.'

'I'd still love to know what his connection to Sarah is,' I tell him.

'Who's Sarah?' Janice asks.

'I've no idea what her real name is. The woman who was sitting slightly apart from the other family members, with the little boy. She lives on the same road as me.' I decide not to mention the parking wars, as it's not a story that shows me in my best light.

'Daughter, maybe?' Alasdair offers.

'No,' Janice says firmly. 'He didn't have any daughters. Two sons, that was it. She might be with one of the sons, I suppose, although she looked quite a lot older than them, and I'm pretty sure he didn't have any grandchildren.'

'How do you know all of this?' Alasdair asks her. I'm not at all surprised, but he hasn't come across the formidable Janice in person before.

'I chat to people,' she says enigmatically.

It's weird, being outside during the day. I keep glancing around me guiltily, as if one of the senior partners is going to pop up at any moment and demand to know why the hell I'm not in the office. Martin was quite clear in his latest missive, though. As a mark of respect to John, anyone attending the service and reception had to keep their phones turned off and invisible until the proceedings were officially over.

'Perhaps she was a family nanny or au pair,' Alasdair suggests after a while. We consider it before I dismiss the idea.

'Too young. She can't be more than ten years older than the sons. Babysitter, maybe?'

'Why would you include a babysitter in the family pew?' he counters.

'You'll be able to ask her yourself in a minute,' Janice advises us. 'We're here.'

There's obviously some sort of receiving line because, although the buses have long since dumped their passengers and departed, there's still a long queue outside the entrance to Skinners' Hall. I'm grateful for the fine weather as we shuffle slowly towards the door; queuing in the rain would have turned my hair into an untameable frizz.

Eventually, we inch our way inside to be greeted by John's widow and two sons. 'I'm so sorry for your loss,' I tell her as I shake her proffered hand before moving on and repeating the process with each of the boys. Up close, I can see that they've both inherited John's light blue eyes but, where his were cold and calculating, theirs sparkle with life. If I didn't know better, it would almost look like amusement.

There are two waiters standing at the end of the reception line, each holding a silver tray with an assortment of drinks. I grab a glass of champagne and scan the room, which is humming with muted conversation. I spot her on the second sweep. She's standing all alone, sipping a glass of champagne, with Rollo beside her holding a glass of orange juice. She looks lost and, despite our enmity, I find myself feeling a little sorry for her, even as my curiosity about who she is grows. I'm still staring at her when she looks up suddenly and meets my gaze. I can see her eyes narrow briefly before she grabs Rollo's hand and begins to cross the room towards me. I glance behind to summon Janice and Alasdair as my wingmen, only to find that they're already engrossed in conversation with other people. Shit. I'm going to have to front this out on my own, as best I can.

'I'm sorry,' she says once she reaches me. 'You look familiar, but I can't place you. Do I know you from somewhere?'

'I live in your road,' I tell her.

'She's the lady you shouted at about the parking space,' Rollo adds, unhelpfully in my opinion.

I can practically see the penny dropping and brace myself for the inevitable onslaught. What happens catches me by surprise. She smiles.

'You got me clamped,' she says, but there's no malice in her tone.

'Only after you reported my car as abandoned,' I reply.

'It's a fair cop,' she admits. 'For what it's worth, I'm sorry. I've been dealing with a truckload of shit over the last year, and I think I've taken it out unfairly on lots of people, including you. I'm Rebecca, by the way.'

'Thea. Nice to meet you, I think.'

'Don't worry, I don't bite. I take it you worked with him?'

'Yes. I'm one of the partners at Morton Lansdowne.'

'Did you like him?'

'I respected him.'

'Nicely sidestepped.'

'Do you mind me asking how you knew him?'

'Not at all. This is Rollo, my son. John is – sorry, was – I must get used to saying that. John *was* his father.'

For a moment, it seems as if time freezes while I try to digest that information.

'You weren't expecting that, were you?' Rebecca says with a grin. 'It's all right. Nobody does.'

'How?' is all I manage, before I run out of words.

'Oh, the usual way. I'm sure you don't need diagrams, do you? Wealthy married lawyer seduces stupid woman who really ought to have known better. It's a classic tale; I think Disney are working on a film version of it. It's a bit like *Beauty and the Beast* except she falls pregnant and the beast gets even more beastly.' She glances down at Rollo, who looks unfazed, as if he's heard this story many times before.

'Darling,' she says to him. 'I think there are some snacks over there. Why don't you put some on a plate and bring them back for Thea and Mummy?'

'Can I have some too?' he asks.

'Of course. Don't wolf them down though; take your time. I don't want you being sick on this expensive-looking carpet.'

'Sorry about that,' she says as Rollo crosses the room towards the buffet. 'I do try to protect him from the worst of it, but I can't always help myself.' She lowers her voice conspiratorially. 'The truth is, I'm glad the fucker's dead. That makes me sound like an awful person, I know, but I can't help how I feel.'

Before I have a chance to even formulate an answer, we're interrupted.

'Rebecca, darling, there you are. Where's dear Rollo?' I turn and come face to face with John's wife. Today just keeps getting weirder and weirder.

'Sorry, how rude of me,' she says seamlessly. 'I don't think we've met except in the receiving line just now. I'm Alice, John's widow.'

'Thea. Junior partner,' I reply.

'Thea lives on the same road as me,' Rebecca explains as Alice puts an arm around her and gives her a squeeze.

'Really? What a small world. I'm so glad you've got someone to talk to, though. I was worried you'd be bored with all these stuffy lawyers.'

'I sent Rollo over to investigate the buffet table,' Rebecca tells Alice. 'Thea was asking about our situation, and there are some things he's not ready to hear yet.'

'Quite right. Poor boy can't help who his father is, can he? Still, now John's dead, we can set about putting things right for both of you. Oh, heavens, I can see Martin the terminally dull trying to catch my eye. I'd better go and play the dutiful grieving wife.'

I'm starting to feel like I've slipped through a portal into a parallel universe. The longer I spend in this room, the less sense the world makes.

'I don't think you were meant to hear that,' Rebecca says with a smile. 'She's doing a terrific job, but underneath it all I think she's as glad to be rid of him as I am. Are you going home after this?'

'I probably ought to go back to the office.'

She grimaces. 'That's what *he* used to say. The way he talked, it was like the world would end if he wasn't at his desk. He thought he was so bloody important, but what will his legacy be, hmm? He's not going to get a star on the Hollywood Walk of Fame because he helped fat cat business A buy wanker business B. All those hours, all those late nights, all that money, and all that's left of him are an indifferent wife, two legitimate grown-up children who barely knew him, an ex-mistress that hates him and an illegitimate son who hopefully won't remember him. As far as his oh-so-precious fucking job is concerned, it's like dropping a pin into a pond. It shines for a moment, but doesn't even cause a ripple as the water closes over it and it's forgotten. Sorry, I probably oughtn't to be saying this to you. Champagne always makes me indiscreet. I'd better grab Rollo and head off before I make a tit of myself.'

As she turns to look for her son, something rebellious stirs in me. Before I have a chance to second-guess myself, I touch her on the arm.

'Sod the office. I've got some wine in the fridge if you fancy coming over.'

She smiles widely. 'Deal. I'll even leave you a parking space.'

8

In the end, we agree to meet at Rebecca's house at 9 p.m., to give her a chance to bathe Rollo and get him settled in bed. I feel a little anxious as I ring her doorbell, a bottle of Chablis tucked under my arm. What if this afternoon's ceasefire was only temporary?

'Thea, bang on time.' She smiles as she opens the door. 'Come on in. I'm just settling Rollo. He's exhausted but refusing to admit it. Go through to the living room and I'll be with you in a moment.'

Rebecca's house is laid out exactly how mine was before I did the renovations, so I don't need directions. Where my house was tired and shabby, however, hers is homely and she obviously loves bright colours. Although the walls are painted in neutral shades, the artwork on the walls bursts with colour, as do the cushions on the sofa.

The sofa. Where John's wife Alice is sitting, swirling a glass of wine the size of a goldfish bowl. Her eyes are slightly glazed, and I suspect this isn't the first glass.

'Thea, isn't it?' she says, slurring her words slightly. 'Nice to see you. Help yourself to a drink.' She waves in the direction of a table in the corner, where an expensive-looking bottle is standing in a wine cooler.

'It's from John's cellar,' she tells me as I pour myself a small glass. 'It seemed appropriate. Oh, for God's sake pour a proper measure,' she scolds as I turn around. 'Keep me company.'

I top up my glass and settle next to her on the sofa. I'm burning with curiosity about her friendship with Rebecca, but can't quite find the words to ask her about it without sounding intrusive.

'It's OK,' Alice tells me after a moment. 'You can ask. I won't be offended.'

'Ask what?'

'How I can bear to be in the presence of my husband's mistress without slapping her.'

'That wasn't quite the question.'

'I'm close though, aren't I?'

'It does seem an unusual setup,' I admit carefully.

She sits up and takes a large mouthful of wine, spilling a little onto her chin. 'OK. Full disclosure. Rebecca was neither John's first mistress, nor his last. I sometimes think he must have had a time machine, because how else could he claim to work pretty much twenty-four-seven and yet find time to screw so many young women? Anyway, I digress. Rebecca was just one in a long procession, and I was indifferent to her because I was used to it by then. But then she did something that made her stand out, that meant John couldn't drop her as casually as all the others when he got bored. She got pregnant.'

'How did that make you feel?' I ask.

'I didn't know. Not to begin with, anyway. John dealt with it in the same way he dealt with everything, by throwing money at

Rebecca to pay for a private abortion and expecting that to be the end of it.'

'But she didn't.'

'She refused. He was absolutely livid. He wasn't used to people saying "no" to him and he didn't take it well at all. Of course, I had no idea what the problem was, but I knew something was up by the way he banged and crashed around on the rare occasions he came home. Ah, there you are, darling,' she says as Rebecca joins us and fills another glass to the brim. 'Is Rollo all settled?'

'Yup. He fought it like a trooper but he's absolutely sparko now. I think we could host a rave and he wouldn't notice. The bed in the spare room is made up if you fancy staying.'

'You're very sweet, but the boys and I are staying at the flat tonight.'

'What are they up to this evening?'

'The usual, I think. Taking advantage of being together in London to meet up with some old friends and make a night of it before we all go our separate ways again tomorrow.'

'It's funny how different they are from him, isn't it?'

'I thank God every day for it. Can you imagine if they were carbon copies of John? One of him was bad enough. Thinking of which, I was just telling Thea how we met.'

'Oh, yes? Where had you got to?'

'John being cross when you refused to abort Rollo.'

It's odd listening to them; they're like a double act as they take turns to explain how John initially tried to wriggle his way off the hook, before Alice found out what was going on and threatened to expose him if he didn't do the right thing by Rebecca. I learn that Rebecca's house, car and all of Rollo's school fees and extra-curricular activities have been funded, with very bad grace, by John. Their mutual hatred of the man borders on the visceral. I mean, I didn't like him, but this is in a whole new league.

'Can I ask you something?' Alice asks me a while later.

'Sure.'

'What is it you like about your job? What's the thing that makes it all worthwhile?'

I consider her question for a bit.

'When a transaction comes together,' I tell her. 'Months and months of labour, late nights, drafting and re-drafting the agreements, and then finally, the all-important signatures that close the deal. It's a buzz.'

'You like to win,' Alice says.

'Yes, of course. Doesn't everyone?'

'Yes, but I think it's pathological with lawyers. It certainly was with him. He was still looking for ways to get back at us, right up until the day he died.'

'I think we've both learned a valuable lesson,' Rebecca adds. 'The fewer lawyers you have in your life, the happier it is.' She obviously realises her mistake as she instantly adds, 'Present company excepted, of course.'

'Of course,' I tell her with a smile. But the damage is done. The events of the day, plus their visceral attacks on John and his profession, have planted a seed of doubt in my mind, and I can feel it taking root with every sip of wine.

9

After a restless night plagued by unsettling dreams, I call Alasdair.

'Hiya. What happened to you?' he asks when he picks up. 'One minute you were there, talking to whatshername, and then I turned around and you'd gone.'

'I got a better offer,' I tell him. 'Anyway, what are you up to this morning?'

'Usual. I've got a stack of emails that need answering. You?'

'Same, but I wondered whether you could spare me a couple of hours. I need some of your wisdom.'

'Is that what we're calling it now?'

'Behave. I'll buy you breakfast.'

'I'm on my way.'

* * *

'So, what's up?' he asks, a little over an hour later. We're settled in a café about ten minutes' walk from my house, sipping our coffees. He's taken full advantage of the fact that I'm paying the bill by ordering a full English breakfast with all the extras, while I've gone for a more figure-friendly avocado on sourdough toast with poached eggs.

'I think I'm just feeling a bit unsettled,' I tell him. 'The combination of the memorial service and my subsequent conversation with Rebecca and Alice.'

'What was wrong with the memorial? It was practically a state funeral. If I get something half as grand when I snuff it, I'll be pleased.'

'Would you though? Let me ask you a question. Of the people who turned out yesterday, how many do you think were there because they genuinely cared about John?'

'I don't know. Does it matter?'

'Let me ask it a different way. Why did you go?'

'Because it was expected. Martin wanted a good turnout from the firm.'

'And that's my point. We were all there because we'd been instructed to go, not because we wanted to pay our respects to a much-loved friend and colleague. All those bigwigs were probably there for the same reason. And, if you think we disliked him, that's nothing compared to the loathing his wife and mistress felt for him. The whole thing was a charade.'

'It was still spectacular though. What's your point?'

'I had a dream last night. I was in a cemetery, watching a burial. It was pouring with rain, you know, like it always is in films. There was a priest there saying some words, and the undertakers, but no mourners. Not one. Even my father had a better turnout than that. It made me sad to think that someone could die and nobody cared enough to attend their funeral. So I moved closer for a better look.'

'Right,' he says, looking baffled.

'I glanced down at the coffin. There was a brass plaque on it with the name of the deceased. It was my name.'

'But this was just a dream, Thea.'

'Yes, but it got me thinking about a phrase, and in the end I had to get up and google it. It turned out to be Charles Darwin, who said "a man's friendships are one of the best measures of his worth". I'd change it for gender-neutral language, of course, but he's got a point, don't you think? None of the people at John's memorial would probably have referred to him as a friend, and I found myself asking who my friends were.'

'I'm your friend.'

'You're probably my best friend, and you're the only person at Morton Lansdowne I've told about my father, but how much do you really know about me?'

'I know lots about you.'

'Go on then. What's my mum's name? What was my favourite TV show when I was growing up?'

'Umm...'

'Let's start with an easier one. What's my sister's name?'

'Ah, I can do that one. It's a herb. Rosemary?'

'Not bad, but it's a spice. Saffron.'

'That's not a measure of friendship though. Friends are there when you need them, like I was this morning.'

I laugh. 'You're all heart. Free breakfast and the possibility of a shag didn't influence your thinking at all.'

'That's a bit harsh, Thea.'

'Sorry. You're right. I'm not myself this morning. Ignore me.'

We're interrupted by the arrival of our food, and the conversation pauses while Alasdair sets about his breakfast with the kind of enthusiasm you'd expect from someone who hasn't had a square meal in ages.

'Why did you go into law?' I ask him as I cut a small piece of sourdough and spear it with my fork.

'You know why. I come from a family of lawyers,' he replies between mouthfuls. 'My father is a lawyer, as was his father. My mother was a solicitor but gave it up when she had children. My brother is a barrister. It's what we do. And you went in because it was hard and you're some sort of weird masochist.'

'Did I tell you I wanted to become a criminal barrister originally? Fighting for justice, pleading my client's case in court, all of that.'

'Why didn't you?'

'Because I quickly realised that I'd either spend a lot of my time defending people who were undoubtedly guilty, or prosecuting people who were probably innocent. Justice might be blind, but there was no way I'd be able to sleep well at night if, for example, I managed to get a rapist acquitted on a technicality. How would I face the victims? And yet, that's exactly what I would have been expected to do.'

'I get that.'

'If I wasn't going to fight for justice then I wanted to be the best of the best, nothing to do with masochism. Everyone kept saying how tough corporate law was, how fiercely competitive, how difficult it was to break into. So, naturally, I set my sights not only on corporate law, but the most competitive of the corporate law firms. And, once I was in, I was 100 per cent focused on getting an associateship, then a senior associateship, and then becoming the youngest ever female partner.'

'And you've achieved all of that.'

I sigh, remembering my dream. 'Yes, but at what *cost*? I've spent my whole life chasing success to prove I'm not like my dad, but what if I've used the wrong yardstick? According to Darwin's quote, I'm an abject failure. Don't get me wrong, you are my friend and I love you to bits, but would we be friends in the outside world if we weren't joined by our profession? What other friends do I have? I've been so totally focused on material success and financial security that I'm scared I've lost sight of everything else that matters. If I died tomorrow, nobody would miss me.'

'Nonsense. I'd miss you, and it sounds like Alice and Rebecca could become friends too,' he offers.

'I wouldn't be so sure. Do you know what they said? "The fewer lawyers you have in your life, the happier it is." Pretty damning, don't you think?'

'Yeah, but that's based on their experiences with one particular lawyer, who was a nasty piece of work. It doesn't extrapolate to all of us.'

'Doesn't it? Name me a happy occasion that has lawyers attached to it.'

He thinks for a moment. 'Buying a home.'

'Uh-uh. If you did a survey of a hundred home buyers and asked them to rate whether the impact of the solicitor on the process was positive or negative, I don't think you'd get a ringing endorsement. Try again.'

'OK, us then.'

'What's so great about us?'

'We oil the wheels of commerce. We make sure that, whatever companies do, it's fair and legal in the jurisdiction where they do it. We hold them accountable.'

I laugh. 'And they show their appreciation by shouting at us, continually complaining about how fucking expensive we are, and generally treating us like slaves.'

'Where are you going with this?'

'Oh, I don't know. Nowhere, probably. I'm just having a wobble. I've been so focused on career progression and being the best I can be that I've never stopped to think whether this is what I actually want. I think, if I'm going to get all psychoanalytical about it, which I certainly was at half past four this morning, it's never been about me.'

'What is it about, then? Your father?'

'Partly, yes.'

'But you're nothing like him, Thea. He was, to be blunt, a waster. Nobody could ever call you that. You're young, idiotically bright and deservedly successful. You've made your point where he's concerned, surely. What else is it about?'

'I don't know if I'll ever completely feel that I've made my point where he's concerned, but thank you. I also wonder whether I've subconsciously been competing with my sister. No, bear with me,' I urge as I can see he's about to snort in disbelief. 'Mum has tried to treat us equally, but Saffy has always been the favourite really. Even when we were small, she got extra privileges because she was older, and she used that to lord it over me. It felt unjust; she may be older, but that doesn't make her a better person. So how do I reverse that?'

'By being the best.'

'Exactly, but it's all meaningless, because I may be more successful than her on paper, be the youngest female partner and all that stuff, but it doesn't matter because it hasn't changed anything. Mum still prefers her because she understands her.'

'You think she doesn't understand you?'

'Oh, she tries to make the right noises, but when I was made partner, it was clear Mum didn't have a clue what that meant, so she just retreated into her comfort zone, which was to talk about Saffy.'

'Have you talked to her about it?'

'Of course not! I'd just come across as whiny and needy. But it does make me wonder if that's another part of the reason why

I've driven myself so hard. There's another quote I had to look up in the small hours. It turned out to come from an American Trappist monk by the name of Thomas Merton, who said: "People may spend their whole lives climbing the ladder of success only to find, once they reach the top, that the ladder is leaning against the wrong wall." And that's the big question, isn't it? Is my ladder leaning against the wrong wall? I've realised I don't want to end up like John Curbishley, where people only come to my memorial out of duty. I want to die surrounded by people I love, and who love me in return. At the moment, I can't see how a career at Morton Lansdowne is going to give me that. I may have proved that I'm not a waster like Dad financially, but I feel like I've clambered to the top of a mountain, only to realise that nobody apart from me cares because I'm completely alone.'

Alasdair studies me for a long time without speaking. I push my half-eaten breakfast to one side, no longer hungry, and sip my coffee, letting my thoughts run wild.

'When was the last time you had a holiday?' he asks eventually.

'What's that got to do with anything?'

'I just wondered if time away from the office would do you good, help you to get some perspective. Are you finishing that?' He indicates my plate, which he slides over to his side of the table when I shake my head.

'I had a week at an all-inclusive in St Lucia last January. I thought I'd give myself a treat before the partnership application process kicked off in earnest.'

'That sounds nice. Was it?'

'No idea. I spent pretty much the whole time in the business centre. Mergers and Acquisitions don't stop just because you're not in the office. I was basically working remotely.'

'But you're a partner now. That gives you more control.'

'It gives me more responsibility. And where do I go from here? Senior partner in X years and then what?'

He sighs. 'You have got it bad, haven't you? Do you need to speak to someone, do you think?'

'I'm talking to you.'

'I meant someone qualified. A counsellor. I'm pretty sure there's something in the company wellbeing policy about them arranging therapy if you need it.'

'And what signal would that give off? I'll tell you. I might as well fix a red flashing light to my head with a sign that says "Look out. Thea's not coping." I'd be downgraded and sidelined faster than you could say "Told you she wasn't up to it." This isn't about whether I'm coping or not.'

'Isn't it?'

'No. It's about whether I *want* to cope.'

'OK, I get you. Final question from me.'

'Go on.'

'Let's say you decide your ladder's against the wrong wall, as you put it, and you chuck it all in. What else would you do?'

'That's the biggest kicker of all,' I tell him. 'I've no idea. But I suspect I'd still need to be the best at it.'

'You're a talented lawyer, Thea. That's why they made you partner. Don't underestimate that, and don't let the events of one day derail you. The junior associates have a nickname for you, did you know that?'

'No. Do I want to?'

'I think you do, because it sums you up nicely. They call you Thearless. Get it? It's the word fearless, but they've substituted in your name. People didn't like John because he was an arse, not because he was a lawyer. People like and respect you, and I'm sure they'll come to your funeral in droves because of that, OK? If it helps, I'll even throw myself on your coffin and wail.'

I smile. 'I'm not sure it does, but thank you.'

'Like you said, this is just a wobble. We all have them from time to time. The trick is to recognise it for what it is, and not make potentially catastrophic career decisions based on it. So, here's Dr Alasdair's prescription. First, I'm going to take you home and use my magical sexual powers to flood you with good mood endorphins. Then, you're going to take the whole of the rest of the weekend off.'

'Your magical sexual powers? Is that what we're calling them now?'

'A guy can hope.'

'The sex sounds fun, but I can't take the weekend off.'

'You can and you must. Go for walks, have a look at the world out there, think about what you want. Maybe even have a chat with your mum. Don't look at your emails; they'll all still be there on Monday morning. Try to imagine what life would be like without the cut and thrust of Morton Lansdowne. I guarantee you'll be in the office champing at the bit come Monday morning, just like you were when they made you partner in the first place.'

'Are you sure?'

'Absolutely.'

'Thank you.'

'What for?'

'For listening to my demented ramblings, I guess.'

He smiles. 'What are friends for?'

10

It's not a wobble. A month has passed since John Curbishley's memorial service and, although I followed Alasdair's advice and I've tried to summon the enthusiasm that I used to feel, it's just not there. In fact, I feel more and more like someone who's trapped on a train that's going in the wrong direction, and there's no sign of a station where I can get off and change tracks. I'm currently sitting in an airless basement meeting room in Paris, trying to find a way over the seemingly endless hurdles in French employment law, which gives workers so much protection it's almost impossible to get rid of them. Normally, this kind of thing energises me; a knotty problem that I can really get my teeth into, but I'm just not feeling it. I'm glad there aren't any windows in here, as I have a horrible suspicion I'd probably let the discussion wash over me while I stared out of them. It's not helped by the fact that the people on the other side of the table keep breaking off into heated discussions in French.

'Shall we take fifteen minutes for a comfort break?' I suggest after one such debate. If I don't get up and move, I'm in danger of going to sleep.

'How do you think it's going?' Laura, one of the junior associates, asks quietly while we're getting coffee. I take a moment to study her; she reminds me of how I was at her stage. I can see the same hunger in her eyes that I used to have.

'Honestly? I have no idea,' I tell her and see the surprise register in her face. Partners aren't supposed to say things like that.

'But we'll get there, right? I mean, there has to be a way to make these people redundant without making the transaction so costly it becomes unviable?'

'If there is, I can't see it. The law is pretty clear. The only way we're going to get rid of these employees will be to be to offer such a ridiculous incentive that it would be frankly cheaper to keep them on and pay them to sit at home and watch TV. On top of that, I get the distinct impression that the guys on the other side of the table are enjoying running rings around us. Time for a change of tack. I'm going to suggest we wrap things up for now. Our client needs to rethink their approach, and it might just unsettle the other side and make them a bit more cooperative if we call a sudden halt.'

'That seems a very high-stakes plan.'

'I don't know about you, Laura, but I can't see any benefit in sitting in that room for the rest of the week while they carry on making us look like idiots. It's not a good use of our time.' I'm already shutting down, looking forward to curling up in my own bed tonight and spending the rest of the week at home. I've always enjoyed travelling, having all the humdrum aspects of life such as food and laundry being taken care of by the expenses policy, but the shine has definitely worn off recently. One hotel room is pretty much like another; yes, they might vary in size and opulence depending on the price, but they all have the same problems. The beds are never as comfortable as your own; the showers always depressingly feeble; the layout impractical for working. I don't know how I never realised this before.

'You're the boss,' Laura says uncertainly.

'I am, and I've decided it's time to get the hell out of here,' I tell her as I pull out my phone to call Janice and get us booked on the next train to London.

* * *

I know pulling the plug like this is a risky strategy, and it seems the senior partners don't think it's the right one if the summons that arrives before we even reach the tunnel is anything to go by. It takes the form of an email from Helen Armitage, the senior partner who has taken the transaction over from John.

> Thea,
>
> I gather you have terminated this week's negotiations prematurely. Please come to my office at 8 a.m. tomorrow for an urgent debrief.
>
> Helen

The phrase 'urgent debrief' is a company euphemism. What it actually means is 'come prepared to have your arse kicked from here to next week'. It's like being invited to a meeting to discuss 'future resourcing', which always means 'you're fired'. Although I've heard of people getting 'urgent debriefing' requests, this is the first time I've received one myself. I stare at the screen for a while, trying to work out why the request hasn't filled me with terror in the way it's supposed to. Although I'm pretty certain I can defend my decision, I know I'm not going to get the chance to do that. The conversations in urgent debriefs tend to be one-sided and loud. After a few minutes, I close my laptop and stare out of the window at the passing countryside.

It's dark by the time I get home. Usually, I'd leave my bag in the hallway to be dealt with later and go straight into the study to get on with some work, but the combination of my despondency about life in general and the impending urgent debrief have robbed me of my usual motivation. Instead, I carry my bag upstairs and unpack it before pouring myself a glass of wine and settling in front of the TV. After a bit of channel hopping, I settle on *Grand Designs*. Tonight's couple have embarked on an ambitious project to convert a former Welsh Methodist Chapel into a family home for them and their three young children. We're only ten minutes in, but already Kevin McCloud is confidently predicting that it's all going to end in tears. Just the kind of schadenfreude I need on a day like today.

By the time we reach the end of the programme, the wine bottle is two-thirds empty and I've also polished off a chicken madras with rice that I found in the freezer. The chapel conversion is stunning; after a few false starts, the couple realised that the best way to get around all the various planning restrictions and other issues thrown up by trying to convert what was basically a poorly insulated barn with pretty windows into a home was not to convert it at all. Instead, they put an entire new 'skin' inside the chapel, ensuring they didn't compromise the structure in the process, and then constructed their home within the skin. They are, of course, horrendously over budget and there were times when their marriage hung by a thread, but even the famously gloomy Kevin can't fault it. I particularly like the way they've aligned the glazing on the inner layer with the stained-glass windows on each side of the chapel. Their other stroke of luck came when the east end of the chapel, where the altar was, proved to be in such a poor state that the only option was to demolish it and replace it. After a bit of to and fro with the council, and yet more overspend, they've installed a glass wall that floods that end of the house with natural light.

For a moment, I'm tempted to see if I can find another episode on catch-up, but I can feel my eyelids beginning to droop so, after clearing away the remains of my meal, I head upstairs to bed.

* * *

Initially, it seems as if Helen doesn't seem to have got the memo on how to conduct an 'urgent debrief' because she's not shouting. Instead, her voice is suspiciously calm and reasonable.

'I was a little surprised,' she begins, 'to be informed by Monsieur Duchamp that you had cancelled the remainder of this week's sessions and pulled the entire team off site. Talk me through your decision process.'

'It's a genuine impasse,' I reply. 'As you know, the deal is only viable to our client if they can shift the software development offshore to their team in Hyderabad.'

'Yes. They've been very clear about that.'

'Unsurprisingly, the French aren't very happy about their developers facing the axe, and the law is on their side. The only way they can get redundancies approved by DIRECCTE, the work inspectorate, is to prove that the company is having economic difficulties that can only be resolved by reducing the workforce. Even then, the workers have to consent. The books clearly show that the company is healthy and they've made it clear there's no way the workers are going to consent. We're out of options and there didn't seem to be any point in sitting there while they said the same thing over and over again. They were enjoying humiliating us, so I decided to take back control the only way I could think of, by calling a halt to the negotiations while we re-grouped. I didn't really see what else we could do.'

'But you made an executive decision to pull our client out of the process without even consulting them. How do you think they feel about that?'

Uh-oh. Here we go.

'Here's my problem,' she says, and her voice is positively saccharine, making me jump when she suddenly starts shouting. 'It wasn't your decision to make, you *fucking imbecile*. Do you have even the first idea how much damage you've done? Quite apart from the loss of billing revenue, you've made a laughing stock out of both us and our client. If you think I'm angry, I'm not a patch on them. They're not only threatening to ditch us for literally any other law firm, but they're also talking about suing us to recoup their spend so far.'

'I think that's a little—'

'Shut up! I don't want to hear you say another word. You've fucked this so badly, I don't even know if it's unfuckable. What you've done is sailed into the battle of Trafalgar and then promptly run away because the French "looked a bit fighty". How do you think that looks?'

'What was I supposed to do? I told you we were getting nowhere.'

'For starters, it might have been a good idea to talk to me before you went off half-cocked. I'd have told you to stay in that fucking room, nodding and smiling, while the associates worked their arses off behind the scenes to find a way around it and I got new instructions from the client. What you were not, I repeat, *not* supposed to do was pull the fucking plug and flounce off site without consulting anyone. What the hell is the matter with you?'

She's right. I should have talked to her before pulling the

team. Hindsight is a wonderful thing, but now there's nothing I can do except sit here politely while she hurls a torrent of abuse at me. I'm strangely calm about it though, because somewhere between the point where she compares my intellectual ability unfavourably to a woodlouse's and her detailed description of the anatomically challenging things the other senior partners want to do to me, something inside me has very quietly snapped, a bit like one of those strands of mozzarella when you pull a slice of pizza away.

'Do you understand?' she finally concludes. I'm not sure I do, because I've tuned out most of the last five minutes, but I have no desire to prolong this meeting, so I simply nod my head.

'Good. Get out. I've got a deal to save.'

'Are you OK?' Janice is waiting for me in my office. 'I walked past Helen's room a few minutes ago and she certainly wasn't holding back.'

'I'm fine, thanks, Janice.'

'Of course you are. If it's any consolation, she may have barked but she's not going to bite. Not hard, anyway.' She lowers her voice even though we're the only two people in the room. 'She missed a filing deadline once when she was a junior partner. The fines were astronomical, and Martin was so angry we thought he was going to have a stroke.'

I know she's trying to make me feel better, but I just need five minutes alone. 'Janice,' I say. 'I know it's not your job, but would you mind very much fetching me a flat white? I'd rather not be around other people right now.'

'Of course.' She bustles off and I open my laptop and start composing an email. It's brief and to the point, and I read it a couple of times before clicking send. I haven't even finished my coffee before I'm summoned to see Helen again.

'Sit down,' she instructs, closing the door behind me. 'Look.

I realise I may have said some things in the heat of the moment earlier which might be considered upsetting, but I think this is disproportionate.' She holds up a printout of my email.

I stay silent.

'You must have realised that HR would send it on to me,' she continues when she clocks that I'm not going to say anything. 'I've had a chat with them and they agreed not to take it any further until I had the opportunity to talk to you. Obviously, nobody is going to try to coerce you if you genuinely feel this is what you want, but I'm begging you to reconsider. Today is just a bad day in the office; we've all had them. Yes, I'm pissed off, but I think I'm allowed to be in the circumstances, and the good news is that I've already had a couple of phone conversations and it looks like it might just be fixable. Don't do this, Thea. Learn from your mistakes and do better. You're a good lawyer who made a mistake. You're not the first, and like I said, it looks like we might be able to get things back on track.'

I stay silent.

'Why don't you take the rest of today off and think about what you want to do? I can probably sit on this for a day.'

'I have thought about it,' I tell her firmly. 'I'm sorry, Helen, but this is what I want.'

'You realise that the next person to see this will be Martin. He's not going to react well.'

'As someone said to me only a few minutes ago in this very room, I can't go to the battle of Trafalgar expecting a cup of tea and a biscuit.'

'That's not quite what I said, but are you absolutely sure?'

'I am.'

'OK.'

The summons to see Martin comes so quickly that I barely have time to sit back down at my desk. 'What the hell have you done?' Janice asks when she relays the message. 'The office rumour mill is in overdrive. Everyone knows something big is going down, and that you're at the centre of it, but beyond that it's all increasingly wild speculation.'

'I'll fill you in as soon as I've talked to Martin, I promise,' I tell her as I head for the lifts.

'Go straight in,' Margaret tells me when I reach Martin's office on the eighth floor. 'He's expecting you.'

Martin is sitting behind his desk and gestures to the chair in front of it as Margaret softly closes the door.

'What,' he growls, waving the printout of my email, 'the bloody hell is this?'

'It's my resignation.'

'I can see that. Please tell me this isn't some kind of hissy fit because Helen shouted at you. You're made of stronger stuff than that.'

'It's not a hissy fit.'

'What is it then? Someone made you a better offer? I'll warn you now, they'll likely retract it as soon as they hear about the little stunt you just pulled in Paris.'

'Nobody's made me any offers.'

'Then I don't understand.'

'This isn't a knee-jerk reaction to my meeting with Helen, I promise. I get that I fucked up and I completely deserved most of what she said. The truth is that I don't want this, Martin. Not enough, anyway. You've always said that a good corporate lawyer has to be hungry for success. I'm not hungry any more. I'm tired, fed up, and losing interest. I fucked up the Paris deal because I was bored, and that's not good for me or Morton Lansdowne.'

He stares at me for an age, and then sighs.

'I get it. I've seen that look before. Believe it or not, you're not the first person to do this. There was a guy in my intake, absolutely fabulous lawyer who streaked ahead of the rest of us. He was the youngest senior partner ever appointed and then, one day, quite out of the blue, he just decided he'd had enough. I remember desperately trying to persuade him to change his mind, but he had the same look in his eyes that you have.'

'What happened to him?'

'He left, bought a house in Dorset and took up beekeeping. He never looked back. I hope this proves to be a similarly serendipitous decision for you, Thea. We'll miss you.'

'I haven't gone yet,' I tell him. 'I have three months' notice to serve.'

'I don't think it would be in either of our interests to for you to do that, and I'm sure it wouldn't be good for general morale. It's probably best for everyone if we wrap this up quickly. We'll honour our contractual obligations, naturally. I'll leave the HR department to take you through all of that.' He stands and holds out his hand for me to shake. 'Goodbye, Thea, and good luck.'

11

If you ever want to find out if you're as indispensable at work as everyone tells you you are, try resigning. As a partner, I certainly expected the process of offboarding me, as the HR department described it, to take a week or two at a bare minimum. I'm therefore more than a little surprised to be handing in my car park pass and nosing the Porsche out of the parking lot for the final time just as most of the workers in the offices around us are heading out for lunch.

By the time I was finished with Martin, an HR representative was already waiting to take me down for my exit interview. As soon as they realised that I wasn't carrying a grudge or planning to sue, they pretty much lost interest and just took me through the paperwork instead. The only thing that surprised me at that point was that, despite resigning, I'm being put on gardening leave for nine months, during which time I'm not allowed to work for any other law firms. When I queried it, they told me that it was standard practice because I currently have sensitive information that could benefit competitors, so they were protecting themselves. I'm also not allowed to talk to anyone from Morton Lansdowne or any other commercial law firm during that time, which is going to be a bit tricky for Alasdair and me. At the end of the gardening leave, I'll be paid for a further three months in lieu of notice, and the restrictions will be lifted as hopefully any information I have will be out of date by then.

It was a curiously banal process which made me realise that they didn't actually care about me as a person at all. I came away with the distinct impression that none of us are anything more than payroll numbers as far as HR is concerned; what we actually do or the rank we hold is totally irrelevant to them. I was tempted to point out the lack of humanity in Human Resources, but I think the irony would have been lost on them.

After HR had 'processed' me, I had yet another meeting with Helen Armitage. This time, however, she'd also summoned two other junior partners based purely, from what I was able to gather, on the fact that they happened to be in the office today. Laura, the junior associate who'd been in Paris with me, was also there and seemed a little overwhelmed by everything, if the wide-eyed looks she kept giving me were anything to go by. It took just over an hour to hand over the current transaction and then that was it. Janice was summoned to help me clear my office, which took no more than five minutes because I hardly had anything personal in there, and she escorted me down to the parking lot and relieved me of my pass. The most emotional moment came courtesy of Alana, who'd applied and failed to get partner at the same time as me. She marched into my office and delivered an impassioned monologue about how I was a disgrace to feminism and why had I bothered applying for partnership, a role that most people (especially her) would crawl over their dead grandmother's body for, if I was just going to chuck it in the bin after little more than six months? I would have explained, only, having delivered her message, she promptly turned on her heel and stalked out again, leaving Janice and me staring after her in disbelief.

Janice was her typical efficient self, and I've realised that she's probably the only person at Morton Lansdowne that I'm actually going to miss. Apart from Alasdair, of course. I wonder how he'll take the news? He's in Ireland at the moment, so I imagine it will take a while for word to reach him. I would have liked to be able to tell him myself, but the gardening leave ban means I can't. I hope he'll be OK. I guess we couldn't have continued as we were forever, so maybe this is for the best where he's concerned as well.

I did make a vague plan on the way home to knock on Rebecca's door and see if she was free for lunch, but there's no sign of her SUV when I pull into the space outside my house. I haven't seen her properly since we buried the hatchet on the day of John Curbishley's memorial service, but we've waved to each other a few times when I've been working in my study over the weekend and she and Rollo have passed my window on their way to or from one of his activities.

As I let myself into the house, I automatically turn left into my study, before I realise that I have no reason to be in here and no laptop to sit down in front of. This is the moment when the enormity of what I've done hits me properly, and I suddenly feel a bit wobbly. I make my way carefully into the kitchen, where I pour myself a glass of water, holding it with both hands as I drink so as not to drop it. After refilling the glass, I sink down onto one of the sofas in the living space and lower my head into my hands. I don't even realise I'm crying until the first fat, salty tear drops off my chin and makes a wet mark on my blouse. I study the stain with fascination; I can't remember the last time I cried. I've been angry plenty of times during my time at Morton Lansdowne, frustrated too, but I've never cried. I'm not even sure what I'm crying for. It's not as if they sacked me or made me redundant; this was purely my decision. So why the hell am I sobbing like my heart is broken?

My impromptu and unexplained self-pity fest is interrupted by the sound of a key being inserted in the front door. My first thought is that maybe Janice has come to check up on me, but that's obviously not possible as she returned my front door key before I left. Before I have a chance to come up with any other theories, the door swings open to reveal a wiry man who I guess must be in his mid-forties. He's whistling a tune I don't recognise and carrying what looks like a large gym bag. I've never seen him in my life before. He's totally oblivious to me as he closes the front door, but my heart is thumping hard in my chest. *Who the hell is he, and why does he have a key to my house?* The thought has barely registered before my mind conjures up a more sinister scenario. *He's got some sort of weapon in the bag. He's going to murder me, put me in the bag and then bury me somewhere in the woods.* By the time he finally notices me, I've gone into full fight-or-flight mode.

'Who the hell are you, and what are you doing in my house?' I demand, springing to my feet and trying to look as imposing as I can which, given that he must be at least a foot taller than me, isn't very successful.

'I am Lukasz,' he replies in a thick Eastern European accent, as if it's the most obvious thing in the world. 'I come to water your plants.' He points at the hanging baskets and flowerpots on the other side of the bifold doors.

The initial relief that he's not going to attack me after all is short lived, as I now realise how rude I've just been.

'I'm so sorry,' I tell him in a more conciliatory tone. 'It's just that I've never seen you before, and it was a bit of a surprise.'

He smiles. 'I have never seen you before either. My boss, he gives me the key of your house and he says, "Lukasz, you must look after the plants for this lady. She has a very important job and is very busy." So, every few days, I come here and I take care of them for you.'

'Thank you. They do look amazing.'

He nods to acknowledge the compliment. 'I hope you don't mind me asking, but you look sad. Did you receive bad news?'

God, my face is probably a mess. Funnily enough, I never considered how I looked while I was busy being convinced I was facing my untimely end. 'No,' I reply. 'I'm fine. I just had a bit of a shock, that's all. I'll go and sort myself out while you carry on.'

Before he has a chance to say any more, I bolt up the stairs into my bathroom, shutting and locking the door behind me. I look at myself in the mirror and I'm amazed poor Lukasz didn't turn and run. I look like I've escaped from some kind of mental institution. However, before I get a chance to sort myself out, the tears restart. This is ridiculous; I can't spend the whole day crying, particularly as I'm still not 100 per cent sure what it is I'm crying about.

'Pull yourself together, Thea, for God's sake,' I tell my reflection crossly, before turning on the taps and attacking my face with the flannel. The end result is not pretty; my skin is red and blotchy, particularly around my eyes, but at least the sad panda look is gone.

When I tentatively make my way back downstairs, Lukasz has gone but I can tell he's watered everything because the hanging baskets are dripping noisily onto the paving slabs below. What a strange way to earn a living, I think to myself as I watch the droplets of water hitting the ground. I wonder how many houses he has the keys to. How many houses does he visit each day, doing exactly what he does for me? I mean, he was here for, what, ten minutes? Instinctively, I start to do the maths in my head. Assuming he works an eight-hour day and allowing twenty minutes between appointments, that's sixteen houses every day. My mind now switches tack, and I hurry into my study to find the paperwork for my garden contract. It only takes seconds to confirm what I thought; I pay £100 per month for 'gardening services'. Assuming Lukasz is here for ten minutes, three times a week, that translates to half an hour per week or two hours a month, which means his employer is essentially charging me £50 an hour to pour water into some pots. I doubt very much that Lukasz is being paid that much, which means that there's a middleman creaming a fat profit off me.

I'm just about to pick up the phone to call the company and tell them I'm cancelling the contract because their charges are ridiculous when the hypocrisy of the situation hits me. As a partner at Morton Lansdowne, I was charged out at over £500 per hour. I am, or at least I was, corporate Lukasz. The reminder of the sudden loss of my identity overwhelms me as the tears start falling freely once more. I have no idea how long I sit at the desk in my study crying my heart out, but it feels like an age. When it eventually stops, I go back upstairs and give my face another good wash before checking the time. Three o'clock. How can it only be three o'clock when so much has happened today? Normally, I'd be in the thick of things with at least another five hours to go before leaving the office. How on earth do people manage to fill their days if they don't work? At this rate, I'll be stir crazy by six, and that's just today. What the hell am I going to do tomorrow, and the day after that?

Thankfully, before I can go too much further down this particular rabbit hole, my phone pings with a message and I see it's from Alasdair.

> You RESIGNED? WTAF Thea?? I'm in meetings till 8.30 but will call you after.

Shit. What am I going to do? After thinking for a while, I tap out a message that I'm pretty certain won't get me into trouble, even if they find it.

> Turns out it wasn't just a wobble after all. I'm fine, don't worry about me. This is what I want. Plus, I'm not really supposed to talk to anyone from work while I'm on gardening leave – sorry *sad face*. Take care of yourself, won't you. Tx

I am really going to miss him, but the more I think about it, the more I think it's for the best. A clean break for both of us. Although I enjoy his company and the sex is fun, he probably needs to meet someone who can give him more than I can and, after nine months of enforced no contact, he's bound to have moved on. As for me, who knows? I do sometimes wonder if my 'one' is out there, but on balance I doubt it. All my relationships to date have been casual, like Alasdair. On the rare occasions I've allowed myself to contemplate taking things to a deeper level, something inside me has pushed back; proper relationships sound very needy and draining to me.

After staring aimlessly out of my study window for a while, I decide I need to make a to-do list. I rummage in my bag and pull out my notebook and fountain pen. Most of my colleagues take notes with biros, but I've always preferred the feel of a fountain pen, much to their amusement. Turning to a fresh, blank sheet, I start to write:

1. *Update family.*
2. *Figure out what to do now.*
3. *...*

I stare and stare at the empty third item, willing my mind to come up with something, but it's overpowered by item two. What on earth am I going to do with the rest of my life?

12

I'm still staring at the piece of paper when a movement outside catches my eye, and I look up to see Rebecca's SUV pull into the space in front of my car. I smile as she carefully positions it to make sure it's not on the kerb, before opening the back door to allow Rollo to climb out. Feeling the need to hear a friendly voice, I quickly cross to the front door and open it.

'Nice parking,' I call.

She turns and grins. 'You have to be so careful round here. I haven't worked out who it is yet, but some busybody reports you to the council if there's so much as a wheel out of place.'

'Really?' I reply. 'I wonder if that's the same one who reports your car as abandoned if you don't move it frequently enough.'

'Bound to be,' she says, laughing. 'Anyway, how are you? I don't think I've seen you working from home on a weekday before.'

'I'm not working from home,' I tell her. 'I quit this morning.'

'Really? Someone made you an offer you couldn't refuse?'

'Nope. I decided I needed a change of career.'

'Sounds interesting. What's the plan?'

'No idea.'

Her mouth drops open. 'Wait a minute. Are you seriously telling me you've quit a lucrative career without the first clue what you're going to do next?'

'Yup.'

'Bloody hell. You've either got lady-balls of steel or you've lost the plot.'

I smile. 'I guess I'm about to find out.'

Rollo tugs at her sleeve. 'Mum, we're going to be late,' he whines.

'Sorry, darling. Listen, I've got to run but why don't you come over for a glass of wine later if you're not busy?'

'I can assure you I'm not busy. What time?'

'Eight? I'll have fed this one and we can have a proper catch-up.'

'I'll see you later then.'

I stand and watch as Rebecca and Rollo hurry up the road and into her house. I've got something to look forward to now. It's only a glass of wine with a friend-slash-acquaintance, but it's a start, and maybe a proper friendship will come out of it.

Returning to my study, I stare at the paper again for a while, before scratching out number three on the list. Number one is easy to get out of the way, and number two is going to take a lot of figuring out. Everything else can wait.

I pull out my mobile and dial Mum and Phil's number.

'Thea!' my mum exclaims when the call connects. 'What a treat. You never call in the week.'

'I've got some news,' I tell her carefully.

'You've been promoted again, haven't you? Oh, darling, congratulations.'

'I haven't been promoted. I resigned.'

'You what?'

'I quit. I decided I didn't want to do this any more and I handed in my resignation.'

There's an uncomprehending silence. 'But you love your job,' she says eventually.

'I *loved* my job. Past tense.'

'Oh, darling.' Her tone has changed to one of concern. 'Is everything all right? You aren't ill, are you?'

'I'm fine.'

'Then I don't understand, sorry. You've wanted to be a lawyer since forever, and you've worked so hard to get to where you are. Why would you chuck it all away?'

I sigh. This was never going to be an easy conversation, but I'm pleased she's engaged, at least. Normally, she'd have switched to telling me about Saffy's latest achievement by now. I tell her about my wobble after John Curbishley's funeral, and how I just lost the love for what I do.

'Do you think you ought to talk to someone?' she says very carefully when I finish.

'Like who?'

'I don't know, some sort of professional. A counsellor, maybe.'

'What, you think I'm having some sort of breakdown?' I ask incredulously.

'I wouldn't say breakdown,' she replies hurriedly. 'But this is a big thing, and it's very unlike you. I just wondered whether maybe things have all got a bit much for you lately. They do work you ridiculously hard. You might be suffering from burnout or something like that.'

'I'm not suffering from anything,' I tell her robustly. 'I just decided I wanted to do something different with my life, that's all.'

'But you've invested so much in this and you're obviously

good at it. I just wonder, if you talked it all through with someone who knows about these things, whether it might be helpful. How are you sleeping?'

'What's that got to do with anything?'

'I read an article recently about how not sleeping well is linked to depression.'

'I'm not depressed, Mum, and I sleep just fine.'

'OK. Will you do one thing for me though?'

'What?'

'Come and stay, just for a few days. I'm worried about you. You were so thin and pale at Christmas, and now this. Let us look after you for a bit while you recover. I'm sure Saffy would be pleased to see you too.'

'I don't need to recover, because there's nothing wrong with me.' I'm starting to get seriously pissed off now.

'Well, the invitation's there if you want it. Think about it?'

'Fine. I will.'

The conversation wraps up pretty swiftly after that. I think Mum realised that she hadn't handled it particularly well and I didn't really feel like talking to her after she'd effectively questioned my sanity. My mood is a lot darker as I stare out of the window. Am I burnt out? Is this a breakdown? I don't feel like either of those things are true, but all the tears I've shed this afternoon might be telling a different story. As if on cue, they start falling again. What on earth is the matter with me? How can I have gone from high-flying lawyer to weeping wallflower in the space of just a few hours?

'For God's sake, get a grip, Thea,' I mutter angrily as I dab roughly at my eyes.

I unlock my phone again and launch the browser, entering 'Symptoms of depression' into the search box. Most of them I can dismiss easily. 'Low sex drive or low self-esteem' are definite nos. Some of them are just irritating, like 'neglecting your hobbies'. 'I'm a lawyer,' I snarl at the phone. 'I don't have time for hobbies.' However, 'feeling tearful' strikes a nerve, as does 'finding it difficult to make decisions'. In the end, I decide to cut myself some slack on that last one; I've made a pretty life-changing decision today, so the fact that I couldn't put together more than two items on my to-do list shouldn't be a cause for concern.

So I'm tearful, that's all. Nothing to see here; move along, please.

* * *

Things are no better the next day. My drink with Rebecca last night was great fun, and I was tipsily congratulating myself on our blossoming friendship as I made my way home. However, as soon as I got into bed and tried to go to sleep, it was as if my mind had been waiting for just this moment to go into overdrive.

'What the hell have you done?' it whispered.

'It's fine. It's the right thing.'

'Is it? You shot your career in the face without a backup plan? I thought you said you weren't like your father, but this looks exactly like the kind of thing he would have done.'

'He wouldn't have done it, because he would never have got as far as I did in the first place, and I've got a whole year to come up with a plan.'

'Ha. You'll be so intensely bored by the end of next week you'll be crying out to go back. Would they have you back?'

'Probably not, but it doesn't matter. I don't want to go back.'

'You will. Maybe your mum's right. Maybe you're depressed, or burnt out. You should have just asked for a break, rather than burning the whole thing to the ground. You're an idiot, and you've ruined everything.'

'I know what I'm doing. It'll be better once I have a plan.'

'Honey, you patently don't have a clue what you're doing. People who know what they're doing don't nuke jobs they've trained their whole lives for.'

After a sleepless night, I called my mother again and took her up on her invitation to stay. I was surprised how delighted she sounded, and also how good it made me feel. Although I'm still a bit annoyed with her, the idea of home-cooked food and people around me is a lot more appealing than sitting in my house staring at the walls and eating ready meals of uncertain age from the freezer.

I've had to pull off the M20 into Maidstone services because I've been crying most of the way here. If I turn up at Mum and Phil's like this, they'll pack me off to a lunatic asylum before I've even crossed the threshold. At least I'm more prepared today; I couldn't find any tissues at home but I've crammed a load of loo roll into the glovebox so, once I've finished my latest episode, I'll use that to dry my face before sorting out my makeup using the rearview mirror. As I wait for the tears to stop, I turn my attention to the people coming and going around me. I'm reminded a little of how I felt walking to Skinners' Hall after John Curbishley's funeral inasmuch as I feel I really don't belong here, outside, during the day. This is going to take quite a bit of getting used to.

* * *

'Darling! We're so glad you could make it,' Mum exclaims as she opens the door and wraps me in a hug. From the tone of her voice, you'd be forgiven for thinking I was bestowing some enormous favour on her, rather than the other way around. 'I've made up your room and lunch will be on the table soon. Phil's at work, of course, so it'll just be you and me. How long do you think you'll be able to stay for?'

'I don't know. A couple of days? I don't really have any plans but I don't want to get under your feet.'

'You won't be under my feet. You're always welcome here, Thea. Stay as long as you want. It'll be a treat having you around again.'

I can't decide if she's being genuine or just over-compensating for suggesting I'm having some sort of breakdown yesterday. As she gently releases me, I look into her eyes and try to read her, but it's impossible.

'Why don't you take your things upstairs now, and then you can settle in after lunch. I told Saffy you were coming and she's promised to call in after she's finished work.'

Of course, she would have been on the phone to Saffy the moment our call was over. I do feel a flash of irritation as I carry my overnight bag upstairs to my old room. Could I not have had my mother to myself, just for once? I banish the thought as soon as it appears. Now is not the time for childish competition. She's probably a bit anxious because she doesn't know if I'm going to suddenly start acting all erratically, and has called in Saffy for backup. Actually, it will be nice to see her and maybe she can help me manage Mum.

I'm no longer surprised by the tears that spring from my eyes as I open the door of my bedroom. Nothing has changed in here since I moved out to go to university and, as I gaze around the room, it feels a little bit like all the years since have been for nothing. I was so certain what I wanted to do back then, and I'd laid out every step to achieving my goals. I open the top drawer of the desk I spent so many hours at, doing schoolwork and revision. Inside, among various other nicknacks, is the A4 pad I was using for revision notes during my A levels. I turn to the back page and there, in my neat handwriting, is my career plan laid out like a flowchart. My eyes blur as I read it; I achieved every one of those goals apart from senior partner by forty. In fact, I hit junior partner quicker than I'd originally planned; on my world domination chart I'd written that I'd get there when I was thirty-five.

I wonder what eighteen-year-old Thea would make of the soggy mess standing here now. I don't think she'd be very sympathetic. I've always been a fighter and I think she'd feel that I'd let her down by giving up and throwing in the towel like this.

After listening carefully to make sure that Mum's still downstairs, I cross the landing to the bathroom to sort out the mess the latest crying bout will have made, before going down to join her for lunch. A couple of days is all I'll need, I tell myself. Make it clear to them that I'm not mad, enjoy Mum's cooking, and I'll be right as rain by the end of the weekend.

13

So, that worked out well then. Having thought a few days would be all I needed, it's actually four weeks later when I finally point the Porsche back towards London and home. To say it's been intense would be an understatement. Things unravelled as soon as I got downstairs for my first lunch with Mum; she'd obviously been working her socks off between my call and my arrival, as all my favourite foods were on the table. The sight of it set me off, and of course me crying started her crying, and we were still fairly soggy when Saffy joined us late in the afternoon. By the time Phil got home, you'd have been forgiven for thinking that we'd just come back from having a much-loved pet put down, from the state of the three of us.

The other thing, apart from the semi-constant weeping, that caught me by surprise was how tired I was. After the first, very emotional, day, Mum had to wake me and send me to bed just after nine as I'd fallen asleep on the sofa, and I didn't surface again until nearly midday the next day. In fact, for the first week or so, I think I slept more than I was awake. This was probably a good thing in retrospect, because I still spent an awful lot of my waking hours in tears. Mum and Phil were obviously worried, but thankfully salvation arrived in the form of Tim, Saffy's GP husband, who was summoned to examine me after a few days had gone by with no visible sign of improvement. After asking a lot of questions about my general wellbeing and whether I'd had any suicidal thoughts, he pronounced his verdict.

'I don't think you're having a breakdown, Thea,' he'd told me. 'I think you're bereaved.'

'Bereaved?' I'd asked. 'I don't understand.'

'You may not have lost a loved one in the traditional sense, but you have lost something very precious to you. It's not about the job, the salary or the prestige, although I'm sure those things were nice. Your whole identity was tied up in your career. You're grieving for yourself.'

My first thought had been to dismiss what he was saying as gibberish but, rather than jumping down his throat like old Thea would have done, I let his appraisal sit with me for a while and, in the end, I had to agree he was spot on. It was such a relief to have a diagnosis that I could relate to that I burst into tears yet again, but for the first time I knew why I was crying. After that, I started to feel better. I've been very fragile, but I'm feeling much stronger now. Even so, we've agreed that I should only return to London for a few days this time, just to see how I get on.

I do feel totally different, like I've shed my armour and I'm suddenly soft and vulnerable. There are still flashes of 'old' Thea; she hasn't departed completely, but the constant drive to do better, to chase after the next life goal, has gone. I still have no idea what I'm going to do next, but I'm much more at peace with that. I've also taken a surprising amount of enjoyment in things that would have horrified 'old' Thea, including a rapidly developing addiction to the daytime TV programme *Homes*

Under the Hammer. If you've never seen it, it's a similar concept to *Grand Designs*, inasmuch as every episode follows two or three people who have each bought a run-down property at auction. Unlike *Grand Designs*, the participants in this show generally transform the house or flat on a comparatively modest budget before selling it on for a fat profit. There are occasional disasters, but it's generally feel-good viewing that reminds me how lucky I was with both my house and Brian the fabulous builder.

I feel unexpectedly anxious as I pull up and get out of the car. After the intense emotional journey I've been on, to be confronted with 'old' Thea's life is challenging. The first thing that strikes me as I let myself in is how cold it is in here. I'm never usually here at this time on a weekday, so the heating doesn't kick in automatically until six. I'm shivering as I hit the override button on the boiler control, before running upstairs to find a thick jumper to put on until the house warms up. Mum insisted on washing my clothes before I came home, so I unpack them into the chest of drawers and sit down on the bed. This would have been a dangerous manoeuvre a couple of weeks ago, as I would almost certainly have crawled under the covers and gone straight to sleep, but now I take the opportunity to look around. I've spent countless nights in here, mostly on my own and sometimes with Alasdair, but the thing I notice now is the lack of pictures. There are a couple of prints on the wall, but no photos. In fact, there aren't any photos in the whole house. It's my home, and it's nicely furnished and decorated, but there's actually nothing of *me* here. It could be an Airbnb for all the personality I've injected into it.

Feeling the need for a cup of coffee to help warm me up, I make my way back down to the kitchen. What I find in there is just as depressing. The cupboards aren't completely bare, but again it looks like the kind of thing you'd find in a holiday home. A small bottle of olive oil that I don't even remember buying, salt and pepper and a barely used bottle of vinegar that I got ages ago because Alasdair kept complaining that the local chippy never put enough vinegar on his fish and chips. There is a tin of some fancy ground coffee that I probably bought when I first moved here, but a quick sniff of that is not encouraging. I try to remember the last time I made my own cup of coffee, but I can't. Anytime I've wanted it before, I've just popped to the excellent coffee shop round the corner for a takeaway.

The fridge is completely bare apart from another bottle of milk that I can tell has gone solid without needing to open it, and the freezer contains nothing except a small bag of peas that have definitely seen better days, two ready meals, and some furry ice cubes in the tray. After four weeks of Mum's cooking, the ready meals look unappetising to say the least. Did I really live on this stuff? Of course, the truth is that I hardly ever ate here except for Saturday and Sunday nights when I wasn't travelling. I can't even remember the last time I cooked a meal from scratch.

This is enough to energise me, and I pull out one of the cookbooks that I bought as part of the kitchen décor and start leafing through it, searching for inspiration. However, I'm quickly put off by the lists of weird-sounding ingredients that I've never heard of. What even is za'atar, anyway? I push the book back into the rack and take out another one that looks more user friendly. After a while, I come across a recipe for shepherd's pie. Perfect, warming comfort food. I take a picture of the ingredients on my phone before writing a list of everything else I think I need, including coffee. I've hardly touched a drop of alcohol while I've been at Mum and Phil's as Tim thought it would probably be better to avoid it while I was so vulnerable, but the idea of a nice glass of red to go with the shepherd's pie is very appealing, so I add a bottle to the list.

* * *

I'm feeling very pleased with myself a few hours later. The house is warm, I've stocked up on the essentials, and the onion and carrots I've lovingly chopped are sweating nicely in the pan. I've peeled potatoes and cut them into chunks ready to boil at the right moment. I'm just about to add the lamb mince to the vegetables when the doorbell goes.

'Hi,' Rebecca says when I open the door. 'I saw your car. You haven't been around for a while.'

'Yeah, I've been away,' I tell her.

'Anywhere nice?'

'Just spending some time with my family. How are you?'

'Yeah, I'm all right.' Her tone is surprisingly downbeat.

'You don't sound it. Is everything OK?'

'It's been better, but I'll live. I'm a fighter.'

Her final sentence resonates hard with me, and I decide I can't let it go.

'What's up? Talk to me, Rebecca. It's not Rollo, is it?'

'Oh, no, he's happy as a lark now that he knows he's not going to have to go to boarding school. We've had a long chat about his extra-curricular activities too, and dropped all the ones he didn't like, so he's like a pig in clover. The issue is the house. I haven't told him yet, but I'm going to have to sell.'

'Why? I thought Alice said she was going to make everything all right.'

'It's not her fault. Well, not really. I wasn't surprised to find that John didn't leave anything in his will for me, but I was pissed off that he didn't leave anything to Rollo either. I mean, he's just as much John's son as the other two. Alice is doing what she can, but her priorities are obviously going to be herself and her boys. I'm sure it won't surprise you to know that my house is in John's name. So, legally, Alice could turf me out anytime. However, what she's said is she'll sign the house over to me as soon as probate is granted, but I'll have to take on the mortgage from that point as well.'

'That seems generous and fair. What's the issue?'

'How am I going to get a mortgage? There's plenty of equity in the house, but I'd still need to borrow something in the region of half a million pounds. Even if I had a job, it wouldn't earn anywhere near enough to get that. Sorry, what's that smell?'

'Oh, shit. Come in for a minute.'

I hastily turn off the heat but it's too late. My beautiful vegetables are charred, smoking crisps and there's thick acrid smoke billowing out of the pan.

'Is there oil in there?' Rebecca asks.

'Yes. I was softening the vegetables.'

'It looks like it's about to ignite. Quickly, grab a tea towel and rinse it under the tap, then cover the pan with it.'

I follow her instructions and I'm alarmed by the hiss as the wet material makes contact with the metal.

'God, I'm *so* sorry,' Rebecca says. 'I didn't realise you were cooking or I would never have distracted you.'

'It's my fault,' I tell her. 'If I'm honest, I completely forgot that it was there. I'm not sure cooking is my forte.'

'What were you making?'

'Shepherd's pie, at least that was the plan. I'm not sure what to do now, as I only bought one onion and a couple of carrots like the recipe said.'

'Can I see?'

I show her the book. 'My mum's an excellent cook,' I tell her. 'So I thought I'd have a go at making something from scratch myself.'

Her eyes widen. 'You mean you've never cooked before?'

'Well, I have, but it was a long time ago.'

'How long?'

I blush. 'University.'

'Bloody hell! Sorry, that's rude. Can I ask what you've been living on?'

'Well, when I was at work, I could just order stuff in. When I was travelling I'd eat in whichever hotel I was staying at, and when I was here I'd either get something delivered or have a ready meal.'

'OK, look. The least I can do is replace your ruined ingredients.' She carefully lifts the tea towel and inspects the blackened vegetables. 'I think this is probably safe now. You might need a new pan though. I really am sorry.'

'Like I said, it's my fault,' I tell her as inspiration strikes. 'Actually, how do you feel about being my guinea pig? Rollo too.'

She laughs. 'You do like to make life hard for yourself, don't you? Your first time in the kitchen in however many years and you decide to throw a dinner party?'

'It's hardly a dinner party. The recipe says it serves four. I was just going to portion the rest up and freeze it, but if you don't have anything else on, I'd love to cook for you both. If it's a disaster, we'll order in. What do you say? I owe you, so it's the least I can do.'

'How did you figure that out?'

'You've had me over twice. It must be time I returned the favour.'

She smiles. 'OK, you're on.'

14

Another six weeks have passed and I'm pretty much back to my old self. What I'm struggling to understand now is how on earth I ever found time to work, let alone put in the long hours and late nights that I don't miss at all. I seem to have embraced a life of leisure with surprising ease and, although I know I need to figure out a plan at some point, the cushion of my gardening leave and pay in lieu of notice means I'm in much less of a hurry than I was.

A lot of it is doubtless down to my blossoming friendship with Rebecca. Our weekdays tend to follow a pattern where she takes Rollo to school in the morning, and then we hit the gym together for an hour or so, always making sure to be back in time for *Homes Under the Hammer*, to which we're both completely addicted. One of us will then make lunch, or some-times we go out, and then she potters off to collect Rollo from school and I take care of any chores I need to do. I'm turning into a bit of a domestic goddess, even though I say so myself. Although I can still easily afford both Lukasz and Ramona, the cleaner from the same agency, I've decided to dispense with them and look after these things myself while I'm not working. It hasn't been a complete success; in my enthusiasm, I over watered the hanging baskets at first, but a bit of online searching helped me to understand why the plants were looking considerably less healthy than they did under Lukasz's care. Most of them have recovered reasonably well, but I did have to replace a couple and invest in some plant food to put back some of the nutrients I'd unwittingly leached out of the soil.

My cooking has improved in leaps and bounds too. The initial shepherd's pie wasn't a total disaster, but I didn't season anything and the mash was underdone and lumpy. However, Mum and Rebecca have both taken me under their wing, and I'm developing quite an impressive repertoire. The freezer is now stocked with home-cooked meals for the rare nights when I don't fancy preparing something from scratch, and my fridge and cupboards are full to bursting with healthy, fresh ingredients, along with an array of spices and seasonings. If Alasdair could see me now, I don't think he'd recognise me. I do still think about him in idle moments, of course, but I expect he's so busy he's already forgotten about me.

It's Wednesday today, or at least I think it is – weekdays tend to blur a bit now – and Rebecca and I are at mine, enjoying our post-gym cup of coffee in front of the TV. Today's episode of *Homes Under the Hammer* features an ex-council flat (always a good investment, we agree, because they're generally spacious and well built), a three-bedroom end-of-terrace house with a serious damp problem, and a detached house that the previous owner literally stripped back to a shell before promptly going bankrupt.

'That's a hell of a project,' Rebecca remarks as the camera pans round, showing bare brick external walls and nothing else. 'Where would you even begin with something like that?'

'It could be fun,' I reply, writing my estimate of how much the new owner is going to spend on my pad. This is a game we play every day. Each of us writes down how much we think it will cost to renovate the property, and the closest guess wins. There aren't any prizes, but it keeps us entertained.

'It doesn't look like fun to me,' she retorts. 'It looks like it could fall down at any minute.'

'Yeah, but you could put any layout you wanted in there. You literally have a blank canvas to play with.'

'Go on then, what would you do?'

'Assuming the external walls would take the load, I'd keep the downstairs fairly open plan, with a floating staircase against the right-hand wall. So, kitchen-slash-diner on the left there with living area on the right.'

'I'm not sure about that. If you were cooking something like a curry, the whole house would smell of it.'

'You'd need a powerful extractor fan, yes, but at least whoever's cooking wouldn't feel cut off from the rest of the family.'

'Good point. And upstairs?'

'Main bedroom with en suite. That's a must these days. Depending on space, I'd put in two or three more bedrooms and a family bathroom.'

'Sounds good. Can I make a suggestion?'

'Of course.'

'I think you'd need a study downstairs that was separate from the open-plan area. Lots of people work from home now, so you'd need to have that covered.'

'Good point. Two and a half months out of a job and I'd completely forgotten that people work!'

We carry on watching as Gary, who owns the shell, outlines his vision for it. He's going for some structural internal walls that will allow him to take part of the rear wall out and install bifold doors.

'I mean, that could work too,' I say to Rebecca. 'I wonder if you could have the best of both worlds though, if you put in some massive RSJs to support the walls.'

'Listen to you,' she says, laughing. 'Miss Construction Expert of the year.'

'Technically, I'd be Ms Construction Expert, and anyway, you're no better.'

The programme switches back to the flat for a while, and we watch in silence. However, it's not a peaceful silence. Rebecca is chewing her lip thoughtfully, and glancing at me every so often.

'What?' I ask.

'We should do this,' she says, and I notice that her eyes have lit up.

'What do you mean?'

'OK, bear with me because I've only just had the thought and it's not fully fledged yet. I have to sell my house once probate comes through, right?'

'Yes,' I say carefully.

'And you don't know what you want to do with your life, but I'm guessing it's not going to be another high-flying city job.'

'That's a fair assumption, yes.'

'So we both sell up, buy something at auction like these guys have, do it up, make fat profit, rinse and repeat.'

'Are you mad?' I ask her incredulously. 'These people have all got experience, well, most of them. If we tried something like this, we'd probably end up with a *Grand Designs*-type disaster.'

'You've got experience,' she counters.

'What?'

'You did this place. And it's stunning; you know how much I love your house.'

'Yes, but I was lucky because I knew exactly what I wanted, and I had a good architect and a superb builder.'

She stares at me, excitement written all over her face.

'You're serious, aren't you,' I sigh.

'There's no harm in looking into it, right?'

It's hard to refuse her when she's this excited. 'OK, let's talk through how it might work,' I offer. 'Part one is we both sell up, right?'

'Yes. It shouldn't take long. Do you remember me telling you about the guy who came and valued my house a couple of weeks ago?'

'Oily Pete?'

She giggles. 'If you'd seen him, you'd realise how well that nickname fits him. Anyway, he was saying that there's a lot of demand for properties round here at the moment. He reckoned he could even get a bidding war going on for my house, and it would probably sell in less than a week. And my house isn't a patch on yours. He'd wet himself if he saw this.'

An image of a smarmy man in a suit with a damp patch at the crotch comes into my mind, and I hastily push it out.

'OK, so Oily Pete has done the business and we've sold up. Where do we live while we're tracking down this holy grail of a building project?'

'I don't know. Like I said, this idea isn't fully fledged yet. We could rent somewhere, I guess.'

I think about her suggestion for a moment. 'I don't think that would work.'

'Why not?'

'Because the letting agency would want to do credit checks and stuff. Neither of us being in any form of employment is going to be a red flag, I reckon.'

'OK, park that one. I'll think about it some more.'

'Fine. Up pops the perfect property. We do our homework, we go to the auction and, incredibly, we win without going over our set budget.'

'God, we're good,' Rebecca enthuses, punching the air. 'Totally winning at life already.'

'Slow down, tiger,' I tell her with a smile. 'Now we've got to find an architect who can turn our vision into drawings, get the relevant permissions if we need them, and find a builder who's actually going to turn up and not charge us so much that we walk away with a thumping loss. A lot of the people on the programme are already in the trade, or have people who will do the work for mates' rates. And we'd probably need to live there while the work was being done, to save money. I remember what it was like when I was doing this place up. It's not a lot of fun. Oh, and we've got to do all of this without falling out.'

'We won't fall out.'

'We might. My experience is that wherever there's money and investment, there's huge risk of conflict. What if I have my heart set on gold taps for the bathroom, but you want to spend the money on mood lighting in the kitchen?'

'We have both.'

'We've only got the money for one.'

'Then we discuss like rational people and reach a compromise.'

'Which is?'

'The mood lighting, obviously. Gold taps are naff.'

Our laughter is short lived as the programme switches back to Gary and his shell of a house. It's our favourite part of the show now; the camera focuses on various parts of the original house before a screen wipe to how it looks now. The screen wipe is always accompanied by a swishing sound that Rebecca and I imitate religiously, swiping our hands in front of our faces as we do.

'Oh, that's stunning,' I breathe as feature after feature is revealed. 'He must have gone over budget though, surely. There's no way you could do that for sixty thousand.'

'So, how much did you spend?' the presenter asks on screen, and we both lean forward. I've written £100,000 on my pad and I reckon we're going to be much closer to that than Rebecca's estimated £55,000.

'Well, I called in a few favours,' Gary says, 'and Bobbie and I did a lot of the decoration and stuff ourselves during the evenings and weekends, so we actually came in under budget at £52,000.'

Rebecca and I sit in breathless anticipation as two estate agents are brought in to value the property now the work's been done. They're both full of admiration for the high standard of fit and finish, and Gary and Bobbie are delighted to discover that they could make a potential pre-tax profit of £80,000 if they were to put it on the market.

'I was hoping for sixty, so that's a real bonus,' Gary tells the presenter.

'It's a great result,' the presenter agrees. 'So, what now?'

'Oh, Bobbie and I have already got our eyes on our next project,' Gary says with a grin.

'So there we are,' the presenter concludes. 'Join us tomorrow for another episode of *Homes Under the Hammer*.'

I turn off the TV and turn to Rebecca, who is still grinning manically.

'That could be us,' she says. 'Eighty grand. Not bad, eh?'

I decide not to tell her that the salary Morton Lansdowne is still paying me is considerably more than that.

'What about Rollo?' I say, in my final attempt to defuse her.

'He needs stability. You can't keep pulling him out of one school and shoving him in another every time we start a new project.'

This does, thankfully, have the desired effect. 'That's a good point,' she admits. 'I guess we'd need to agree on the general area up front, so I could get him into a school and know he could stay there. Look. Nothing's cast in stone, but it's not a bad idea, is it? Think about it, at least?'

I smile at her. 'I suspect it might be a totally crazy idea, but I promise I'll think about it, yes.'

* * *

I'm in a reflective mood as I tidy up after lunch. Rebecca has headed off to collect Rollo from school, and I've got a pile of laundry that I'm planning to clear this afternoon. I don't know how serious she was about her plan, but it certainly put a sorely lacking spring back in her step. The whole business with the house and her uncertain future has been preying on her mind a lot, particularly as Alice has informed her that probate is due to be granted in a week or two. Alice has offered to cover the mortgage for three months to give her time to sell, as they both agreed that was her only viable option. I've tried not to think about her moving away; she's become such a big part of my life that I'll really miss her.

As I load the washing machine, I replay our conversation in my head. Her idea is crazily impetuous, of course it is, but like all crazy, spur-of-the-moment ideas, there is a tiny nugget of genius in it. And, I have to admit, the idea of being my own boss really appeals.

We can't do this, can we?

15

If I wasn't having a breakdown after I left Morton Lansdowne, I'm surely having one now. That's the only logical explanation, I think to myself as I sign the paperwork authorising an ecstatic Oily Pete to sell my house. Not only has Rebecca's enthusiasm for property development infected me, but my whole family think it's a brilliant idea too. The plan, as much as there is one, is that we sell up and move into Mum and Phil's in the short-term while we look for a suitable property near them to renovate. We've decided to focus on Kent, partly because it gives us cheap accommodation while we're looking, but also because that will enable Rebecca to enrol Rollo in a school knowing that we're going to be staying in the area. Rebecca, who Mum has practically adopted, will go in Saffy's old room and she's clearing out the spare room, which has become a bit of a dumping ground for things that don't have a home anywhere else, for Rollo.

'I think what I'm going to do,' Oily Pete tells me conspiratorially as he stuffs the signed paperwork into his document holder, 'is hold an open house for both yours and Rebecca's properties simultaneously. It's a psychological trick, but it works pretty well.'

'What kind of trick?' I ask.

'Nothing sinister. But, if people see that there's a lot of interest, which I'm sure there will be, it encourages them to put in a higher offer to have a better chance of securing the property. It sifts out the low ballers who just want to waste everyone's time in search of a bargain. To be honest with you, it wouldn't surprise me if we sell both of them on the day, and get a premium on the asking price as well. How does a week on Saturday sound? Gives me a bit of a chance to get the word out.'

'What do I have to do?'

'Nothing, if you don't want to. I'll bring one of my colleagues along so there's someone in each property. You can go out for the day, or you can be here to answer questions. Whatever suits.'

That's an easy decision. I wouldn't trust Oily Pete not to go upstairs and start rifling through my drawers if he's unsupervised. I'm sure he's good at what he does, but he's the kind of person who makes you want to wipe down every surface he's touched afterwards. His shiny grey suit doesn't fit him very well, has a few suspicious-looking stains, and looks like it might have come from a market stall. On top of that, he leaves a lingering aroma of cigarette smoke and cheap aftershave wherever he goes.

'I'll be here, Pete,' I tell him.

'Great. You might want to have some biscuits or something in the oven. The smell of baking makes a place feel homely – encourages the punters to think positively about it, know what I mean?'

'I'll see what I can do.'

'Perfect. I'll be in touch after I've checked that day suits Rebecca as well, yeah?'

As soon as he's gone, I open all the windows and spray air freshener in all the rooms to get rid of the scent of Oily Pete, before calling Rebecca myself.

'How did you get on?' she asks the moment she picks up the phone.

'I can see why you gave him the nickname,' I tell her.

'Yeah. He's a bit creepy, but apparently he gets results. He's lived around here all his life and knows the place like the back of his hand.'

'How do you know him?'

'He was the agent John bought my house through. He described him as "a slippery bastard, but he gets the job done". So, are you all set?'

'Yes. Are you sure we're doing the right thing though?'

'I know *I'm* doing the right thing,' she says, laughing. 'I don't really have any other options, do I? You can still pull out if you're not sure.'

'What, and leave you living with my mum without me there? Can you imagine what that would be like? She'd probably disown me in favour of you and Rollo. I'm sure she already sees him as a surrogate grandchild.'

'Nonsense. Your mum adores you, she just didn't really understand your old job. I'll let you into a secret if you like.'

'What?'

'Nobody outside a law firm understands your old job. John used to try to explain it to me, back in the days when I actually gave a damn about anything he said, but it used to send me straight to sleep.'

'Thinking of my old job, I've started work on the contract between you and me. I'm going to get it all finalised and then, when we find somewhere to buy, we just need to fill in the amounts we're each putting in and sign it.'

'Don't we need to get it notarised or something?'

'Nope. As long as all the necessary legal elements are there, it's binding. It doesn't even have to be a document. Did you know that you could legally enter into a contract using Morse code or semaphore? Even nodding your head could enter you into a contract in some instances. We studied it when I was training.'

'Bloody hell, I'd better be careful not to nod at anyone then. I think I'm pretty safe on the Morse code and semaphore. I'm so excited. I've been scouring the online auction sites to see what's coming up in central and East Kent, and there's loads.'

'Anything promising?'

'Nothing has grabbed me so far, but the fact that there are so many has to be encouraging, I reckon. I'm trying to be as hard headed as possible. We're looking for something to make a profit, not something to love.'

'You sound like a consummate professional already. *Homes Under the Hammer* would be proud of you.'

'Ha. I'm doing my best. Did I tell you that I've also found a school for Rollo near your parents' house? We're going down to visit on Friday.'

'It's not St Justin's, is it?'

'It is, actually. Why, is there something I should know? Is it dodgy?'

'It's fine,' I reassure her. 'It just happens to be the school that Saffy and I went to when we were kids.'

'You could come with us if you like. Unless you have a better offer, of course.'

'Oh, yeah. I'm flooded with social engagements. Sure, why not? It'll be a chance to exorcise some old ghosts.'

'Is that the school you were at when your dad...?' she asks tentatively.

'Yup.'

We've shared pretty much our entire life stories with each other, so I wasn't surprised by the question. I've told her about Dad, and in return she's been candid about her difficult relationship with her now estranged mother, and how that made her vulnerable when John Curbishley turned on the charm. I still struggle to grasp the concept of John being at all charming, but she's assured me he could bring it when he needed to. To be honest, the idea still makes me feel a little queasy.

* * *

Oily Pete evidently does know his stuff, if the stream of people who are traipsing through my house is anything to go by. I did a bit of research and, in the end, I decided to have coffee on the go as well as the biscuits. I've also cleaned from top to bottom so the house is looking its very best. Oily Pete is so confident that he's decided to take sealed bids, and I notice he's collected a fair number of envelopes already, so I'm optimistic as I take advantage of a brief lull to call Rebecca.

'How's it going?' I ask when she picks up.

'Bedlam,' she tells me. 'There's one couple that must have been round five times, and I've had to bribe Rollo with biscuits to stop him trying to "help". At one point, I caught him telling someone that they could only buy the house if they kept his room exactly as it is now.'

I laugh. 'I guess seven-year-olds have different views of how to sell a house.'

'Rollo certainly does. Anyway, we've got a decent pile of envelopes building up despite that. You?'

'Yeah, looking good.'

* * *

'I've been doing the maths,' Rebecca tells me the following Friday as the three of us head towards Maidstone in her SUV. 'Assuming the sale goes through in Oily Pete's predicted two months, and nothing comes up in the survey to make the buyer try to force the price down, I'm going to walk away with just over £300,000 once I've paid Alice back. That's even better than I'd hoped.'

'What are you paying Alice back for?' I ask her.

'She's covering the mortgage on condition that I repay her when I sell the house.'

'Blimey. For someone who seemed so nice, she sure knows how to play hardball.'

'Comes of being married to John all those years, I expect. It's fine. I'm still getting a third of a million quid out of the deal so I don't really have anything to complain about. Anyway, tell me about this school of yours.'

'There's not much to tell. I doubt that any of the people who taught me are still there. It's a good school, or at least it was. They were really supportive of Saffy and me when Dad left. The head did a whole assembly on how children weren't to blame for their parents' mistakes, and I think we actually ended up with more friends than we'd had before. If I had to criticise them for anything, it would be that they were perhaps a little heavy on the religion stuff.'

'I did wonder why the head teacher asked me if Rollo had been baptised. She said it wasn't an entry criterion, but they did strongly encourage it. She also wanted to know about Rollo's father.'

'What did you tell her?'

She glances in the rearview mirror to check that Rollo isn't listening in before lowering her voice conspiratorially. 'I led her to believe that I was a widow.'

'You what?'

'It's not a complete lie. John's dead, after all. She assumed that I was married to him and I didn't see any reason to correct her. It's not as if he's going to be coming to any parents' evenings and contradicting me, is it?'

'And what about the baptism thing?'

'I fudged that. I told her that I'd always been keen but Rollo's father wasn't a believer.'

'Nice.'

'I thought so. Ah, here we are. Rollo, darling, best behaviour for Mummy, OK? If this goes well, I'll treat you to McDonald's for lunch.'

That seems to have the desired effect, as Rollo is all smiles as he climbs down from the back seat. The receptionist informs us that the head teacher is in an overrunning call, but will be with us as soon as she's finished.

'It still smells the same,' I murmur to Rebecca after a few moments. 'Sweaty feet and cabbage. How is that possible?'

She doesn't get a chance to answer, as we're joined at that moment by a formidable-looking woman who I'd guess is in her mid-fifties.

'I'm so sorry for keeping you waiting,' she begins. 'I'm Margaret Steadman, the head teacher of St Justin's. Which one of you is Mrs Kennet?'

'That's me,' Rebecca replies.

'Lovely. And this must be Rollo. Pleased to meet you, young man.' She looks at me quizzically. 'And you are?'

'Thea Rogers,' I tell her.

'And I gather you're moving down from London?' she asks, turning her attention back to Rebecca.

'That's right. We're moving in with Thea's parents to start with, until we find a property of our own.'

'I see.' She glances at me again uncertainly. 'Well, we might not be as, aah, *modern* as some of the London schools, but I'm sure Rollo will thrive with us nonetheless. Let's start the tour with the hall.'

I follow mutely as Mrs Steadman walks us round the school, showing us classrooms full of happy-looking boys and girls engaged in various tasks, while making sure we're in no doubt as to the school's outstanding OFSTED results. It's familiar, yet different. The institutional green paint of the main corridor has been replaced with a much cheerier pale yellow, and the classrooms all sport an impressive array of technology, although I note that imposing crucifixes still dominate every one. The playground, which I remember as being huge, seems comparatively small to my adult eyes, which automatically seek out the corner where Reuben and I shared a French kiss in year five. We did it for a dare, and it wasn't very pleasant, but I remember feeling terribly grown-up afterwards.

'Your application has come at a very opportune moment, Mrs Kennet,' the head teacher tells us when we're settled in her office at the end of the tour. 'We're normally heavily oversubscribed, but it just so happens that the family of one of the children in Rollo's year is moving abroad, so we have a vacancy.'

'I'm sure Rollo will be very happy here, won't you, darling?' Rebecca says, earning an enthusiastic nod from Rollo who, I suspect, has his mind firmly on the promised McDonald's.

'Great,' Mrs Steadman says with a smile. 'Now, you'll have to forgive me as I'm not as experienced in these matters as I should be, but how does Rollo refer to you?'

Rebecca looks perplexed. 'He calls me Mum,' she says warily.

'OK, and Miss Rogers?'

'He calls me Thea, but I don't really understand why that's relevant.'

'I just like to get these things right. We do have a couple of other children from blended families here, and it's a bit of a minefield. I didn't know if you were both Mum, or—'

'Mrs Steadman, we're not in a relationship,' I interrupt as I realise the assumption she's made. 'We're just friends.'

Now it's Mrs Steadman's turn to look perplexed. 'I'm sorry, I thought you said you were moving in together?'

'Yes, but as friends. Separate bedrooms. I only came with Rebecca on the tour because this is my old school.'

Mrs Steadman's face turns puce with embarrassment. 'I'm so sorry. I will confess I was a little confused because of Mrs Kennet's previous marital status, although I have heard of people who are surprisingly flexible in matters of the heart. I can only apologise.'

'Don't worry,' I tell her, trying desperately not to catch Rebecca's eye. 'I should have been more clear.'

* * *

'Some people are *surprisingly* flexible in matters of the heart,' Rebecca says through tears of laughter as we pull out of the school gates and onto the road. 'Don't get me wrong, I love you to bits, but not like that.'

'Why not?' I ask, trying to stifle my own laughter and sound mock-affronted. 'What's the matter with me? I think you're being surprisingly *inflexible* in matters of the heart, frankly. After all, we know you have a thing for corporate lawyers, and I tick that box. Plus, not to blow my own trumpet, but I'd like to think

I'm a rather more attractive prospect than John Curbishley. What else do you need?'

'Stop, I'm begging you!' she howls.

'I don't understand what's so funny,' Rollo complains from the back.

'It's OK, darling,' Rebecca tells him, still snorting with laughter. 'Mrs Steadman just got the wrong end of the stick, that's all.'

We're still breaking out into occasional fits of giggles when we pull onto Mum and Phil's driveway after lunch. As soon as he climbs out of the car, Rollo makes a beeline for Mum, who wraps him in a hug.

'How did you get on at the school?' she asks Rebecca once Rollo is ensconced in front of the TV and she's put the kettle on. 'I don't know what it's like now, but both Thea and Saffy thrived there.'

'Yeah, good,' Rebecca tells her as we both start laughing again.

'What's so funny?'

'The head teacher thought Rebecca and I were a couple,' I explain.

To my surprise, Mum doesn't join in the laughter. 'It's not an unreasonable assumption,' she remarks. 'You two are very close. I've known Thea all her life and I've never seen her bond with someone the way she has with you, Rebecca. In fact, Phil and I were also wondering whether it was more than just friendship. It wouldn't matter, of course. We just want you both to be happy.'

'Mum!' I exclaim in horror.

'What? You'd make a lovely couple, and you've been single for so long I can't remember whether you're attracted to boys or girls.'

'We're just friends,' I tell her strenuously. Of course, she never met Alasdair, as our relationship wasn't really the 'come and meet my parents' type, and I don't think she'd have approved of how casual it was.

'Have it your way,' she sighs. 'I quite liked the idea, actually. It'd be one in the eye for Bridget down the road. She thinks she's so modern because her son's in a civil partnership, but I reckon an unemployed lesbian daughter going out with an equally unemployed single mother trumps that any day of the week.'

'I'm so sorry to disappoint you yet again,' I reply sarcastically.

'Oh, you've never disappointed me,' she says with a smile. 'You're just a bit of a mystery sometimes, that's all.'

16

'What about this one?' Rebecca asks, passing the tablet that she's welded to these days across to me. Oily Pete came good and my current account is now a worrying sum in credit. I look at the property on screen. It's a three-bedroom end-of-terrace in Ashford that's definitely in need of some TLC. The auction guide price is £230,000.

'I'm thinking lose a bedroom, move the bathroom upstairs and extend the kitchen. The rest probably just needs a lick of paint and a tidy up. The garden's a mess, but that shouldn't be too difficult to sort out.'

I zoom in on some of the pictures, and something catches my eye.

'The wallpaper's peeling away here, can you see?' I say, handing the tablet back.

'Oh, well spotted. You're thinking damp?'

'It's definitely a risk. What are the modernised houses in that area going for?'

'Two sixty to two ninety.'

'Mm, not a lot of margin even if we get it for the guide price.'

'Yeah, but I think we have to set our sights a little low, at least to start. We both know that we could have made much more in London, but we'd need to spend much more up front and we wouldn't have the luxury of living here pretty much rent free. However, I agree. This one is too tight, especially if there's damp. I'll keep looking.'

'How is the cut-throat world of property development this morning?' Mum asks as she brings in three mugs of tea and settles herself on the sofa next to Rebecca.

'I'm just looking at the properties coming up next month, Cath,' Rebecca tells her.

'Can I see?' Rebecca hands her the tablet and Mum starts scrolling slowly.

'They're all a bit run-down, aren't they?' she observes.

'That's the point, Mum,' I explain for what feels like the thousandth time. 'If they're not run-down we can't add value to them and make a profit.'

'I don't know. Saffy reckons her house is probably worth a lot more than they bought it for.'

'Yes, but they've been in it for years. The aim for us is to get in and get out fast.'

'So you say. It all seems very risky to me, but I'm sure you know what you're doing. Oh, this is nice.'

She hands the tablet to Rebecca, who takes her time looking at it. 'It is pretty, I agree,' she remarks after a while. 'I love the pond.'

'You could have ducks on it,' Mum observes.

'Blimey, it's got ten acres of land. That's practically a whole county! I wonder why it's so cheap?'

'What are you looking at?' I ask.

'This,' Rebecca tells me, handing over the tablet. The property in question is a pretty two-bedroom stone cottage with a large pond next to it and, as Rebecca pointed out, an awful lot of land. The guide price is £800,000. That's not what catches my eye though. Attached to the cottage is a second building, on the side of which is a massive, tatty-looking tarpaulin that, although it's hard to see because it's partly obscured by a fallen tree, appears to be covering something large and round.

'Is that a watermill?' I ask as I hand the tablet back. 'What on earth would you do with something like that?'

We're interrupted by the arrival of Saffy and a very excited Louis. Since we moved here, Louis and Rollo have become firm friends. Louis, being already settled at St Justin's, was initially happy to take Rollo under his wing and show him the ropes, but now Rollo is definitely trying to turn the tables a bit in his favour by periodically reminding Louis that he's a whole year older and in the class above Louis's. Now that summer is here, they spend most of the time when they're together outside in the garden, usually having water fights.

'How's it going?' Saffy asks once the boys have changed into swimming trunks and had the usual lecture about not aiming for each other's faces.

'What do you think of this?' Rebecca asks her, handing her the tablet.

'Oh, that's gorgeous,' Saffy breathes, after she's studied the pictures.

'Isn't it?' Mum agrees.

'It's also bound to be a lot of work,' I tell them before they can get too excited. 'We're supposed to be looking for something that doesn't need too much doing to it, so we can cut our teeth and turn a quick profit, remember? I might be tempted if it came up after we'd already done five houses, but it's way too much work for a first project.'

'I reckon you'd make a killing on it though,' Saffy tells me, undeterred. 'Tim's addicted to those property porn programmes on Channel 4, where experts help people find their ideal homes, and there was a converted watermill on one of those not that long ago. It was well over a million, and it wasn't half as nice as this could be. Have a look online, there's bound to be one for sale somewhere.'

With a sigh, I get up and perch on the arm of the sofa so I can see the screen. Rebecca has pretty much every property website bookmarked, so it doesn't take her long to find a converted watermill for sale. It's in Worcestershire and is on the market for just under two million pounds.

'This is obviously the old mill building,' she says as we look at pictures of a beautifully appointed kitchen with a light, airy bedroom above and a room that's currently set up as a studio on the top floor. There are nods to the building's industrial past in each room; the kitchen has a massive cog mounted on a plinth at one end, and the studio still has a part of the mill machinery suspended from the ceiling beams. The rest of the house has also been sympathetically upgraded, keeping the period features but with modern touches.

'It is nice,' I agree. 'But how much do you think we'd have to spend to get the other one to that standard? Show it to me again.'

Rebecca switches back to the auction listing and hands me the tablet.

'Right, for starters, you've either got to remove all this heavy machinery in the mill, or relocate it. That's not going to be cheap.' I swipe through the photos until we get to some of the house. 'This has potential, I'll admit. Wait a minute, is that a coal-fired range in the kitchen?'

'It's just a cooker,' Saffy observes. 'You could take it out and replace it easily enough.'

'I bet it isn't just a bloody cooker. Ten to one it's the cooker, central heating and hot water system all in one. So you've got to start from scratch with that, putting in a modern boiler, radiators and all the pipework to join them together. The windows look rotten too, and what the hell are you going to do with the outbuildings, the barns and all that land?'

'I don't think you'd need to do anything to the barns apart from clear them out and spruce them up a bit,' Rebecca argues. 'The new owners can decide what they want to use them for. And the land can just be parkland. That's privacy, and people will pay a lot for that, I reckon. I'm not saying it isn't a bigger job than we were originally planning, but Saffy's right. The profit potential is also much higher.'

I study the pictures some more. It's a world away from what I thought our first project would be, but she has got a point. And, on the plus side, the house may be ridiculously outdated with rotten windows, but it does look structurally solid. I zoom in and can't spot any nasty telltale cracks in any of the walls.

'It's scary, but also tempting,' I say to Rebecca after a while. 'Do you think there might be a bidding war though? We might not even get a look-in.'

'We definitely won't get a look-in if we don't even try.'

'OK. Let's look at it in more depth and make a list, shall we?' I grab my pad and move to sit next to Rebecca so we can examine the pictures together. Sensing that the entertainment is over, Saffy and Mum wander off to supervise the boys.

'I can't see a radiator anywhere,' I observe after a while. 'We'd definitely need to put central heating in.' I make a note on my pad.

An hour or so later, we've got a list that includes installing the heating, replacing the rotten-looking wood-framed windows with new ones, putting in a new bathroom upstairs and ripping out the old ground-floor one. Rebecca thinks we should relocate the kitchen into the mill, like the converted one we looked at earlier, and we've decided we're more than capable of ripping the old one out ourselves, although we've budgeted for some replastering afterwards.

'Forty thousand so far, give or take,' Rebecca observes.

'That's pretty good, but the big unknown is still the cost of converting the mill, and getting that wheel removed isn't going to be cheap. I wonder where you go to get estimates for something like that?'

'Why remove it? You could make it a feature. You know the buckets on a water wheel? You could fill them on one side with soil and then have flowers cascading over them. Like a nod to its past.'

'Wouldn't it just rotate and dump all the soil on the ground?'

'You'd have to fix it so it couldn't move, obviously.'

'It's a nice idea, but it's probably just as rotten as the windows,' I tell her. 'I wouldn't get your hopes up too high. Let's budget to either remove or renovate it.'

'OK,' she agrees. 'Here's the thing though. Even if we had to spend, I don't know, £200,000 on the conversion, that's a total outlay of a million. If we only sold it for £1.25 million, that's still a clear quarter of a million in profit, and I reckon we could make more than that if we do this well. What do you think?'

I ponder the question for a while. There's no doubt that it's a much bigger project than either of us were looking for, but the more I look at it, the more potential I see.

'Here's how I see it,' I tell her eventually. 'We could do what we originally planned but, as you showed with that house in Ashford earlier, there aren't the margins in those types of houses. Yes, this is riskier, but I agree with you that it has the potential to make us a fortune if we play our cards right. Let's go and look at it, at least. If we decide it's too much for us, we can always walk away.'

Rebecca looks like she's won the lottery, and I have to confess that I feel quite excited myself.

* * *

My buoyant mood sinks a little as we bump down the rough track to the mill a few days later. 'This will all need replacing too,' I point out to Rebecca. 'I'd never get my car down here.'

'You're right,' she agrees. 'Add it to the list. What's the name of the guy we're meeting?'

'Ben Simmonds.'

As we lurch around the final bend and pull up outside the house, a man steps out of the Land Rover that's already parked there.

'Well, hello, future husband,' Rebecca murmurs as she drinks him in with her eyes. She's almost salivating.

'Are you all right there?' I laugh.

'Oh, never better. I mean, you've seen him, haven't you? I always thought Rollo would be an only child, but I swear I can hear my ovaries singing that song from *Snow White*.'

'What, "Someday My Prince Will Come"?'

'No. "Heigh-Ho, It's Off to Work We Go".'

I study the man for a moment, trying to work out what's got Rebecca so worked up. He is good looking, in a rough and ready kind of way. He's tall, with wavy dark brown hair and dark eyes. He has a bushy beard, wide shoulders and his checked shirt is rolled up to reveal thick forearms. He's pleasantly rugged, I suppose, but I can't get past the beard. I've never been into beards.

'Shall we get out of the car then?' I prompt after a moment.

'Yes, of course.'

'Hi. You must be Rebecca and Thea. I'm Ben,' the man says. He has a deep, resonant voice and his hand is so large that it completely engulfs Rebecca's and mine in turn.

'I'm Rebecca,' she announces. 'Before you ask, Thea and I are purely business partners and friends.'

Ben looks momentarily confused, which I don't blame him for at all.

'I see,' he tells her. 'Well, I've got the house key if you want to look in there first.' As he turns away, crossing the courtyard to unlock the door, Rebecca leans close to me so she can whisper without him hearing.

'Oh, shit,' she murmurs. 'Did I make a tit of myself? I think my knickers just melted. Does he come with the house, do you suppose?'

'Behave,' I snigger. 'Do I need to hose you down before we go in?'

'No.' She pulls herself up straight. 'Professional game face on. Ready?'

We follow Ben into the house, which is cold even on this warm summer day. He obviously notices me shivering as he says, 'It's the thick stone walls. They keep you cool in the summer and, once you get some heat into them, they'll keep you warm in winter too. My house is just the same.'

'Do you live locally then?' Rebecca asks.

'In the cottage at the end of the drive.'

So much for professional game face. Rebecca looks like all her Christmases have come at once.

'Did you know the previous owners?' I ask, keen to keep the conversation focused on the property while Rebecca tries to recover her composure.

'Very well. They were my grandparents. My mum and dad

were, well, they weren't good parents so I grew up here. However, my grandad died two years ago and Nan passed away just after Christmas, so it's time to move it on to someone new.'

'I'm so sorry,' I tell him.

'Don't be. Frankly, I'm surprised she lasted as long as she did after Grandad died. They were devoted to each other and she was lost without him.'

'How come you're not taking it on?' I ask after a moment.

'Lots of reasons. The main one is that I'm not the only heir, so I'd have to buy the others out. Plus, and I probably shouldn't say this to prospective buyers, it's an awkward size.'

'How so?'

'Ten acres. Too much for a garden but not enough for a farm. Grandad used to mow it with a tractor and Nan tried to keep the place neat after he died by letting one of the local farmers graze his sheep here, but the pittance he paid wasn't even enough to maintain the fences, so that petered out last summer.'

'Have you had a lot of viewings?'

He smiles. 'How am I supposed to answer that? I have a vested interest.'

'It'll all come out at the auction anyway.'

'I guess so. A few people have come to look, but I don't know whether they'll bid. What are your plans, if you don't mind me asking?'

'We're going to convert it into a modern home but keep the period features,' Rebecca blurts before I have the chance to stop her. 'You don't mind, do you?'

He laughs. 'Why would I mind?'

'Because this is your family home.'

'I wouldn't worry about that,' he tells her. 'I'm a realist. I know this place is hopelessly outdated, and I reckon Nan and

Grandad would have been happy to see it renovated. Knock yourselves out. Now, why don't I wait in the car while you have a good look round. I'm sure you'll want to talk without an eavesdropper. When you're ready, I'll show you the mill and the grounds if you like.'

'Thanks,' I tell him.

'Sorry,' Rebecca says as soon as he's gone. 'I don't know what's the matter with me today.'

'Really? I reckon I have a pretty good idea,' I tell her with a grin.

'Oh, bollocks, I think I'm in love,' she replies.

17

An hour later, I feel quite optimistic. Despite the musty air in the house, I couldn't detect any signs of damp and, although they look very tatty and desperately need sanding down and repainting, the window frames felt reassuringly solid when I prodded them with the screwdriver I brought with me for the purpose. As I feared, though, the coal range is the only current source of heat. Ben described how his grandmother would lug an enormous pot of boiling water from the range and pour it into the bath, adding just enough cold to make it bearable, and then the three of them would take turns to wash as quickly as they could before the cast iron of the tub sapped the warmth out of it. The mill had been his grandfather's domain, although Ben admitted he'd never seen it running, as it had been mothballed before he was born when his grandfather realised he couldn't compete with the new mills.

The machinery in the mill looked rusty and unloved to me, even though Ben assured me it had been checked and maintained regularly every year until his grandfather died. However, I found it easy to imagine what the building could look like once all the milling paraphernalia was removed; if we put glass in the large doorway, it could be a light and airy space.

As we pull off the bumpy track onto the road, I can sense Rebecca fizzing with excitement next to me.

'What's got you more revved up, Ben or the property?' I ask.

'Both, but the property mainly. It has so much potential, and it's not nearly as bad as we thought it was.'

'I agree. There's one possible red flag though. Did you spot it?'

'No. What?'

'What Ben said about the land. "Too big for a garden but too small for a farm." Do you think we could split it into smaller plots?'

'Not a bad idea, but sometimes there's covenants and things dictating what you can do. If there was any hope of getting planning to develop it, I reckon the price would be way higher, don't you?'

'Good point. Something to check.'

'Anyway, even if we can't split it into smaller plots, there's the tractor and that thing in the barn to keep the grounds under control. What did Ben call it?'

'A gang-mower.'

'That's it. Stick that on the back of the tractor and you'll have the place mowed in no time.'

'Assuming the tractor works, the mower isn't seized solid and the owners don't mind spending their weekends cutting the grass.'

'I think it's a small price to pay. Plus, it's all about perception, isn't it?'

'How so?'

'Describe it simply as a ten-acre plot and it falls flat.

Describe the house as “set in ten acres of idyllic parkland with a lake” and it suddenly sounds aspirational. Basic marketing.’

I laugh. ‘You’ve got a point. So, what do you want to do?’

‘I think we should go for it. I didn’t see anything there that I felt was beyond us and I still think the potential returns are massive, way bigger than anything else we’ve looked at. What about you?’

‘I think so too, even though I’m worried about the mill and how much it will cost to get all that dilapidated machinery out. We’ll probably have to take the roof off and hire a crane.’

‘That’s the big expense, I agree. But it’s the only one. We don’t even have to knock through the wall between the house and the mill because there’s already a door.’

‘We might need to extend it though, otherwise it’ll still feel like two buildings rather than one.’

She smiles. ‘What?’ I ask.

‘We’re doing this, aren’t we?’

‘It would seem so.’ I smile back. ‘I need you to promise one thing though.’

‘What?’

‘If we bid for it, and we get it, you’ll be 100 per cent focused on the renovation, not distracted by the man who lives at the end of the drive.’

‘From nine to five, Monday to Friday, I solemnly swear I’ll be focused.’ She grins. ‘Outside those times, I’m making no guarantees. Take it or leave it.’

‘He might have a girlfriend, or a wife.’

‘No wedding ring.’

‘Men don’t always wear them.’

‘Ben would.’

‘How on earth have you figured that out?’

‘I just have a feeling about him.’

'Is this your ovaries again? What are they singing now?'

'Easy. Michael Bublé, "Feeling Good".'

'I do think he was a little blindsided by your need to clarify our relationship,' I observe after a while. Rebecca is humming the song as she drives.

'Yes,' she agrees. 'It wasn't my finest hour, but I couldn't risk a repeat of the school mix-up. Not when there's so much at stake. Anyway, distract me from my pornographic thoughts. What happens now?'

'We need to get a survey done before auction day. Let's get that organised first.'

When we get back and study the listing again, I'm pleased to find that the mill is one of the lots in a live auction, rather than an online one. The idea of entering our maximum bid and then having to wait up to a month to learn if we've won doesn't appeal to me at all. I'd rather be in the room, gauging the competition and ready to move on immediately if we're unsuccessful. Rebecca and I have agreed that we'll go up to £850,000 if the bidding exceeds the guide price, which gives us a buffer of £50,000 from our combined pot to spend on anything vital that a mortgage company would want fixed before lending against the mill.

'So,' Rebecca says on auction day once I've parked my car. 'Most important rule?'

'Don't go above the price we've agreed, whatever happens.' Although I bought my house in Walthamstow at auction, we've been doing lots of research online to hone our techniques, and this has become our mantra.

'And rule number two?'

'Don't suddenly get tempted to bid on something else that we haven't looked at.'

'Absolutely. And we'll sit tight to begin with, see who else is interested in the mill before we start bidding.'

'Sizing up the competition.'

'Exactly.'

I'm buzzing with adrenaline as we collect our bidding paddle and take our seats in the busy hall. I'd forgotten how exciting auctions are. It hasn't even started yet, but there's a real sense of anticipation in the room as people mill about, chatting to one another and finding places to sit. I've bought a few things on online auction sites over the years, and it is satisfying to win, especially when there's a flurry of last-minute bidding, but you can't beat a live auction. It's the fast pace of the bidding, the patter of the auctioneer and the slam of the gavel to announce the winning bid. I've never been interested in gambling, but I reckon this must come as near as dammit to the kind of rush people get from that.

Silence falls as the auctioneer makes his way to the podium, but the first few lots attract little interest and don't reach their reserve price. As we make our way steadily through the catalogue, my heart begins to thump hard in my chest. All these people are obviously here for something, but we don't seem to have reached it yet. I just hope it's not the mill.

'Lot twenty,' the auctioneer announces. 'A three-bedroom end-of-terrace property in Ashford. Who'll start me at £230,000?'

'That's one of the ones we looked at,' Rebecca whispers to me, in case I'd forgotten.

No paddles go up, but the auctioneer seems unfazed. 'Fine,' he says. 'Two ten. Any takers?'

In the end, he has to drop another £10,000 before a bid

comes in, but then they flow in quickly and the property quickly climbs back to the guide price before finally selling at £240,000.

'They're all playing the same tactics,' Rebecca observes. 'Not revealing their hand until they absolutely have to. Ah, here we go.'

'Lot twenty-one,' the auctioneer calls. 'A disused watermill with attached cottage and grazing land. Who'll give me £800,000 for it?'

Again, no paddles go up and he progressively drops the price to £700,000. At £650,000, you can tell he's starting to get frustrated but a paddle goes up near the front.

'Finally!' the auctioneer exclaims. 'Right, six-sixty anyone?'

Another paddle goes up and I can sense Rebecca twitching next to me. 'Hold your nerve,' I encourage her.

The two current bidders push the price back up to £700,000 fairly quickly, but one of them drops out at that point.

'Seven-ten,' the auctioneer calls. 'Can I get seven-ten from anyone? I have to tell you we're still below the reserve here, so we aren't selling.'

No paddles go up.

'OK, if that's how it is,' the auctioneer continues. 'Seven hundred thousand. Once, twice—'

'Go!' I whisper to Rebecca, and her hand shoots up.

'Seven-ten from the back of the room!' the auctioneer announces with renewed enthusiasm, and I see the other bidder turn around with an annoyed look on his face, trying to locate his competition.

'Yeah, buddy, we're coming for you,' I murmur under my breath as I smile sweetly at him. From that point on, the price climbs in increments of £10,000 until, at £750,000, the other bidder throws in the towel.

'We could be there,' Rebecca murmurs excitedly. 'The

reserve has to be within 10 per cent of the guide price, so that's anywhere from £720,000 upwards.'

'OK. We're still not at the reserve,' the auctioneer announces, puncturing our optimism. 'But seven-fifty is the final bid. Any more for any more? No? Seven-fifty once, twice, and not sold. Contact the team afterwards if you want to make an offer. Paddle number 604. Right, lot twenty-two, four acres of land with planning permission for three detached houses.'

This is obviously the lot that everyone has come for, as the bidding is fierce and it ends up going for substantially more than the guide price. Although it's entertaining, I feel spent and just let it wash over me. Everything depends on Ben now, and whether he's prepared to accept our offer. If he does, we've got ourselves a bargain.

'The suspense is killing me,' Rebecca mutters. 'How many more lots?'

'A few, I'm afraid.'

'I don't think we should offer any more than £775,000,' she says firmly. 'We were the only bidders left, so I don't think we should have any competition now.'

'I agree,' I tell her. 'Let's wait and see what happens though.'

After the flurry of enthusiasm for the building plot, the rest of the auction is fairly lacklustre, and I'm glad when the final lot grinds its way up to the reserve price and the gavel falls for the last time. When I bought my house in London, there was fast-paced bidding for every property, so this has been a bit of a let-down in some ways.

'Let's go and find someone to talk to,' I tell Rebecca, heading for the cashier desks. Although a large number of lots went unsold, the area is still busy and we have to wait for nearly an hour before a desk comes free.

'How can I help you?' the woman behind the desk asks.

'It's lot number twenty-one,' I explain. 'We'd like to see if we can make an acceptable offer for it.'

She taps at her screen for a while. 'OK,' she says. 'I have to inform you that there has already been an offer put in from another bidder. Let's see the status of that.'

My heart sinks as she taps some more. I know it's not the end of the world, but we've put enough work into this that it will still be disappointing to lose it.

'I can see that offer hasn't been accepted yet,' she says eventually.

'Can you tell me how much it was?' I ask.

'No, sorry. I can take your offer and put it to the vendor though. Or, if your offer happened to be above the reserve price, I can authorise the sale myself.'

'We'd like to offer £775,000,' Rebecca tells the woman behind the desk, and I find myself mentally crossing my fingers.

'Great. Let's see then.' She makes some entries on the screen and smiles.

'Congratulations,' she says. 'It's yours.'

18

The purchase of the mill went through very quickly, and we've spent the last two months getting on with as many of the jobs on the outside as we could. The fiddliest, and most time consuming, has undoubtedly been the windows. Our initial efforts were slow and incredibly frustrating until Ben showed us how to remove the window frames from the hinges so we could lay them flat on a workbench. In fact, Ben has been a surprisingly regular visitor and helper. He's one of those guys who seems to know how everything works and is so well plugged in to the local community that, on the rare occasions that something is beyond him, he knows exactly who to contact to sort it out. We've learned that he doesn't have a regular job, preferring to earn his keep doing bits and pieces for friends and acquaintances as required. He explained that he doesn't have a mortgage on his cottage and lives quite frugally, so he doesn't need much. I have no reason to doubt him as his invoices, when I can persuade him to submit them, are ridiculously small in comparison to the work he's done.

Thanks to him, the tractor is up and running and the gang-mower (which proved to be seized) has been thoroughly overhauled. Under his patient instruction, Rebecca has learned how to attach it to the tractor and mow the area we now refer to jokingly as 'the park'. To my mind, it seemed to take her a long time to learn such a simple-seeming task, until I realised that she was getting to spend extended time with him in a hot cab, necessitating them to strip down to the bare essentials to try to keep cool.

'God, the way his arms glisten when he's hot and sweaty,' she confided in me when I called her out on it. 'I was so distracted by them the other day, I nearly drove straight into the lake. And then there are his thighs. Dear Lord, I've never seen thighs like that before. I reckon you could attack them with a chainsaw and it would just bounce off.'

Unfortunately for her, Ben either hasn't noticed her dialling up the flirtation or is so far impervious to it. We've been completely up front with him about our plans, so my gut feel is that he's either not attracted to her, or he's protecting himself because he knows we'll be moving on as soon as the renovations are done and the mill is sold. However, Rebecca is growing increasingly frustrated, and I think the only reason she hasn't jumped on him is because she has just enough presence of mind to realise that we'd be a lot worse off if he took it badly and stopped helping us.

Rollo, on the other hand, has had an idyllic summer and totally idolises Ben, especially since he pitched up one day at the end of August with a slightly dilapidated-looking wooden boat in tow.

'The people I got it off were glad to see the back of it,' he'd explained when I asked where it came from. Since then, whenever he hasn't been helping us with something, he and Rollo have been working on it, sanding it down and re-waterproofing it. Ben has promised to teach Rollo and Louis how to row as soon as they've finished it. Saffy and Louis are regular visitors and, although she doesn't help with the house, having someone keeping an eye on the children has been a huge plus. They've built various dens around the place, had picnics and water fights, and generally enjoyed the kind of summer you'd expect to find in an Enid Blyton novel before school started again at the beginning of this month.

Although I'm sure I could have found someone local who would charge less, in the end Rebecca and I agreed to play it safe and re-use the architect who'd drawn up the vision for my house in London. It's paid off, with a stunning set of plans submitted to the council, showing sympathetic conversion of the mill. We've put an open-plan kitchen-diner on the ground floor, a bedroom with en suite on the first, and a second bedroom and shower room on the top, accessed by an exquisite oak staircase that promises to be one of the most expensive single items on the build. We looked at a number of cheaper options, but nothing else fitted so naturally. We've opened up the doorway on the ground floor to make the space flow better into the adjacent cottage, and also added an opening on the first floor. Every so often, we spread out our copy of the drawings on the dining room table and Rebecca and I stare at them, sighing with pleasure.

The email arrives one particularly hot afternoon. Ben and Rollo are working on the boat while Rebecca and I paint another in the seemingly endless series of window frames. My hands are sweating as I press to open it, and that's not just because of the heat. Although our application is strong and well researched, you can never tell which way the council is going to go, and the fact that they write to the architect rather than us with the decision just adds another layer of bureaucracy.

'I've got an email from the architect,' I tell Rebecca.

'Read it out then.'

'OK, there's some standard text letting us know that they've heard from the council, and an attachment.' I scan the text. 'It seems like we're not quite there, we need to get a certificate of some sort. Let's have a look.'

I open the attachment and begin to read.

To: Hutchinson and Roberts, Architects
Ref: The Mill
Mill Lane
Little Mappington
Ashford

Thank you for your application in regard to obtaining permission to convert the above property from commercial to residential use. We have examined the plans submitted, and agree that they are sympathetic to, and in keeping with the character of the current building.

'That's pretty encouraging, isn't it?' Rebecca interrupts.

'Wait, there's more,' I tell her, before continuing to read.

However, industrial buildings such as this form an important part of our cultural heritage, and the council has a responsibility to preserve them in their current state wherever possible. Therefore, in order for us to proceed with your application, we require you to supply certification that the mill is beyond economic repair. Such certification can be acquired through the Historic Industrial Buildings Trust, details of whom we have included below.

We look forward to hearing from you in due course.

Yours sincerely,
Barbara Evans (She/Her)
Ashford Borough Council Planning Department

'That's not too bad,' Rebecca says encouragingly after I've closed the attachment and read the rest of the mail from the architect asking if we're happy to sort out the certificate. 'I mean, it would have been better if they'd just said yes, but at least it's not a blanket no. All we have to do is contact these historic people, get them to agree the mill has had it, and it sounds like we're there.'

'I guess so,' I agree cautiously.

'You don't sound convinced.'

'I am,' I reassure her. 'I just don't like unknowns, and when I read "historic trust" my mind says "fanatics".'

'What's up?' Ben asks as he and Rollo wander over from the barn. They're both covered in fine sawdust, apart from clear patches around their mouths and noses where they've evidently been wearing masks.

'We've got to get certification from some historic trust that the mill can't be fixed, but then we're there,' Rebecca tells him, looking him up and down appreciatively.

'Uh-oh.' Ben's face falls.

'What? First Thea and now you. It's a formality, that's all,' she stresses.

'I hope you're right,' Ben tells her. 'It just reminds me of all the hoo-hah when the local vicar wanted to take the pews out of the church to make it into a multi-purpose space.'

'What happened?' I ask.

'Most people were broadly supportive. The pews aren't original and, by all accounts, they're horribly uncomfortable. But then the Victorian Trust got involved, arguing that they were historically important and one thing and another, and eventually sucked all the life out of the idea.'

'That's not going to happen to us,' Rebecca assures him. 'It's a rubber stamp in our case, no more.'

'Let's hope so,' he agrees, but I can see the doubt in his eyes.

I sent my email to the Historic Industrial Buildings Trust before Rebecca and I set off for the mill this morning. I took care to explain that we're planning to convert it sensitively and that the council broadly approve of our plans, deliberately couching my request for the certificate in terms of it being a mere formality. Although I did have a slightly sleepless night, including the usual 4 a.m. wide awake spot when everything seems calamitous, I feel more positive this morning and I'm humming along to the radio as I carefully apply primer to the latest window frame when my phone rings.

'Is that Thea Rogers?' The female voice on the other end sounds brisk and efficient.

'That's me,' I confirm.

'Great. I'm Charlotte, and I'm calling from HIBT.'

'HIBT?'

'Sorry, the Historic Industrial Buildings Trust. It's a bit of a mouthful so we generally just use the initials.'

'Wow, I didn't expect to hear back from you so quickly.'

'You caught us in a lull,' she explains. 'So, you've got a watermill, I understand?'

I explain the situation to her, and she sounds reassuring.

'That's common,' she says. 'Councils don't know what they're looking at, and they're terrified of approving an application and someone coming after them later. If your mill is anything like most of the ones we see, it's not going to be an issue. People generally worked them into the ground, only giving up on them once they really couldn't be fixed any more, so the chances are the poor thing's had it. However, we'd better do as the council says and give it the once over. Let me see who's available and I'll call you back, OK?'

'Thanks, Charlotte.' Her pragmatic approach has lifted my spirits no end, but it takes me a while to share the news with Rebecca and Ben. Rebecca is mowing the park, and typically is at the far end when I go to check, and Rollo is at school today, so Ben has been taking the opportunity to test the boat on the lake without putting him at risk. We've agreed that we won't say anything to Rollo about it, so he thinks he's on the genuine maiden voyage when he next comes.

'That's great news,' they both agree when I finally manage to get them together at lunchtime.

'I am relieved, I'll admit,' I tell them. 'I was worried we'd be crawling in beardy enthusiasts, spilling real ale everywhere while banging on about flange gaskets or whatever.'

'Is that what happens, then?' Ben asks with a mischievous twinkle in his eye. 'I've got a beard, quite like a pint of real ale, and I expect I could get enthusiastic about a flange gasket if I knew what one was. Maybe this is my tribe.'

'You know I didn't mean you,' I say hurriedly. 'I meant, you know, *old* people. The type who like Morris dancing. Oh, God. You're not into Morris dancing, are you?'

'What have you got against Morris dancing?' Ben asks, evidently enjoying my increasing discomfort. 'It's a centuries-old tradition. If you're going to succeed outside the Big Smoke, you're going to need to learn to be a bit more accepting of our customs, Thea.'

'Oh, come off it!' Rebecca laughs, punching his arm playfully. 'You're no more a Morris dancer than I am.'

He grins. 'I had you going for a moment though, didn't I?'

His eyes meet hers for a second and, although I'm no relationship expert, I definitely see something pass between them. Maybe Rebecca is in with a chance after all.

19

'So, we've got two guys coming to look at the mill on Friday,' I tell Rebecca and Ben a couple of days later. We're taking a break from painting the window frames, as we're expecting a plumber friend of Ben's to give us a quote for putting a modern boiler into the cottage. Even though it's late September, the weather is fine, with more in the forecast, so we're confident that we'll have them done before winter hits.

'What qualifications do they have?' Ben asks, a mischievous expression on his face. 'If they can't pull off a convincing "hey, nonny, no", we'll have to send them packing.'

'OK, I admit I was perhaps stereotyping them a bit with the whole Morris dancing thing, but with names like Ernest and George, I doubt very much they're in the first flush of youth.'

'You don't know that,' Rebecca counters. 'Old names are making a comeback. There's a girl in Rollo's class called Mabel. I didn't think anyone was called Mabel any more. Apparently, there's a Constance in reception as well.'

'Oh, that's unkind,' Ben observes. 'What if she turns out not to be constant at all? We had a girl called Felicity in my class at primary school. She was the most deceitful little cow I think I've ever met.'

'Really? How so?' Rebecca leans forward as if interested, but the puppy dog eyes she's giving Ben are very clear. From his expression, he's not only picking up the signals, but he's pretty happy with them too.

'I'll give you an example,' Ben tells her, lowering his voice conspiratorially so she has to lean even closer. I notice she's now positioned herself to give him the maximum benefit of her cleavage. Subtle, she is not.

'There was another girl in our class, called Alison. Felicity absolutely hated her, for some reason, and was always trying to get her into trouble. Anyway, one day Alison couldn't take it any more, and she apparently attacked Felicity in the girls' toilets. There was a tussle and a mirror got broken. Felicity went straight to the headmistress in floods of tears and reported it. Alison was suspended for a week. I've never seen Felicity so happy.'

'That's nasty,' Rebecca says.

'Oh, it gets worse. I mean, it seemed out of character for Alison, but what we didn't know at the time was that the incident never happened. There was another girl in Felicity's gang called Olivia, who had a bit of a crush on me. She told me that it was Felicity who broke the mirror, and she made up the whole story about Alison attacking her.'

'What a cow!' Rebecca exclaims, somehow managing to look outraged and lovestruck at the same time. 'What did you do?'

'I urged Olivia to tell the headmistress what she knew, but she was scared of Felicity. That pissed me off, so when Alison came back, I made a point of being friends with her and looking out for her. Felicity and Olivia were livid, but I was more popular than they were, so they didn't dare come after me.'

'Aww. You're so nice. Any girl would be lucky to have you as a friend.' Rebecca has turned the flirtation up to the max, and it's making me feel a bit queasy. Ben, I notice, is lapping it up. Thankfully, before this little scene can get any more nauseating, we're interrupted by the arrival of Ben's plumber friend, Chris.

* * *

'Your best bet's going to be oil,' Chris observes after we've shown him round. He's looked at the architectural drawings and made copious notes in scrawling writing on his pad. How he deciphers it later is anyone's guess.

'We were hoping for something a bit more eco-friendly,' I tell him.

'Yeah, no good here. Most of the eco stuff needs a really well-insulated house, and I think we can all agree this ain't it. The only way you're going to get this place warm is to pump a shit-load of heat into it until the walls warm through, and heat pumps won't do that.'

'What about wood pellets?' I persevere, keen to prove that I've done my research.

'A few problems there. First, the boilers are bloody massive. You'd need to build an outhouse just for the boiler and the wood pellet hopper. Have you got planning for an outhouse?'

'No,' I admit. 'But we could probably get it.'

'Fine. But then you've got to keep filling the hopper. House like this, you'd be filling it every few days in winter. And after all that, you've got to empty out the ash. Ben says you're developing this to sell on?'

'That's right.'

'Steer clear of wood pellets then. They smell nice, but they're a pain in the arse in every other way. Nope, as there's no gas here, I reckon old-fashioned oil is your best bet. It still won't be cheap, mind, even at mates' rates. You need the boiler, the oil tank, radiators, all the plumbing. It's a big job.'

'Oil's OK,' Ben assures us. 'It's what most of the village has.' He turns to Chris. 'Can you run us up some numbers?'

'Sure. I'll have something with you by the end of the day.'

'What's the latest with you and Ben?' I ask Rebecca as Ben walks Chris back to his van.

'What do you mean?' she replies guiltily.

'Oh, I don't know, I felt like I was a bit of a third wheel earlier. You were practically dry humping him, and he didn't seem to be resisting.'

'I don't know what you're talking about!' she says archly.

'Any girl would be lucky to have *you* as a friend, Ben,' I say in a saccharine voice. 'Will you be my special friend, Ben? Look at my cleavage, Ben, it's all for you.'

'It wasn't like that.'

'It totally was. But it seems to be working.'

Her face transforms instantly into an expression of hope. 'Do you think so?'

'Why don't you ask him out? The worst he can do is say no.'

'He's supposed to ask me out. That's how it works.'

'What is this, the 1950s? What happened to female empowerment? If you want to go on a date with him, then ask him.'

She suddenly looks terrified. 'Oh, I don't know, Thea. Anyway, I've got Rollo to think about.'

'Rollo adores Ben nearly as much as you do,' I point out. 'Plus, I'd take advantage of the on-hand babysitting service at Mum and Phil's while you can.'

'I'll think about it, OK?'

'Do. I don't think I can stand the way things are for much longer.'

* * *

I was half right about Ernest and George. When they climb out of the battered Volvo estate and introduce themselves, Ernest is exactly as I imagined he would be. He's bald, with a thick white beard covering half of his ruddy face and a pot belly poking out of his overalls. His actual age is impossible to guess; he could be anywhere between sixty and eighty, I reckon. It wouldn't surprise me if he has a second career moonlighting as Santa in a garden centre somewhere each Christmas.

The surprise is George. He may have an old person name, but he's our age or possibly a little younger. His blond hair is a strange mismatch with his eyes, which I would expect to be blue, but are actually such a dark brown that they're almost black, but that's not the main thing that I notice about him. What I notice is that he's absolutely, 100 per cent, the most beautiful man I think I've ever set eyes on. I mean, Alasdair was pretty good looking, but George is properly hot. As he comes closer, I notice that his eyes are framed by the kind of lashes that no man should be allowed to possess, and his full lips part to reveal even, white teeth when he smiles in greeting. His voice is soft but his grip is firm as he shakes my hand, and a quick glance down reveals that his hands are as beautiful as the rest of him, with neatly cut nails on the ends of his thick, strong fingers.

'Would you like a cup of tea or coffee before we begin?' I manage to stammer as I reluctantly let go of George's hand.

'That would be perfect, love, thank you,' Ernest replies, making me bristle slightly. 'Tea, white with two for me. George?'

'I'm a coffee man. White, no sugar. Would you like a hand?'

If I'm impressed by his manners, that's nothing compared to the very graphic train of thought that is coursing through my mind as I contemplate various ways I'd like George to give me a hand. It's like a switch has flicked in my head, and all rational thought has been turned off.

'No, it's fine,' I say hurriedly.

'I wouldn't mind using the loo, if you have one,' Ernest continues. 'My bladder isn't what it used to be.'

'No problem, let me show you the way.'

They follow me into the house and Ernest disappears in the direction of the bathroom when I direct him, leaving me alone with George. I concentrate very hard on not looking at him as I busy myself with filling the kettle and switching it on.

'This is quite the project,' George observes, glancing around him. 'Are you doing it all yourself?'

'No, I have a partner – a business partner. She'll be here any minute actually, they've just popped out for more paint,' I gabble. What is the matter with me? Thankfully, before I have the opportunity to make a complete idiot of myself, Ernest reappears.

'That's better,' he informs us unnecessarily. 'So, Charlotte in the office informs me you're after a certificate to say your mill is beyond economic repair. Is that right?'

'That's it,' I tell him as I hand him his mug.

'I expect it's just a formality; sadly, most of the mills I've seen lately are completely shot, but we have to dot the i's and cross the t's, don't we.'

'There isn't anything Ernest doesn't know about watermills and windmills,' George informs me, his soft voice making my insides quiver.

'I come from a long line of millers,' Ernest explains. 'Sadly, I'm the last one as neither of my children have any interest. They say their childhood was spent being dragged round various mills, and if they never see another one, it'll be too soon.'

'And what about you?' I ask George. 'How did you get into the milling business?'

'I started out as a regular mechanic, but modern cars are basically just rolling computers and I'm a sucker for old-school engineering,' he says, treating me to another flash of his beautiful smile. 'Steam engines, mills, basically if there's heavy cogs, I'm into it.'

'George is restoring a traction engine,' Ernest adds.

'Not on my own,' George clarifies. 'It's a group project. The idea is that we'll take it to shows and stuff once it's done.'

A picture of George on the platform of a massive traction engine, sweat glistening on his strong arms as he shovels coal, forms in my mind. Dear God, I'm going to need to lie down if this continues for much longer. Seven months without Alasdair to keep my libido under control and I'm in danger of turning into some kind of sex pest. Thankfully, Rebecca and Ben choose this moment to appear and save me from total meltdown.

'This is Rebecca, my friend and business partner,' I tell Ernest and George. 'And this is Ben, who lives at the end of the drive and has been helping us out.' I spot Rebecca sizing George up, and a niggle of irritation forms in the pit of my stomach. *Leave him alone*, I silently project at her. *You've already got Ben, don't be greedy.*

'The kettle's just boiled if you and Ben want a cuppa,' I tell her instead.

'I'd love one, I'm parched,' Ben says, thankfully diverting Rebecca's attention back onto him. A look passes between them, and I wonder if she's plucked up the courage to ask him out. An awkward silence descends while we watch her getting mugs out of the cupboard and fiddling about with the teabags.

'George was just telling us about a traction engine he's restoring,' I tell Ben, keen to get the conversation flowing again.

'Really?' Ben's interest is clearly piqued, as I'd hoped it would be. 'That's a big old thing, where are you keeping it?'

While the three of them chat about the intricacies of traction engine restoration, I take the opportunity to sidle over to Rebecca.

'Did you have a conversation with Ben?' I enquire gently.

'Have I asked him out, do you mean?' She smiles. 'We're going to the pub on Saturday evening, as it happens. Are you sure you don't mind looking after Rollo?'

'Of course not. I'm pleased for you,' I say, suppressing a sigh of relief. 'George is a bit of a surprise, isn't he?'

'Hmm. Definite gay vibe there, if you ask me.'

'Do you think?' I hadn't considered that, and it's definitely an unwelcome thought.

'He's too beautiful to be straight,' she says simply.

Before I can think of a suitable comeback, Ernest sets his mug down on the side with a thump.

'Right then,' he says. 'Shall we take a look at this mill of yours?'

20

'Overshot, nice,' Ernest comments as we walk around the side of the mill and the external components come into view.

'I'm sorry?' I say.

'He's talking about the flow of the water,' George explains. 'It flows in from above the water wheel, see? It's the most efficient way to drive a wheel because you're using the weight of the water to turn it. Undershot wheels are the opposite; they have paddles that dip into water flowing beneath them, a bit like a paddle steamer in reverse. They're nowhere near as efficient though.'

'Why aren't they all overshot then?'

'You need a good drop from the pond to the tail race to drive an overshot wheel.'

'Sorry, you've lost me again. What's a tail race?'

'OK, let's start at the top and work our way down. To drive a watermill you need water, right?'

'Which comes from the pond.'

'Yes, but if we're looking at the whole picture, you need

something to refill the pond, otherwise you'd run it once, empty the pond, and that would be it.'

'I hadn't thought about that.'

'So what usually happens is you have a river nearby, and part or all of the flow from the river is diverted into your mill pond. River levels are unpredictable and mills like this one work best with fairly constant water flow, so think of the mill pond as a kind of battery. When you run the mill, you're depleting the battery, and the stream or river recharges it.'

'But if you have a stream or river constantly flowing into your pond and you don't run the mill, wouldn't it flood?'

'It would, but that's where the spillway comes in.'

If I were talking to anyone but George, I would have given up on this conversation by now, but the sound of his voice and the way his mouth moves as he talks are holding me spellbound.

'I'll bite,' I tell him with a smile that I hope isn't openly flirtatious. 'What's a spillway?'

'Basically it's a mini dam that acts like a safety valve. If the level in the pond rises above the level of the dam, it flows safely over the spillway back into the stream below, bypassing the mill completely. Yours is over there.' He points to the waterfall that I'm definitely not going to tell him I thought was just a water feature.

'OK. I get that.'

'So that's what's happening at the moment. All the flow from the river is coming into your pond and going straight over the spillway to rejoin the river. But, if you open the sluice gate to let water into the mill, it flows down the raceway, which is the trough you can just see through the tree, over the water wheel, causing it to turn, and then down the tail race, which is effectively just a mini stream, until it rejoins the river lower down. It's a simple mechanism, but like a lot of these things, pure genius.

More reliable than a windmill unless you have a drought and, back in the day, you'd have had daisy chains of watermills all along a river, with the water passing from one to the next.'

'It's a shame about the tarpaulin,' Ernest complains. 'I can't see the wheel at all. I've never come across someone covering a wheel up like that.'

'My grandad was a stickler for looking after it, even though it wasn't running,' Ben tells him. 'Every year, he'd re-treat the wheel and then cover it back up to stop the weather getting to it.'

'How long since it was last treated?'

'Probably three or four years. He was too frail to do it at the end of his life.'

'Hm. If it's well treated and the weather's been kept off, it might be OK. Let's have a look inside.'

'Oh, my word,' Ernest breathes as I open the door and follow him and George into the mill. 'This is a lot better than I was expecting.'

I stare around in bemusement. Is Ernest looking at the same thing as me? Because all I can see are rusty bits of metal and manky-looking wood.

'Right, let's start at the beginning,' Ernest continues, getting a torch out of his bag and shining it at an enormous cog that's half-submerged in the floor. 'Pit wheel looks solid and the wallower is also in good condition apart from a little surface rust.' He prods the wooden column that rises through the ceiling with his screwdriver. 'Shaft feels nice and firm here, no evidence of woodworm or rot.'

'We do like a firm shaft,' Rebecca murmurs in my ear, causing us both to snort with laughter. Thankfully, Ernest and George are too engrossed in the mill machinery to notice, but I spot Ben looking at us quizzically.

'Sorry,' I mouth at him, and bite my lip to prevent any more inappropriate giggles escaping while Ernest continues to inspect the shaft approvingly.

'Smut aside, what does this all mean, do you suppose?' Rebecca whispers to me as Ernest and George move to the staircase to continue their inspection.

'I'm not sure, but it sounds like our mill might not be as knackered as it looks,' I whisper back.

We follow George and Ernest up the stairs to the middle floor, where Ernest makes more encouraging noises about various incomprehensible-sounding bits of machinery before wandering over to a round wooden tub and lifting the lid.

'George, come and look at this,' he says excitedly. 'We've got French Burr stones by the look of it.'

'I'm sorry, what?' I ask.

'There are essentially two types of stone you find in a mill like this,' George explains in his smooth-as-chocolate voice. I reckon he could read the dictionary to me and I'd find it fascinating. 'Derbyshire Peak stones are the most common, but French Burr stones, which is what you have, are harder and grind finer. It's a good thing.'

'Umm. I'm not sure I want good things, George,' I tell him. 'We're supposed to be certifying that it's beyond repair, remember?'

'I know, but you heard what Ernest said, didn't you? So far, it's all looking pretty good in here.' He obviously registers my look of dismay as he quickly continues. 'Look, although it's been covered up, the water wheel will degrade pretty fast if it's not looked after, and while this machinery all looks in reasonable condition, it might well be seized solid for all we know.'

'I hope you're right,' I tell him grimly. 'We need that certificate.'

There are more noises of delight when Ernest reaches the top floor, and my mood plummets further. After an hour or so, we congregate on the ground floor, or the 'machinery floor' as Ernest insists on calling it.

'Well, ladies, you've quite made my day,' Ernest says happily. 'It's a long time since I've seen a mill in such good condition. You're very lucky.'

'So what happens now?' I ask, feeling anything but lucky.

'OK. I can't give you a certificate today, I'm afraid. What I need you to do is get rid of the fallen tree outside so we can have a look at the water wheel. If that's as good as the rest of it, I reckon we might be in business.'

'What do you mean, "in business"?'

'The bearings need to be greased, and there are probably a few adjustments that need to be made, but I reckon this mill could be a runner. Good news, eh?'

I stare at him as my heart falls through the floor. He's obviously completely forgotten how we wanted this to go. Ernest is chatting happily with Ben, but George obviously picks up on it, as he gently pulls Rebecca and me aside as we walk back round to the cottage.

'Look, I know this isn't what you wanted, but I'm sure you'll find a way to adapt your plans if you don't get the certificate.'

'I can't think how,' I tell him gloomily as Ben pulls out his mobile phone and dials a number.

'Dave,' I hear him say when the call connects. 'I'm calling to ask a favour. Yeah, there's a tree that I need moving. No, at the mill. As soon as possible really.'

There's a long pause, presumably while Dave, whoever he is, checks his availability. 'Wednesday?' Ben says eventually. 'Perfect. Thanks. Yeah, see you then.'

'Dave will come and deal with the tree on Wednesday,' he announces unnecessarily.

'Perfect,' Ernest says happily. 'I'll call Charlotte and give her the news. I can't speak for George here, but, assuming nothing urgent comes up in the meantime, I'll be back on Wednesday too with a large pot of grease. All being well, and assuming the water wheel is OK, I reckon we might be able to fire it up as soon as the tree is out of the way.'

* * *

'Well, that couldn't have gone much worse,' I mutter darkly as we watch the Volvo bounce back down the track.

'What are we going to do if we can't get the certificate?' Rebecca asks. 'I guess we could adapt the plans and do up the mill instead of converting it. It would certainly be a talking point for the new owners. "Come next door and have a look at my fully functional mill."'

'Sounds like the ultimate dinner party bore to me. It was bad enough listening to Ernest wanging on about wallowers and pit wheels. Honestly, if George hadn't been there to translate and explain, I think I would have gone to sleep.'

'Hmm. I did notice you were paying rather close attention to him,' she says with a half-smile. 'I still think he's gay, but I'm sure the idea of him getting hot and greasy with the mill machinery isn't the worst mental image you'll ever have had.'

I allow the image to form in my mind, sitting it alongside the earlier one of George on his traction engine, and I have to admit it does improve my mood. I file them neatly away for future use before returning my focus to our predicament.

'Ben?' I ask, after thinking about it for a while. 'I don't

suppose you have any mill saboteurs in your extensive contact list, do you?'

He smiles. 'Sadly not. In fact, I don't have anyone with any form of mill expertise, I'm afraid. I do agree with Rebecca though. It might actually be a selling point.'

'I doubt it,' I tell them. 'It's like a swimming pool on steroids.'

'What have swimming pools got to do with it?' Ben asks, confused.

'Having a swimming pool generally devalues a house and makes it harder to sell,' I explain. 'Having a fully functional bloody watermill is going to be even worse.'

'I'd have thought swimming pools would increase the value,' Ben persists. 'They're aspirational, aren't they?'

'Maybe, if you were in a hot country and had an outdoor pool you could use a lot. But here, you either need an indoor pool if you're going to want to use it year round, or you get to use it on the three nice summer days when you're not working. And, for the privilege of doing that, you lose a fat chunk of garden and have to spend a fortune on chemicals and what have you to maintain it. Oddly, very few people see that as a plus when looking for a house. How much do you think it costs to maintain a sodding mill? And you're never going to get any benefit out of it unless you're some kind of psychotic uber-baker who's obsessed with milling their own flour. I don't know about you, but that sounds like a pretty niche market to me.'

'I've just had an idea,' Rebecca remarks thoughtfully. 'If this mill is so historically significant, or whatever, there are probably grants and stuff you can get to pay for its upkeep. So, you get your dinner party talking point, the government coughs up to maintain it, and every so often you bring in someone like Ernest to mill some flour and charge for entry. It could be a win-win.'

'Hmm. Maybe, but I reckon it's still going to need a very

specific type of buyer. One who appreciates the privacy the park gives them, but is also happy to invite a load of strangers round every so often to watch Ernest strut his stuff. In fact, you're going to need specific strangers too, because listening to Ernest talk about milling is guaranteed to send most people to sleep.'

She sighs. 'You're right. Back to plan A.'

'Which is?'

'Hope like hell that Ernest finds a fatal problem when he tries to run it.'

'Are you sure you don't know any mill saboteurs?' I ask Ben again.

He smiles. 'Not one, sorry.'

'Right, well, I guess there's nothing we can do but crack on for the time being. We're not going to learn anything more until your mate Dave gets rid of the tree.'

As I settle back into the familiar task of painting the window frames, I allow various images of George to play through my mind. I know I'll probably never see him again after he and Ernest have sorted the mill out, but I've never reacted that viscerally to a man before, even Alasdair. To be fair, the only other eligible man I've seen since leaving Morton Lansdowne is Ben but, even if Rebecca weren't chasing him for all she was worth, the beard would rule him out for me. I tell myself firmly to get a grip and focus on solving the problem at hand.

Not until after I've enjoyed these mental images for a little while longer, though.

21

It's Wednesday morning and I'm feeling nervous. Ernest is due to arrive at any moment to start greasing the mill in preparation for its (hopefully fatal) test run, but there's no sign of Ben's mate Dave yet. If the tree doesn't go today, this whole fiasco is just going to drag out, and I want to know where we stand so we can make a plan. At least we've finally finished the windows, which I have to say look particularly good now in their fresh white paint, and Ben's other friend Chris is cracking on at an impressive rate installing the new central heating system. I'm conscious that I've only got a few more months where I'm actually going to be paid a salary, but living at Mum and Phil's has been ridiculously cheap because they flatly refused to charge more than a peppercorn rent, so I'm actually pretty flush with cash and relaxed where day-to-day living expenses are concerned. I also managed to offload the idiotic Porsche, which I've replaced with a much more sensible SUV. Rebecca also seems fairly relaxed where money is concerned, no doubt in part because Alice relented and didn't ask her to pay back the three months of mortgage cover. I did think it was odd that she seemed to be playing hardball over it, given how she'd promised to make everything all right, so I was pleased for Rebecca when she changed her mind.

Rebecca and Ben's date night at the pub obviously went better than expected, as I caught her trying to creep in early on Sunday morning. We normally make a point of staying away from the mill on Sundays, so there's one day of the week where we're free of it, but she insisted on making a picnic and taking it down there, so we all trolled along too. It was actually a lovely day. Ben spent a lot of time trying, with various degrees of success, to teach Rollo and Louis to row on the lake while the rest of us observed from the safety of the shore. To my mind, the splashing-to-progress ratio was definitely heavily weighted towards the splashing side, but they did manage to make it all the way around by the end of the day, coming ashore completely soaked. Mum offered to bring Rollo home with us so Rebecca and Ben could have some more time alone, which was obviously well used if the flushed and happy expression on her face when she turned up a few hours later was anything to go by.

Thankfully, any apprehension I might have had about their burgeoning relationship getting in the way of progress at the mill has proved unfounded. They are openly affectionate with each other, but we're working as hard as we ever have. Today, we've finally started to rip out the tired old kitchen as, even if we don't get permission to relocate it into the mill, we need to do something with it. Ben is currently dismantling the coal-fired range, a messy job because every interior surface of it is thick with coal dust and it seems to be putting up quite a fight, so he looks a little like a miner at the end of a particularly mucky shift. The telltale smudge of coal dust on Rebecca's nose that I've chosen not to mention indicates that they've managed to find a moment together already this morning, despite the heavy workload.

The sound of an approaching engine makes me glance out of the window, just in time to see a covered pickup truck pull up and park outside the door. The words 'D. Lodge, Tree Surgeon' are emblazoned on the side along with a phone number and email address, so I'm guessing this must be Ben's mate Dave. I'm therefore rather surprised when the driver's door opens and a stocky woman with short, ash-blonde spiky hair hops out. She's dressed all in black except for her boots, which are Dr Martens with a riotous floral pattern. Another woman emerges from the passenger side; she's tall and athletic looking, with dark brown hair pulled back in a ponytail.

Ben has obviously heard them arrive too, as he's on his feet and outside to greet them before they've even had a chance to close the doors.

'Bloody hell, Ben!' the stocky one exclaims when she sees him. 'Did you lose a fight with a coal scuttle? You can keep well away from both of us, thank you very much.'

'Nice to see you too,' he says warmly as Rebecca and I walk out to join them.

'Thea, Rebecca, this is my mate Dave,' Ben tells us before turning back to her. 'Thea and Rebecca own the mill. I'm just helping them out.'

'Of course you are,' she says, laughing. 'I'm Dave, which is short for Davina if you hadn't already worked it out. This is my partner Brooke, which isn't short for anything. Ben tells me you've got a tree that needs moving?'

'Yes, round the corner. Would you like me to show you?'

'Nah, you're all right. A tree surgeon who can't find the right tree isn't going to be in business for long. There isn't any chance of a cup of tea though, is there?'

'We're pulling the kitchen apart at the moment, but we still have a kettle,' I tell her. 'How do you like it?'

'White without, please. Do you want one, Brooke hun?'

'Yes, please. Same as hers if that's OK.'

'Why didn't you tell me Dave was a woman?' I whisper to Ben as we make our way back indoors. Rebecca has elected to stay outside, chatting to Dave and Brooke while they change into their work gear and pull various harnesses and massive chainsaws out of the back of the pickup.

'Does it make a difference?' he asks, clearly amused.

'Of course not! It's just that I kind of assumed that a tree surgeon with a name like Dave—'

'Would be a man. Everyone does. It's part of her USP. If you got in a bloke, let's call him Terry, who fit all the stereotypes of a tree surgeon, you'd probably forget him before he even reached the end of the drive. You won't forget Dave, will you?'

'And Brooke, is she...?'

'Brooke is Dave's everything. Business partner, life partner, the lot. They met when we all started secondary school and have been inseparable ever since. They live in the village and got married four years ago. I think Brooke would like to start a family, but Dave's worried about how she'll cope on her own with the business. Anyway, they're great friends of mine and they'll do an excellent job.'

'Thinking of friends, we probably ought to chat about you and Rebecca.'

He grins. 'Are you going to ask me what my intentions are?'

'Not at all. She's very smitten with you though, so I just wanted to check whether you feel the same way, or whether I'm going to be mopping her up with boxes of tissues in a month or two.'

'I think she's incredible,' he says simply. 'To come through everything that she's been through and still be as optimistic as she is, that's amazing. Look, I know you two are going to sell this place and move on, but you'll still be in the area, won't you? She's been very clear that she's not going to keep yanking Rollo out of one school to stuff him in another.'

'So you're thinking this could be a long-term thing?'

'I'd like it to be, yes.'

A thought comes to me. 'And, just for the sake of argument, if we were to buy another property not too far away, would you be as helpful as you have been here?'

'My God!' he exclaims theatrically, clapping a hand to his forehead. 'This is a honeytrap. I should have known!'

'What?' I have no idea what he's talking about.

'This is how you operate, isn't it? Find a handyman and get Rebecca to seduce him so he'll willingly work himself to the bone for you. She's the honey and you're the trap.'

'I'm pretty sure that's not how a honeytrap works, and you're miles off course,' I tell him with a laugh. 'I was just curious, that's all. Oh, that must be Ernest arriving now. I'd better go and greet him.'

'Before you do, let me just tell you in all seriousness that you have nothing to fear from me where Rebecca is concerned. I know it's early days, but I've got a good feeling about her, and I'll do everything I can to make her happy.'

I smile as I pick up the mugs of tea. 'I know you will, Ben. You're one of the good guys.'

'I like to hope so.'

* * *

My day is brightened considerably when I realise that Ernest is not alone. Once more, George is with him, looking frankly edible in dark blue overalls. I wonder if he'll get hot and have to peel them off his top half, tying them round his waist so I can appreciate his biceps as he works.

'Look at that, George,' Ernest exclaims as he levers himself out of the driving seat. 'Our tea is waiting for us. That's service, that is.'

'Sorry, Ernest,' I tell him. 'These are for the tree surgeons. I'll get you something in a minute.'

'They're here then?' he asks.

I don't reply, nodding at the pickup truck instead. As if on cue, the telltale sound of chainsaw motors suddenly fills the air, and I round the side of the cottage to find Dave and Brooke already hard at work in the branches of the tree. Rebecca is watching them with an awed expression on her face.

'It's extraordinary,' she yells over the din. 'Kind of like ballet but with massive power tools.'

I stand and watch with her for a few moments and I see what she means. Dave and Brooke are in their harnesses working their way confidently through the tree, as bits of branch fall regularly onto the ground below. After a few minutes, I catch Brooke's eye and wave the mugs, before settling them on the ground to go and deal with Ernest and George. It looks like I'm not a moment too soon, as Ernest has cornered Ben and appears to be giving him a detailed lecture on some aspect of mill mechanics. Ben is trying to look interested, but I can tell he's desperate to get away so he can carry on fighting with the range.

'Ernest, I've been meaning to ask you a question,' I say to him in one of his rare pauses for breath. 'It's very kind of you to come and do this, but we haven't talked about finance and what your time costs.'

'Oh, you don't need to worry about that,' he replies. 'We're still in the discovery phase, so HIBT picks up the tab. If we find it's not viable, I think there's a fee for the certificate, but Charlotte will tell you all about that. If, as I suspect, it's a runner, then there are various things we can offer to help you get the most out of it. But let's not jump the gun, eh? George and I have a lot of work to do before we get to that stage.' He glances uneasily at Dave and Brooke. 'I hope they know what they're doing,' he observes unhappily. 'Women wielding power tools make me uneasy. It's like women driving buses or lorries. Unnatural.'

'I won't hold you up,' I tell him, forcing myself to remain civil. 'If you want to make a start, I'll bring your tea round to you in a few minutes.'

'Perfect. Right, come on, George. We've got greasing to do.'

By three o'clock, the tree has been reduced to a pile of logs, and the rest of us are watching as Ernest and George carefully ease the tarpaulin away from the water wheel. It's brittle from being out in the sun, and they're being careful not to leave any pieces on the ground, in case they get washed into the river when we open the sluice. I've got my fingers metaphorically crossed, hoping that the holes in the tarpaulin have let in enough weather to make the wheel underneath unusable, but Ernest's shout of triumph when they finally get all the tarpaulin away to reveal a depressingly solid-looking wheel is enough to assure me that the mill has played another bloody ace.

'OK,' Ernest calls. 'We're ready. George, have you tentered the stones?'

'Yup.'

'What the bloody hell does that mean?' Dave asks Ben.

'No idea,' he replies.

'Right,' Ernest shouts again. 'I'm going to set our remote camera up inside the mill. The rest of you, stand well back, all right?'

'Why?' I ask. 'What are you expecting to happen?'

'I'm hoping it will start running normally, but there's a lot of heavy machinery in there that could make quite a mess if it breaks loose, so best to play it safe and keep clear to begin with.'

We've all seen the heavy machinery he's talking about, and respectfully take quite a few steps back. Ernest disappears inside the mill, reappearing a few moments later and leaving George alone at the top of the channel leading down to the water wheel.

'How come George gets the dangerous job?' I ask Ernest.

'Simple. He can run faster than me,' Ernest replies with a smile, before giving George a thumbs up.

'He'll open the sluice gate to start the water flowing,' Ernest tells us all. 'We'll be able to see what's happening on my phone screen.'

We all watch in silence as George turns the handle to raise the gate. Even at this distance, we can clearly hear the clack-clack of the ratchet mechanism, and my heartbeat quickens as water begins to pour over the wheel. George, having done his job, sprints over to join us.

'Well, this is a bit of an anticlimax,' Dave observes a few moments later. She's right. The water is pouring over the wheel but there's no sign of motion.

'It takes time,' George tells her. 'We need to fill enough buckets in the wheel to overcome the inertia.'

We stand and watch as nothing continues to happen. I'm just beginning to hope that maybe Ernest's diagnosis was wrong and the whole mechanism is seized after all when the wheel suddenly lurches and starts to turn. We all crowd round Ernest's phone to see what's happening inside, and I can clearly see the massive cogs turning and meshing with each other. Ernest's face lights up.

'Ladies and gentlemen,' he announces. 'We have a runner!'

Fuck.

22

'Now what?' Rebecca asks gloomily once the others have left and it's just the three of us once more. After its successful trial, Ernest got George to shut the mill down again fairly quickly, and they've promised to return next week to inspect the wheel more thoroughly and perform any adjustments needed, including dressing the stones, whatever the hell that is. I think this is probably Ernest's equivalent of winning the lottery, and George seemed pretty excited too. In my mind, the only upside of this disaster is that we might see more of George, as he's assured us that he and Ernest will help with any work the mill needs, and HIBT will be on hand to make sure we're aware of the various grants on offer. What HIBT absolutely won't give us, however, is the one thing we really wanted, namely the certificate that would have enabled us to proceed with the conversion.

'I don't know,' I sigh. 'I mean, we'll have to finish the renovation of the cottage, because nobody will buy it in its current state, but if the council and HIBT slap a preservation order on the mill, which Ernest seems to think they might, that's literally a millstone round the neck of whoever owns the property.'

'Ha ha.' Rebecca smiles grimly. 'I see what you did there.'

'For what it's worth, I'm really sorry,' Ben offers.

'What have you got to be sorry for?' Rebecca asks him.

'I feel kind of responsible. It was me that sold you the mill, after all.'

'It's not like you forced us to buy it,' she tells him reassuringly, laying her hand on his forearm. 'Thea and I jumped into this hole all by ourselves.'

'Maybe George would like it,' she continues after a long, morose silence. 'He's into all that kind of thing, and he could keep his traction engine in one of the barns.'

'I don't think George is going to be able to give us the return on our investment that we're looking for,' I say sadly.

'What makes you say that?'

'Unless he's a secret millionaire, I very much doubt a charity like HIBT is going to pay him the kind of wage he'd need to buy this.' In the silence that follows, I do allow myself a brief fantasy where George is in fact a secret millionaire who buys the cottage, declares undying love for me, and I spend the rest of my days watching him hurling sacks of wheat around in the mill as effortlessly as if they were filled with feathers, his muscles rippling as he does. I'm just getting to the bit where he picks me up as if I'm similarly weightless and takes me upstairs for some thrilling sex when Ben's voice punctures my reverie.

'Maybe it would be more attractive to a buyer if you could find a way to make it earn its keep,' he suggests.

'But how would we do that?' I counter. 'It's not commercially viable; it's basically a museum piece.'

'Exactly,' he replies. 'Open it as a working museum.'

'Sorry, Ben, but I think that would make it even more unattractive to a potential buyer. Even if the council let you do it, it would be a load of aggro. You'd need to provide car parking, you'd have strangers permanently wandering around the place and, oh God, you'd probably have to have some sort of gift shop selling overpriced tat. Plus, and this is the killer, this is just a two-bedroom cottage without the mill conversion. Who's going to want to pay top dollar for that, even when we've renovated it?'

'You could extend the cottage in another direction. It might even be cheaper than converting the mill and it's not like there's a shortage of space.'

For the first time since Ernest pronounced the mill operational, a flicker of hope stirs in me. The mill itself is still a problem, but if we got permission to extend the house in another direction, we could still make something desirable out of it.

'Do you know what, Ben?' I tell him. 'I think you might be on to something with that.'

'You're a genius,' Rebecca agrees, giving him a kiss and earning herself a dark smudge on the cheek to go with the one on her nose.

* * *

By the time George and Ernest return the following Wednesday, it feels like we're back on track. The architect has visited and is drawing up new plans for us to extend the house backwards, which will include knocking through the current rear wall to create the all-important open-plan kitchen-diner, with space for the extra bedrooms that were originally going to go in the mill above. As a bonus, it means we're going to be able to install bifold doors that will not only let in a lot of light, but also give a beautiful view of the pond. I hesitate to say it, but I think it might even be better than our original plan. Plumber Chris, despite being initially frustrated that his original piping diagrams for the mill were going to have to be redone, is now also on board and trying to persuade us to install underfloor heating in the extension.

We've looked at the possibility of splitting the plot into several subplots and applying for permission to build multiple houses, with the aim of selling it on to a developer, but Rebecca was right that there's a covenant to stop us doing that and, having done a quick straw poll in the pub, Ben told us that there would be quite a lot of objection from the village as well, so we've abandoned that idea. We do have an extensive list of questions for Ernest and George though, and I'm looking forward to sitting down with George and grilling him. Rebecca has agreed to distract Ernest because she thinks I deserve a bit of one-on-one time with George, although she's admitted that she still thinks he's gay and she's also worried about listening to Ernest drone on about tentering and all his other strange little milling terms. I have done my absolute best to resurrect enough of 'old' Thea to remind me that mooning around over men is not what modern, self-sufficient women do and I'm not some fifties housewife who isn't complete without a man. It hasn't been a complete success.

'Morning, ladies,' Ernest says happily after he's wriggled free from the driving seat of the Volvo. 'Have we got some treats in store for you. Any chance of a cuppa first, though?'

Without waiting for a response, he strides through the open door into the house, carrying a large folder under his arm. 'Doesn't look like you've made a lot of progress in here,' he observes, staring at the blank walls where the kitchen units used to be.

'Yeah, we're having to adapt our plans because of the mill,' I tell him, trying not to sound annoyed as Rebecca and I set about making the tea. 'So everything's up in the air a bit at the moment.'

'That mill is a real beauty. I've been telling everyone at HIBT about it.'

'I bet that was a delight for them,' Rebecca murmurs in my ear, causing me to snort with laughter.

'Yes, well, we've got a lot to do,' Ernest continues, shooting us a suspicious look. 'There's rather a lot of paperwork, but I'm happy to take you through it.'

'I expect you're anxious to get out into the mill,' Rebecca says hurriedly. 'Can't George take us through the paperwork?'

Ernest looks at us suspiciously again, evidently trying to weigh up whether we're up to something or not.

'You have been saying it's time I stepped up on the admin side of things,' George chips in. 'I'm happy to do it if you like.'

'Hmm,' Ernest says doubtfully. 'I could use a second pair of hands really, but someone's got to do the forms.'

'I'll help you,' Rebecca tells him.

'But you don't know anything about watermills,' Ernest protests.

'I seem to own one, so I probably ought to learn, don't you think?' she replies smoothly, giving me a surreptitious wink as she adds milk to the mugs.

'Very well. Let's have our cuppa and then I'll show you what's what. I just need to pop to the loo. You really ought to do something about your track. It plays havoc with my bladder.'

'He's a bit eccentric, but he does know what he's talking about,' George assures us once Ernest is out of the room. 'At HIBT, they call him the mill whisperer. He'll have that thing purring like a kitten in no time. Have you given any more thought to what you're going to do with it? Mills are happiest if you run them pretty much every day.'

'We're still trying to figure that part out,' I tell him honestly as we sit down at the table and he pulls a fat wad of papers out of the folder that Ernest brought in.

'OK, well, the good news, at least I hope it's good news, is that there are lots of ways that the Historic Industrial Buildings Trust can help you, if you want us to. I think I mentioned that last time we were here.'

Although he's taken up a lot of my fantasy time over the last week, some of which has been shockingly graphic, having him here in the flesh is way better. My eyes linger on his long lashes as he blinks. In fact, even the way he blinks is sexy: it's not merely a functional down and back up like most people, it's more languid, like a cat. It's as if his eyelids are aware how special his lashes are and don't want to rudely hurry them.

'The first thing we need to do,' he continues, seemingly totally oblivious to the effect he's having on me, 'is get you to sign the agreement with HIBT.'

'Make sure you get her to sign the agreement,' Ernest says as he emerges from the loo, tugging up his zip and totally ruining the moment.

'I'm already on it,' George reassures him.

'Good.' Rebecca hands him his mug of tea and he takes a long, loud slurp. 'That,' he observes in a solemn tone, 'is a damn fine cup of splosh. I don't know what you ladies do, but it always tastes better when you make it. It's the same with the missus. She makes a cracking cuppa too. It must be something in your genes, like you're born with the ability to make great tea. Right, Rebecca, would you like to accompany my good self to the mill?'

There's so much wrong with what Ernest has just said and done that I can't stop myself from staring at him aghast as he leads the way to the door. As Rebecca follows him through, she turns and mouths, 'You so owe me for this,' at me, drawing her hand across her neck dramatically.

'Like I said,' George murmurs once they've closed the door behind them, 'he is an eccentric.'

'How the hell does his wife put up with his rampant sexism?' I exclaim. 'I'd have killed him by now.'

'I couldn't possibly comment,' George says conspiratorially, flashing me a smile that combines with the tone of his voice to do frankly unnecessary things to me. 'What I can tell you, having met her, is that she's very encouraging of any projects that take him out of the house. Now, back to the agreement.'

'What am I agreeing to?'

'HIBT is a charity, so we need income from somewhere. A lot of the buildings we've been involved with over the years are open to the public, and the owners generate revenue from them. In return for the help we can give you, we ask you to agree to a 5 per cent contribution from any profits you might make from the mill.'

'What if we don't make any profit?'

'Then you don't give us any money. However, if you sell the mill and the subsequent owners decide to make an income, we would still expect a contribution from them.'

'And how long does this agreement last?'

'We ask for a ten-year commitment, but we have many HIBT partners who are still happily contributing decades after the official agreement ended, because they recognise the value that we bring. I think it's important to explain that this is about relationship. We want you to get the best out of your historic building, so we're not just going to get you up and running and then disappear. Any time you have an issue, or even if you just want some advice, you can call on us. Think of it like a subscription.'

The idea of regular visits from George is almost enough to make me sign on the dotted line immediately, but I manage to rescue my rational lawyer brain from wherever it's been sleeping and read the small print carefully. It's all pretty standard stuff and seems like a fair deal, so I sign at the end without any qualms.

'Welcome to the HIBT family,' George says with a smile as I push the document back to him. 'We're really excited to be working with you on this project.'

Not half as excited as I am, but that's got nothing to do with the mill. My mind is already conjuring up excuses to get him on site regularly. So much for 'old' Thea and her self-sufficiency.

23

Although we've been fantastically lucky with the weather so far, with a warm and dry September, October has decided to make up for it by being exceptionally cold and wet. Ben has pulled the boat out of the lake and put it in one of the barns to keep it dry over winter, much to the boys' dismay. They're both well on the way to becoming reasonably proficient rowers, although there is still a lot of splashing, which I suspect is now largely deliberate. It's early on Saturday morning and we're cooped up at Mum and Phil's, with the boys plonked in front of the TV watching a children's channel.

Mum, Rebecca, Saffy and I are sipping coffee in the kitchen and chatting about the latest developments at the mill when Saffy suddenly puts her hand on my arm.

'I know it's not going as well as you'd hoped, but I think this project has been good for you,' she tells me.

'How did you work that out?' I ask.

'You're different, somehow. Don't take this the wrong way, but I was always a bit scared of you before.'

'What's the "right" way to take a remark like that, Saf? And why were you scared of me? You're older than me, for starters.'

'Yes, but you were…' She tails off.

'I was what?' I prompt her.

'I'm trying to think of the right word. Hard, I guess. There was a hardness to you.'

'Thanks a lot!'

'You were very driven, love,' Mum adds gently. 'Always working, never taking a proper break. Even when you visited us here, we kind of got the impression you were only here in body, that your mind was somewhere else. And you were so thin and pale. Look at you now, you're glowing with good health.'

'What is this? Gang up on Thea day?' I ask crossly. 'Rebecca, do you want to add anything? Let's get it all off our chests.'

'Absolutely not,' she says with a laugh. 'I'm staying well clear. All I will say is that it's been a journey. I don't think either of us covered ourselves in glory when we first met, but now it feels like we've been friends forever. I can't imagine my life without you in it.'

That's enough to stop me in my tracks. I think back to our fierce rivalry over the parking space in Walthamstow, and I just can't connect with it at all.

'You're right,' I tell her, feeling mollified. 'It has been quite a journey.'

'We always loved you,' Mum says, and I sense another well-intentioned but misjudged remark is on the way. 'You're just easier to understand now.'

'And softer,' Saffy offers, compounding the issue.

'So what you're saying,' I tell them with my hackles up once more, 'is that, rather than being proud that I was out there making a success of my life, you just saw me as a hard frosty bitch that you couldn't relate to. Well, thanks for sharing. I feel so much better now.'

'That's not what we meant,' Mum soothes. 'Of course we were proud of you, even if we didn't understand what you did. We're just saying that your new life seems to suit you better.'

'I don't know. I thought it was quite a good summary, actually,' Saffy interjects, nudging me playfully.

'You can sod off,' I tell her. I don't know whether I'm annoyed because I feel attacked, or because I don't want to admit that Mum and Saffy might have a point. Rebecca's and my first foray into property development may not be the smooth sailing that we'd planned, but there's no doubt that I'm way happier than I would have realised was possible when I was working at Morton Lansdowne. I'm sleeping better than I have in years and, although it would have been a lot easier if the mill had been beyond repair, the constant problem solving is certainly keeping me from being bored. And then, of course, there's George.

Ernest may be boring and sexist, but George was right that he knew his stuff and, although it seems very noisy in there to me when we start the mill up, that's apparently how it's supposed to sound. Rebecca and I did a good job of feigning dismay when Ernest was called away to deal with a temperamental windmill in Norfolk, but we were both relieved, particularly as George promptly stepped up to fill his shoes. No sooner was Ernest out of the way than Rebecca decided it was high time I started to learn about the mill and disappeared to help Ben with other projects in the house, leaving George and me alone together.

Under his patient guidance, I've been sanding, painting and generally sprucing up the mill. We've retreated the water wheel, a messy job that I normally would have hated and done anything to avoid, but which turned out to be surprisingly enjoyable with George there. The only slight niggle is that, although we seem to get on well, he hasn't given anything away about his relationship status, or whether he finds me even remotely as attractive as I find him, which is a bit frustrating. However, despite the fact that Rebecca swears she can't see it and that I'm imagining it because I want it to be true, I reckon there are a few promising signs. I've caught him watching me a few times when we've been working together, and I don't think it's always because he's making sure I'm doing it right. There was also the 'sanding incident' where he covered my hand with his when showing me how to rub down a tricky-shaped piece of wood in the mill. The warmth of his hand on top of mine made my insides melt, and I still feel a bit unnecessary every time I think about it, which I do a lot. It's just a shame he doesn't visit as often as I'd like. He has, at least, given me his phone number so I can contact him if I get stuck and need to ask him something urgently. So far, I've managed to resist. I'm not that desperate, yet.

'Any progress with you and that young man?' Mum asks, as if reading my thoughts.

'Do you mean the gay one?' Saffy adds.

'Why do you all think he's gay?' I demand, getting ready for the next round of what appears to be 'lay into Thea' day.

'I've no idea whether he is or he isn't,' Saffy says blithely. 'I'm just going with what Rebecca told me.'

'I know you really like him,' Rebecca interjects, obviously keen to get her point across before I jump down her throat, 'but I'm going to stick my neck out and say I don't think he's right for you, even if he isn't gay.'

'Why not?'

'Look,' Rebecca says carefully, obviously aware that she's on dangerous ground. 'He's a nice guy and I can see he's very good looking, but I just don't think he'd be *enough* for you.'

'What's that supposed to mean?'

'Tell me about your last boyfriend.'

Shit. What am I supposed to do now? The closest thing to a boyfriend I've had recently would be Alasdair, but Mum and Saffy don't know about him, and they'll grill me from here to next week if it comes out.

'Thea's not good at boyfriends,' Saffy tells her with a smile. 'She frightens them.'

'I don't!'

'You do. Who was that poor boy you dated briefly at uni? He was terrified of you.'

'Harrison, and it's not my fault he was spineless.'

'What's George's spine like?' Saffy asks Rebecca. 'Up to the job, do you reckon?'

Rebecca eyes me thoughtfully for a moment. 'I have my doubts,' she murmurs. 'Sorry, Thea. I think you need someone more robust, who's not afraid to challenge you.'

For some reason, my mind takes me back to the breakfast I had with Alasdair when I was having my wobble before leaving Morton Lansdowne. He was never afraid to challenge me, but then we were purely friends with benefits so he didn't really have skin in the game in the same way. Am I really that terrifying? I might have been once, but I'd like to think 'new' Thea is softer. I push Alasdair back into the 'old' Thea box in my mind. He doesn't belong in my new life; nothing from my old life does.

'We're bored.' My reverie is interrupted by the arrival of Rollo and Louis, looking disgruntled.

'I thought you were watching TV,' Rebecca says to them.

'TV's boring. It's all stuff for babies. Can we have a water fight in the garden?'

'No, because it's pouring with rain and you'll catch your death,' Mum tells them firmly.

'You could go and tidy your room,' Rebecca tells Rollo. 'That's what I had to do if I was bored when I was little.'

'Yeah, but you probably didn't even have TV back then,' Rollo quips, before turning to Louis. 'She'll start talking about dial-up internet in a minute, just you wait and see.'

'What's that?' Louis's eyes are wide.

'I don't know exactly, but it's how they did internet in the olden days, apparently.'

'I tell you what,' I say to them before we can go too much further down the path of making me feel like some kind of dinosaur, as I clearly remember dial-up internet. 'Why don't we go to Drusillas? My treat. I'll even buy lunch. Saffy? Rebecca? What do you say?'

'I say you're going to make a terrible parent,' Saffy mumbles grumpily as the boys immediately start asking, 'Can we? Please?'

'You and Phil can come too, if you like,' I tell Mum. 'We could have a proper outing.'

'I think,' Mum replies with a smile, 'this sounds like a trip for the younger generations, rather than those of us who are so old we can remember a time before the internet even existed.'

'That's not possible, Nanny,' Louis tells her firmly.

'Yeah,' Rollo agrees. 'How did you google stuff if you didn't have the internet? Nobody would have known anything.'

'Boys, go and find your raincoats while I look to see if I can magic up an extra treat for us,' I tell them, keen to avoid going down this particular rabbit hole.

'You may have been scary as a sister, but you're useless with children,' Saffy scolds after the boys have scampered off in search of their outdoor gear. 'If you just give in to them every time they complain they're bored, you'll turn them into spoilt monsters.'

'It's not about giving in. I fancied a day out and it'll be fun. Did you have other plans?'

'No.'

'So where's the harm? I won't do it every time, I promise.'

She sighs. 'It is a good idea, I suppose. I haven't been to Drusillas since Mum and Phil took us when we were teenagers.'

'What is it?' Rebecca asks.

'It's a zoo,' I explain. 'Well, it's a conservation place really, but as far as the boys will be concerned it's a zoo. They'll love it, and I have another idea brewing as well.'

As Saffy and Rebecca go off to marshal their children, I pull out my phone and call George. Spending an hour or two with him is bound to push any residual thoughts of Alasdair firmly out of my mind.

* * *

My prediction was correct; the boys are absolutely enchanted by Drusillas. It was a bit of a trek to get here, but we've seen all sorts of different monkeys and lemurs, although the boys' absolute favourite was the meerkats. Saffy and I are very taken with the penguins, so graceful underwater and so comical on land, but Rebecca has been unusually quiet.

'Are you all right?' I ask her gently as we head into the café to get out of the rain and have something to eat before unleashing the boys on one of the indoor play areas.

'Yes, just thinking. How big do you think this place is?'

'No idea. Why?'

'Nothing.' She pulls out her phone and seems engrossed, so I turn to Saffy and the boys.

'We're going to have a little detour on the way home,' I tell them. 'A friend of mine called George is restoring a traction engine, and he's very kindly said we can stop in to see it.'

'What's a traction engine?' Rollo asks, looking completely nonplussed.

'It's a big steam engine that they used on farms, years ago,' Saffy explains. 'It's probably nearly as old as Thea and Rebecca's mill. Let me show you.' She finds a YouTube video of a traction engine and hands over her phone so the boys can see.

'Wow, that's *so* cool,' Rollo exclaims as the video shows the engine powering a huge saw that's currently making mincemeat of a tree trunk. 'Does your friend George's engine do this?'

'I don't think it does anything very much at the moment,' I tell him. 'But I expect it will, one day.'

There's definitely something up with Rebecca, I decide as we make our way over to the soft-play area after lunch. I've pretty much given her an open goal to tease me about making such a blatant excuse to see George, but she's still totally absorbed in her phone and the conversation seems to have bypassed her completely. In fact, nearly an hour goes past before she lifts her gaze from her phone and, when she does, her eyes are shining.

'I've got an idea,' she tells me excitedly. 'It's a bit off the wall, but hear me out.'

'Uh-oh.' I raise my eyebrows at Saffy, who clocks the expression on Rebecca's face and suddenly decides she needs to go and check that the boys are OK.

'Go on,' I tell Rebecca, who looks like she's about to burst.

'You know I asked how big this place was?'

'Yes.'

'I found out. Do you want to guess?'

'Not really.'

'Ten acres. The same as we've got.'

'Right.' She's not making a lot of sense. It can't possibly have taken her this long to find that piece of information, and I can't see why she'd be so excited about it either.

'So, you know our plan has always been to do up the mill and sell it on.'

'Yes.'

'What if we didn't do that?'

'What do you mean?'

'What if, instead of trying to find the one person in the world who probably always wanted a watermill and sell it to them, we keep it and develop it ourselves? We could turn it into something like this.'

I stare at her, waiting for her to tell me the punchline of the joke. She's joking, she must be. The more I look, the more I see that she's serious and my heart begins to sink.

24

'Please, tell me you're kidding.'

'I'm deadly serious. Think about it. How many people will come through here today, do you think? Five hundred? A thousand? Multiply that by the entrance price and you're looking at a serious amount of cash, and that's before they buy any drinks or lunch, or their children go mad in the gift shop.'

To my mind, there's so much wrong with this plan that I don't know where to start, but I know I have to tread carefully so as not to upset her.

'There are a couple of snags though,' I say carefully.

'Such as?'

'Well, I don't imagine you can pick up animals like these at the pet shop, for starters. Plus, I don't know about you, but I don't have the first clue how to look after monkeys or lemurs, or even meerkats and penguins.'

'I wasn't thinking we'd have animals like this,' she tells me, undeterred. 'I was thinking more of a farm-type vibe. You know, chickens, pot-bellied pigs, pygmy goats, those kinds of things. We could open the mill as an attraction, sell flour in the gift shop. We could even have an on-site café and a soft-play area in one of the barns.'

'Let me get this straight. You're proposing, based on a single visit to a zoo in the pouring rain, that we completely change our business plan and do something neither of us knows the first thing about?'

'Look, I know it sounds crazy when you say it like that, but you're forgetting the aces up our sleeves.'

'What aces?'

'Ben and George. I bet Ben knows all about keeping animals, or he'll know someone who does. George knows all about the mill, and I bet we wouldn't be the first HIBT partner to do something like this.'

'OK, but even if that's true and they're willing to help, where is the money going to come from?' I persist. 'We've just about got enough to build the extension on the cottage, but this would cost a fortune. The cost of the fences alone is making me feel faint, and that's assuming the council will let us do it, which I'm almost certain they won't.'

'We don't extend the cottage.'

'I'm sorry?'

'We get it up to standard but don't extend it. That's where we're going to live. It's like it was meant to be, Thea. Our plot may be "too big to garden, too small to farm", but it's just the right size for something like this.'

I study her for a while. Her face is lit up with enthusiasm, and I just don't have the heart to pop her bubble. Her plan is so full of holes that I'm confident it will sink quite happily on its own, so I decide to humour her.

'OK. I'm not buying into this yet,' I tell her. 'But I'm happy for you to talk to George and Ben to see what they think.'

I'm certain they'll both think the same as me, that this is the worst idea ever. Rebecca evidently doesn't see it that way, however, as she leaps up, comes round the table we're sitting at and envelops me in a massive hug.

'Thank you,' she breathes after a few moments.

'What for?'

'For being such a good friend and listening to me. I know you think it's bonkers because I can see it in your face, but it's got to be worth a look, hasn't it?'

'There's certainly no harm in finding out more,' I tell her as she releases me. I feel like a terrible coward for not saying no straight away, but maybe it's kinder to let her discover the flaws in her idea on her own.

* * *

George's traction engine turns out to be located in an industrial unit not far from Tenterden. It's nearly four in the afternoon when we get there, so we've told the boys this will be a flying visit. Despite their earlier enthusiasm, that seems to go down well as they're both flagging after running rampage through the soft-play area for over an hour.

I was expecting to be confronted with a load of rusty-looking bits of metal when I stepped through the door, but the engine appears to be almost complete, and it's absolutely massive.

'Wow,' Rollo breathes as he takes it in. Louis appears to have lost the power of speech completely.

'Hello?' I call, my voice echoing in the large chamber.

'I'll be with you in just a sec,' George's voice calls back, and a few moments later his head pops up in the area where the driver would stand. His smile is wide and, even though he's dressed in the filthiest overalls I think I've ever seen and he has grease smudges on both cheeks, my stomach still flips at the sight of him.

'What do you think?' he asks the boys once he's climbed down and greeted us properly. This is the first time that Saffy, Rollo and Louis have met him, and I can sense Saffy sizing him up.

'It's awesome,' Louis practically shouts. 'Can we climb up on it?'

'I'm not sure that's a good idea,' Rebecca says quickly. 'It looks dangerous.'

'It's OK,' George tells her. 'They'll be fine. You'll be careful and do exactly what I say, won't you, boys?'

Rebecca and Saffy look on nervously as George carefully guides Rollo and Louis up onto the traction engine, before showing them around and explaining how it all works. I was expecting this to be a ten-minute visit, tops, but George is doing that thing he does so well, which is pitching his explanations at just the right level to keep the boys interested, so nearly half an hour goes by before they reluctantly climb down again. While we wait, I allow my fantasies of George and the traction engine free rein in my head, with the result that I'm feeling nearly as jittery as Rebecca and Saffy by the time they rejoin us, although the reasons are very different. I was right. Seeing George has pushed Alasdair back into his box.

'That was the best thing I've ever seen,' Rollo enthuses.

'Say thank you to George,' Saffy prompts the boys.

'Thank you,' they chorus obediently.

'Ah, you're welcome,' he tells them. 'I always like showing off my engine, so thank you for being so interested.'

'I bet you'd like to see his engine,' Rebecca murmurs to me suggestively. 'Go on, ask if you can climb on top of it. It's so big, you need a ladder to get all the way up.'

'Stop it,' I whisper back before turning to George.

'It's certainly impressive,' I tell him, causing Rebecca to snort with laughter next to me. 'How many of you are involved with it?'

'There are four of us,' he explains. 'We each own a quarter share and we spend every weekend working on her. The others would normally be here, but I explained I had some VIP guests coming, so they decided to give themselves the afternoon off.'

'It's quite an undertaking. When do you think it will be finished?'

'We're going as fast as we can. This place costs a fortune, so that's quite an incentive. We'd like to be ready for the summer show season next year, but a lot of that will depend on whether we can get the remaining parts and the necessary certifications in time. Oddly, you can't just pick up bits in your local auto centre, and the health and safety people aren't keen on the idea of a catastrophic explosion, especially if there are members of the public nearby, so she has to pass a boiler inspection before she's allowed out.'

'I notice you refer to it as "she",' Saffy says. 'Does she have a name?'

George smiles again. 'Indeed she does.' He walks over to a stack of metal sheets leaning against one wall, pulls one out and turns it so we can see.

'Harriet. Nice,' Saffy tells him.

'We didn't give it to her. It's the name she came with.'

'Where do you even go to buy something like this?' Rebecca asks. 'It's not exactly the sort of thing you'd pick up on eBay, is it.'

'No, but there are online marketplaces for pretty much everything, including traction engines.'

'Is there a traction engine equivalent of HIBT?' I ask. 'I can imagine this being the kind of thing that would attract hordes of Ernests.'

'There is,' he says, laughing. 'But it's more of a club than anything else.'

'So they're advisory Ernests rather than mandatory Ernests,' I continue.

'Something like that.' There's a twinkle of mischief in his eyes as we banter and he's grinning. I'm going to need a cold bath at this rate. How does this man manage to have such a mesmeric effect on me?

'George,' Rebecca begins tentatively, popping the bubble George and I seem to have found ourselves in. 'Can I ask you something about the mill, quickly?'

'I'm afraid not,' he tells her. His voice is serious, but the twinkle is still there as he glances back at me. He's definitely flirting.

'Oh. Why not?' Rebecca sounds mildly affronted.

'It's the weekend. I don't know anything about mills at weekends.'

'That's ridiculous,' she scoffs. 'You know about your traction engine during the week. I've heard you talking about it.'

'I always know about traction engines because they're my passion. But mills are work, so I only know about them during office hours.'

'OK, how about I tell you something about the mill instead,' she says after considering his reply for a moment, and I have to admit I'm impressed with her ability to think on her feet. 'I don't expect it to make sense now, but it might on Monday morning when you know about mills again.'

'I might not remember,' he warns her, still grinning.

'I'll take the risk. Thea and I are thinking about opening the mill as a tourist attraction, with a sort of petting farm thing attached, and maybe a soft-play area, café and shop. What do you think?'

His expression turns serious as he pivots his gaze to me.

'I haven't signed off on it yet,' I say defensively. 'I've just suggested she talks to you and Ben. Nothing to do with me.'

'Why does it matter what I think?' he asks cautiously.

'Because you've probably got other HIBT people who've done similar things with their historic buildings,' she tells him. 'You might have useful advice for us.'

'I see. Well, it does sound interesting. Shall I give you a call on Monday?'

'Do you think,' I say, sensing an opportunity, 'it's the kind of thing that might warrant a site visit? Big plans like this are best discussed face to face, don't you agree?'

'I can certainly ask,' he replies, and his expression is unreadable. I don't care though. Rebecca's plan may be mad, but if it gets George on site for a day, that's a big plus in my book.

* * *

'This is more than you just fancying him, like Rebecca said,' Saffy says matter-of-factly later that evening. 'I'm smelling full-on crush here. Am I right?'

Rebecca's gone to spend the night with Ben so I've agreed to help settle Rollo at Saffy's for the night and stay for dinner with her and Tim. The boys have had baths and are currently totally engrossed in a PlayStation game, and we're sitting at the kitchen table with glasses of wine while Tim cooks.

'You've seen him, right?'

'Oh yes, and he's undoubtedly good looking, but I'm afraid I agree with Rebecca. He's like a cardboard cutout of a beach hunk. Beautiful, but lacking in substance.'

'No, he isn't.'

'He is, sorry. He's nice enough, but I think he'd bore you long term. You need someone with more oomph.'

'Maybe I don't want oomph.'

'You might not want it, but you need it and I'm afraid I don't think he has it. Not enough, anyway. You're welcome to prove me wrong, of course.'

'Why, thank you,' I say, slightly petulantly. 'I might just do that.'

Annoyingly, Alasdair chooses this moment to escape from the box I pushed him so firmly into earlier. I wonder what Saffy would have made of him, if she'd met him. I have no doubt that he would have charmed her, because he's unable to do anything else, but would she have decreed him to be 'enough' with the same certainty that she's now dismissing George? It's all academic, I decide as I mentally shove Alasdair back into his box once more. He belongs in the past with 'old' Thea and I don't want any crossover from my old life contaminating the new. As far as George is concerned, there's only one way to find out if Saffy and Rebecca have a point or not, and that's to spend more time getting to know him. I just need to engineer more ways to do that.

25

It's Monday morning and I'm feeling decidedly twitchy. Rebecca came home even more upbeat than usual after her night at Ben's but, although she's admitted that they talked about her plan, she flatly refused to tell me what he said, saying it was better to hear it from the horse's mouth. If, as I'd hoped, he'd pointed out the folly of her proposal and shot it down in flames, I can't see why on earth she'd be in such a good mood. I'm also waiting to hear from George, who needs permission from Charlotte for a site visit. I've pondered a lot on what Saffy said, and I've decided that the only way to prove her wrong is to stop faffing about and find out how he feels, so I'm planning to invite him to the pub after work and up the ante a little. It's just the right level of pressure, I reckon. Dave and Brooke are often in there, along with a number of other local people we've got to know through Ben, so it won't be as intense as taking him to a place where it's just the two of us.

It's another cold, rainy day, but the cottage is pleasantly warm when Rebecca unlocks the door and we step into the bare kitchen, the new boiler humming quietly in the corner. I hesitate to use it, because it's a word I hate, but it's almost cosy in here. At least, it would be if it wasn't for the boxes of tools on the floor and the industrial-looking bright copper pipes snaking along the walls to the radiators and up through the ceiling to the floor above.

'Ben should be bringing the materials so we can lag the pipes and box them in today,' Rebecca tells me happily. 'Then we can replaster and decorate.'

As if on cue, I spot Ben's Land Rover pulling up outside, with a covered trailer attached to it.

'Morning, Rebecca, morning, Thea,' he says as he strides through the door, bending to give Rebecca a kiss as he passes. 'Wow. It's warm in here, isn't it? We might need to turn that off when we start work or we'll boil to death. Shall I put the kettle on for a cuppa?' His mood is also worryingly buoyant, although, to be fair to him, it usually is.

'Right,' Ben announces once he's made his cup of tea and we've settled ourselves at the rickety table that serves as our meeting space, dining area and site office. 'Rebecca told me there's a new plan on the table.'

'I think calling it a plan might be a bit premature,' I say carefully. 'I would say it's more of an idea at this stage.'

'She also warned me that you weren't completely on board.'

I sigh. 'It's just a massive swing from what we originally agreed, neither of us have any experience or the required animal knowledge, it's going to cost a fortune and it ties us down. With the original plan, we get a quick return on our investment and can move on. Also, if we decide we don't want to do it any more, it's easy to extricate ourselves. If we go into this, we're stuck with it. Everything we have is ploughed into it and we stand to lose it all if we get it wrong.'

'OK,' Ben replies. 'I hear you. But I reckon it's still got lots of potential. In fact—'

Before he gets any further, we're distracted by the sound of someone else pulling up outside the cottage, and I'm both relieved and delighted to see that the cavalry has arrived in the form of George.

'Hang on a minute, Ben,' I tell him. 'We might as well do this with everyone in the room to save repeating ourselves.'

'What have I missed?' George asks once he's been furnished with a cup of tea and we're all sitting around the table again.

'We were just about to start discussing Rebecca's idea,' Ben explains. 'Thea isn't on board.'

'Right. This is the family farm idea, is it?'

'That's it,' Ben replies.

'Well, Rebecca,' he tells her. 'Now that it's Monday morning and I know all about HIBT's business again, I can tell you that you're right. Lots of other HIBT property owners have found ways to monetise their industrial buildings, and I think a farm would work well here. We'd certainly be able to help you with applications to the council and so on if you wanted.'

'OK, hang on.' I raise my hands to try to slow this down. 'Can we just step back a bit, to the point where this is all going to cost a fortune and we don't know what we're doing? I kind of feel that's central here.'

'Sure,' Ben concedes. 'Let's start with the money side of things. You're right that this won't come cheap, so I suspect you're going to need an investor.'

'Tricky,' George tells him. 'Corporate investors tend only to be interested if you're doing something charitable that makes them look good. I imagine the purpose here is to make a profit.'

'Absolutely,' Rebecca agrees.

'You're going to struggle then,' George continues. 'You might be able to find a private investor, but they'll want a slice of the pie. The other option is to borrow the money, but a lender is going to want collateral.'

'I happen to know of a private investor who would be very interested, if the terms were right,' Ben says mildly.

'Oh, come on!' I say exasperatedly. 'I mean, I know you're good and everything, but Rebecca only came up with this idea on Saturday. How can you possibly have lined up an investor so fast? Do you have a little black book of contacts with entries like "Call Sean if anyone wants money for a family farm"?'

'Nothing so shady,' he replies simply. 'It's me.'

'What?' Whatever I was expecting him to say, it wasn't this. Beside him, Rebecca looks like she's about to burst with excitement.

'I wanted to tell you,' she says quickly. 'But Ben felt it would be better to talk to you face to face.'

'I don't understand.'

'It's what I wanted to do with this place when my grandmother died, but I didn't have the money,' Ben explains. 'My cottage isn't worth much so, despite owning the mill and the land, I couldn't raise the capital I needed. In the end, I decided the best thing to do was sell the mill as it was and pocket the money. The irony being, of course, that now I have the money for the farm but nowhere to put it.'

'Hang on,' I challenge him. 'When we came round the first time, I distinctly remember you telling me that you were selling because you were under pressure from the other grandchildren, or something like that.'

He blushes slightly. 'I may not have been completely truthful. I'm the only heir.'

'Why did you tell us you weren't, then?'

'Because I thought it would be easier to dig my heels in and negotiate hard if buyers thought there were other people involved as well. If they knew it was just me, they'd try to push me around. I know it sounds odd now, but it made sense at the time.'

It takes me a while to digest this information. 'I get it,' I tell him eventually. 'Nice windfall, and I can see your logic. Wasn't the money burning a hole in your pocket though?'

'I'm not that fussed by money, generally,' he replies calmly. 'Yes, I could have gone mad and bought lots of stuff, but what would have been the point? I'm quite happy with my life as it is. If it makes you feel better, I did buy a round of drinks in the pub.'

'It's one of the many things I love about him,' Rebecca adds, stroking Ben's arm affectionately. 'After John, who was obsessed with money, being with someone who isn't into it in the same way is refreshing.'

'Anyway,' Ben continues. 'I didn't think any more about it, because you guys came along with your plan to convert it and sell it, and I thought maybe that was a better idea than mine in the end.'

'I still think it is,' I remind them.

'But then, when Rebecca mentioned her idea, and it was exactly the same one I'd had, I felt like it was meant to be. So, if you'll have me, I'm happy to invest.'

'May I ask how much?'

'If I understand correctly, you've put £600,000 in so far and Rebecca has £300,000. Is that right?'

'That's right.'

'So I thought I'd come in with an equal amount to you – £600,000. That should easily get us everything we need, don't you think?'

'And what would you want in return?'

'An equal partnership in the business with you, I suppose.'

This is all moving way too fast and I feel like I've lost control of the situation. I can feel my heart hammering in my chest and my breath is short. Even the normally soothing presence of George isn't doing it for me.

'I need time to think,' I tell them all, pushing back my chair and getting to my feet. This room suddenly feels claustrophobic and, despite the fact that the weather outside is awful, I need to be in the fresh air. Pulling on my raincoat, I stumble outside, slamming the door behind me.

* * *

I have no idea where I'm going, I just know I need to be alone. In the end, I make my way to one of the barns to get out of the rain and plonk myself down on a hay bale. I feel completely blindsided and outmanoeuvred. I was certain that everyone else would feel the same way as me about Rebecca's idea, so finding myself in a minority of one is a very nasty surprise. This whole project feels like it's spiralling completely out of control and I'm powerless to stop it. For the first time in nearly nine months, I'm regretting leaving Morton Lansdowne.

'Are you OK?' I look up to see George standing in front of me.

'No. Not really,' I tell him honestly.

'Can I sit down?'

'Sure.'

'The others thought it would be best if I came to find you, given that I'm a neutral party in all of this,' he says after a while. 'Do you want to talk about it?'

'It's going to make me sound stupid.'

'Thea, if there's one thing I think we can all agree you're not, it's stupid. Come on, what's up?'

'I just feel railroaded, and I don't like it. I feel suddenly like I'm a helpless passenger on a mad rollercoaster that I never signed up to ride. When we bought this place, it was supposed to be with an aim to converting the mill and selling it on. Now we're staying here and opening a bloody petting zoo?' To my horror, a tear splashes down into my lap. I haven't cried since the mini-breakdown after leaving Morton Lansdowne, and crying in front of George is particularly mortifying.

George says nothing, but I'm aware of his arm reaching out, wrapping around me and pulling me into him. Normally, this would set my hormones on fire, but right now it's exactly what I need. I let him hold me as the tears fall.

'You can say no,' he says gently after a while. My head is resting on his shoulder and I'm breathing in the smell of him. It's a soothing mix of soap and fabric conditioner.

'On what grounds, though? I honestly thought this was an idea so stupid that it would bury itself, but not only does everyone else, including you, seem to think it's great, but Rebecca has also found funding through her boyfriend and I suspect bloody Ben is an animal husbandry expert too. I don't want to be a grinch, because I love Rebecca and the way she manages to come up with new ideas every time something goes wrong, but I can't sign up to this. It's spiralling out of control and turning into a monster. It was supposed to be simple, but this bloody mill is biting us in the arse at every turn.'

'I don't remember specifically saying that the family farm was a good idea,' George says gently. 'I just said lots of HIBT partners had done similar things. But you have to do what's right for you. If you don't like it, tell them.' His fingers are lazily stroking my hair and running down my arm, and I'm slowly becoming more aware of the sensation. My tears have stopped and my brain has finally registered where I am and started firing up my hormones. I can feel the heat building inside me as I lift my head from his shoulder and meet his eyes, which are impossible to read beneath those incredible lashes. As if drawn by a magnet, I lean forward and brush his lips with mine. It's not long before his mouth gently opens and our tongues find each other.

This is so much hotter than I imagined in even my dirtiest dream. I'm on fire and hungry for as much of him as I can get.

'Thea, I can't,' he says suddenly, breaking the kiss and releasing me.

'What? Why?'

'I'm so, so sorry,' he says again, releasing me and getting to his feet. 'I think I'd better go.'

'George, wait!' I call, but he's already gone, sprinting back in the direction of the house.

As I plonk myself back down on the hay bale, there's only one thought in my mind, and it has nothing to do with the farm. What the hell just happened?

26

'What on earth did you do to George?' Rebecca asks when I make my way back to the cottage a few minutes later. 'He came tearing in here looking like he'd seen a ghost, grabbed his stuff, made some lame excuse about being called away and then shot off up the drive as if he couldn't get out of here fast enough.'

'Where's Ben?' I ask, noting that she's alone in the kitchen.

'He's gone home. He figured you and I needed time to talk.'

I sink down at the table and bury my head in my hands. 'George came to find me,' I tell her.

'I know. We sent him. We were worried about you.'

'Yeah, well. We had a chat, I had a bit of a cry, and then we ended up kissing.'

'Oh, wow! Wait, why would he be in such a hurry to leave though? Didn't he like it? You didn't bite him or do something weird, did you?'

'Of course not,' I snap. 'It was lovely, if you must know, but then he pulled away, said he had to go and vanished.'

'Maybe it caught him by surprise. Give him an hour or two

to cool down, and then call him. It's funny; I would have sworn he was gay.'

'Based on the way he kissed me, I'm pretty certain he isn't.'

'You don't think he's married or has a girlfriend, do you?'

'I don't think he's the kind of guy who would kiss someone behind a partner's back.'

'What exactly did he say when he broke it off?'

'He apologised a lot, said he had to go, and then ran off. The stupid thing is that, if anything, I took advantage of him. It was me that started the kiss.'

'Hmm. Definitely sounds like he's just spooked.'

'You're probably right.'

* * *

I'm struggling to concentrate on my work as my mind grapples with the events of the morning. I've called George's phone a number of times, but it's gone to voicemail. Ben and Rebecca are wisely working on lagging the pipes and keeping out of my way, but I know I also need to come to some sort of conclusion about the family farm idea and I just don't know what to do. When my phone rings after lunch, I snatch it up hoping that it's George, but I'm instantly disappointed.

'Hi, Thea, it's Charlotte from HIBT,' she tells me when I answer. 'I've just had a call from George to say that he's been taken ill suddenly, but you need help with submitting application forms for a family farm business. Is that right?'

'Umm, I don't think it's hugely urgent,' I reply, unable to summon enthusiasm for either Rebecca's idea or more form filling unless it brings George back. 'It can probably wait until he's feeling better.'

'The thing is,' she continues, 'this isn't really his area of expertise. I suspect he would have leant heavily on Ernest for advice and, as it happens, Ernest has just finished his assignment in Norfolk. I gather the mill restoration is nearly complete?'

'Yes, not far off.'

'Great. This is probably a good time for George to step aside and Ernest to come back on board to get you over the finishing line. I'll ask him to contact you.'

'Oh, OK.' This is disastrous news, and my mind is whirling, trying to think if there's anything else I can do to get in touch with George so we can straighten this out one way or another. 'Umm, Rebecca and I would like to send a get well card and a small token of thanks to George. You wouldn't happen to have his address to hand, would you?'

'I can't give you his home address because of GDPR,' Charlotte tells me firmly. 'You're welcome to send something here though, and I'll forward it on for you.'

'OK, thanks.'

'Fuck,' I mutter vehemently once I'm sure the call has disconnected.

'What's up?' Rebecca obviously heard me on the phone and has come to check up on me.

'That was Charlotte. George has called in sick and she's decided to replace him with Ernest.'

'Sick?' She laughs. 'Bloody hell, that's a bit extreme. Are you sure you didn't bite him?'

'It's not funny,' I tell her crossly. 'How am I supposed to get to the bottom of this if he's not coming back?'

'Call him.'

'I've tried that. Voicemail. I've left messages too but nothing. I don't buy the sickness story for a minute.'

'Me neither. He's avoiding you.'

'So what am I supposed to do?'

'I don't know. Give him time, I guess.'

* * *

By the end of the day, I've called four more times but it's gone to voicemail every time. I didn't leave any more messages, but I'm like a caged animal. My mood wasn't improved when Ernest called late afternoon to say he'd be popping over in the morning to check on progress and have a general catch-up.

'Look on the bright side,' Rebecca had told me when I'd imparted this latest piece of bad news. 'If you don't hear from George by the weekend, at least you know where he'll be.'

That did bring some comfort, and I'd returned to my varnishing in the mill with a little less aggression. Maybe she's right and he just needs a bit of space to process his feelings. If I haven't heard from him by the weekend, I'll go and find him in Tenterden. One way or another, we're going to talk about this. Even if he thinks it's a mistake, I need closure.

* * *

'I'd forgotten what a cracking cup of splosh you make,' Ernest says the next morning, after taking a deep and noisy slurp from his mug. 'The bloke in Norfolk couldn't make a cuppa to save his life. It was like drinking dishwater. Right then, where are we?'

'We were just beginning to explore the idea of opening up as a tourist attraction,' Rebecca says cautiously. 'Nothing's set in stone, but we have a potential investor and were thinking of using the land to put in a family farm.' We haven't discussed her plans any further yet, so I'm pleased that she's soft-pedalling it.

I'm still in a spin about George and not really in the mood to deal with this at the moment.

'Great idea,' Ernest says approvingly, placing his hands behind his head, closing his eyes and leaning back in his chair. For a moment, I vaguely hope it'll collapse underneath him as a punishment both for looking so impossibly smug and also for encouraging her but, although it's creaking alarmingly, it holds firm. After a moment where he seems to be contemplating his own genius, he brings the chair back down and opens his eyes again. 'What about the covenant?'

'Not a problem,' Ben assures him. 'The covenant specifies that the land must be used for the purpose of agriculture or food production, and the family farm qualifies. I checked when I was thinking of doing it.'

'Is there anyone else doing something similar nearby?'

'I don't think so.'

'Good. So your first issue is going to be getting the council on board. They're going to want to know about the potential traffic impact, whether the local residents object, all that kind of thing. It can take a while, so I'd get cracking on that sooner rather than later. I assume you're planning to use the mill as a centrepiece?'

'That's the idea, yes.'

'OK,' he says, suddenly energised. 'We'll need to get the mill certified for food production, assuming you're going to sell the flour. If you're planning on running it for any length of time, we'll also need to check the pond. It might need dredging. Good news is that winter is the best time to do that, because there are bound to be newts using it in summer, and you're not allowed to disturb them.'

'Hang on.' I'm only half listening to Ernest but this seems important. 'How much will that cost?'

'Oh, it's not cheap,' he says breezily. 'But we should be able to get a grant to cover most of it, if we word the application right. We'd probably best crack on with that too so we can get the dredging done before spring. I've got some forms in my car. I'll bring them in shortly and we can get started.'

I'm starting to feel overwhelmed again, but thankfully Rebecca seems to spot it and suggests to Ernest that he might like to check progress in the mill before we start form filling, which thankfully deflects him.

'Are you OK?' she asks once he's pottered off.

'I'm not trying to be difficult, but I haven't agreed to any of this yet,' I tell her.

'I know. But there's no harm in putting in the applications, is there? If the council says no, then there isn't really anything to talk about. If they say yes, well, then we have options. The more options we have, the better, surely? Ever since the mill turned out not to be as knackered as we hoped, we've known this wouldn't be an easy place to sell, so having a plan B can't be a bad thing.'

'I guess not. I'm just worried that you and Ben are completely sold on this farm idea and, if I'm honest, I feel backed into a corner.'

'That's my fault. I let my enthusiasm run away, especially when Ben offered to invest and everything. Look, nothing's changed, OK? You and I are partners, and I'm not going to force you to do anything you're not comfortable with. If you feel you'd rather press ahead with extending the cottage and trying to sell it, I'm sure Ben will understand.'

I sigh. 'But you want this, don't you?'

'I do,' she admits. 'Much as I liked the property development plan, I like stability even more. The idea that this could be a permanent home for Rollo and me, plus a business that could provide a decent standard of living, that's very tempting.'

'And don't forget Ben,' I add.

'I'm trying not to let him be a factor, but yes. I'd like a future with him too,' she agrees. 'But you and I have a contract and I'll happily abide by it. The only way the farm happens is if you're completely comfortable and on board. Ben and I have drawn up some plans, and I'd like you to have a look at them and give your opinion, but that's it. You have total veto. Ben and I are agreed on this.'

'OK,' I concede. 'I'm happy to look.'

'Thank you. Right, you'd better go and see what Ernest is up to in the mill.'

'Must I?'

'I think, after all the work you've put into it, I'd want to make sure he isn't making a mess in there.'

As I round the side of the building, I see that Ernest is not in the mill, but doing something by the side of the pond.

'Everything OK?' I ask him.

'Yes, just trying to get a feel for the depth of the water,' he tells me. 'I'm going to recommend dredging, just to be on the safe side. The downside of these ponds is that they do tend to silt up over time. If the river is flowing fast, it brings all sorts of stuff with it, which then sinks to the bottom the moment the water slows down in the pond. Best to dredge, I think. Right, do you want to show me what you've been up to inside?'

By mid-afternoon, my mood is at rock bottom. Partly because Ernest isn't George, and I have a constant George-shaped dull ache in my chest today, but also because I've spent most of it at the kitchen table with Ernest, filling in forms. We've done an application to Natural England for the dredging of the pond, one to certify the mill for food production and now Ben and Rebecca are taking us through their high-level plans for the farm, which I was a little alarmed to find were considerably more advanced than I'd expected.

'They're the ones Ben originally drew up when he was thinking of doing it himself,' Rebecca explained when I queried it. 'We've just tweaked them slightly. Ben's also done a complete set of cost and revenue projections, which we'll take you through another time.' She flicks her eyes surreptitiously towards Ernest; she's obviously keen not to have him listening in for that part.

Despite my misgivings, I have to admit that the plans are impressive. Although he hadn't included a soft-play area or café, Ben has obviously put considerable thought into the types of animals to keep and how they would best be housed. He's also put together a detailed map of the whole plot including car parking, fences and paths.

'This is just the start,' Rebecca tells me, and I can tell she's trying not to let her enthusiasm run away with her again. 'I'm thinking we could do rowing boat hire on the pond, "adopt an animal" schemes and I've set aside space in the top barn for something that might bring a smile to your face, Thea.'

'What?'

'You know how George said the industrial unit was costing a fortune? I was thinking we could offer them this area for their traction engine. It's win-win. They pay rent, the public get to see a restoration in progress, and they can do demos and stuff with it when it's finished. Plus, you have George on site regularly.'

'Assuming he's speaking to me,' I murmur quietly, so Ernest doesn't overhear.

'Yes. I admit I had the idea before he was taken ill.' She

makes air quotes when she says the word 'ill' but they're lost on Ernest who has closed his eyes again. She lowers her voice to a whisper. 'I'm sure it'll all be fine once you've talked to him on Saturday, if you don't hear from him before.'

I hope she's right. God, I hope she's right.

27

Saturday and still not a peep out of George. I'm actually a little irritated with him now; how dare he make this all about him, as if I was just a passive object he unwittingly kissed? Don't my feelings deserve to be taken into account too? Still, as Rebecca said, there's no doubt where he'll be today, so I'm on my way to Tenterden to confront him.

Despite being a little distracted by the whole George thing, we have made progress on going through Ben and Rebecca's plans, and I am gradually starting to come round to the idea. The way they see it is that Ben will be the animal expert, I'll be in charge of the milling, and Rebecca will sort out the soft play and the gift shop. We have no idea who's going to run the café yet, but they've made a start on putting together our application to the council based on Ben's original plans with a few updates. I've made it clear that I'm not totally sold yet, but I'm happy to explore the idea a bit further. I think, for me, the thing that has reassured me the most about it is that we still have the mill and the land if it all goes wrong and, although we'd probably have to sell it at a loss, we should still get enough to revert to a slimmed-down property development scheme if we needed to.

My heart is banging in my chest as I pull up outside the industrial unit where George's traction engine lives. Although I've rehearsed this moment several times in my head, the reality of what I'm about to do is just beginning to sink in. If I make a complete fool of myself, it won't just be in front of George, but presumably his friends as well. I'm just about to get out of the car when my phone pings with a message. I grab it eagerly, as I have done every time it's made even the slightest chirp since Monday, hoping that George has finally decided to get in touch, but to my surprise the message is from Alasdair.

> 9 months quarantine is officially over and we're allowed to talk again!!! Just been to your house with flowers and champagne to celebrate, but the door was opened by a very angry man who accused me of having designs on his wife! Took a bit of straightening out. Anyway, where are you? Champagne is starting to get warm… Ax

I stare at the message for a few minutes, trying to think how I feel about it. On the one hand, it's nice to hear from Alasdair, and to know that he hasn't forgotten me, but I also feel a tinge of annoyance that he's just rocked up with flowers and champagne, presumably expecting that I'd let him in and we'd just pick up as if nothing had changed. Knowing him, he was probably expecting sex. To be fair to him, I probably would have been up for that if it wasn't for George. That's enough to re-focus me and I slip my phone back into my bag and open the door. Alasdair will have to wait; I've got more important things to deal with right now.

There's a surprising amount of activity going on when I slip through the door of the industrial unit. Two guys are applying black paint to some part of the traction engine, and there's a regular metallic clanging coming from the other side. Neither of the two guys I can see is George, and they obviously haven't heard me over the din.

'Hello?' I call, but my voice is lost in the noise, so I slowly approach the guys who are painting. They have their backs to me but, once I reckon I'm close enough to be heard over the clanging, I try again.

'Hello?'

'Bloody hell!' one of the guys exclaims, whirling round. 'You nearly gave me a heart attack.'

'Sorry. I did call from by the door but you obviously couldn't hear.'

'I know,' he says, softening his tone. 'It's enough to give anyone a headache.' He raises his voice and bellows, 'Oi, Bob! Knock it off for a minute, will you?'

The clanging stops, much to my relief.

'So, can I help you with something?' the man asks.

'I was looking for George. Is he here?'

The man studies me for a moment. 'Are you Thea?' he asks.

'Yes. How did you know?'

'I'm Trevor,' he says, holding out a paint-spattered hand. 'George isn't here today, but he left something for you.' Once again, he raises his voice. 'Bob, where's the letter George gave you?' he calls.

'On the desk in the office,' a voice replies.

'Come with me, I'll show you,' Trevor offers, leading the way across the unit to a small office. Inside, there's a rickety-looking desk covered in messy stacks of paper and a swivel chair that's definitely seen better days.

'It should be here somewhere,' Trevor tells me, beginning to leaf through one of the stacks. 'Ah, here we go.' He pulls out an envelope and hands it to me. On the front, in George's neat handwriting, is my name.

'Look,' Trevor says carefully. 'I don't know what's going on between you and George, and I don't need to know. What I will say is that I've never seen him this upset before, and I've known him for a long time. If he's done something to hurt you, then you must do whatever you need to do, but I just hope, for all our sakes, that this is a misunderstanding.'

'Don't worry, he hasn't done anything wrong,' I tell him. 'Which is why I'm struggling to understand why he's so obviously avoiding me.'

'Let's hope that letter will help to clear things up then,' he replies. 'Whatever's happened, I think you can be sure he's very sorry for his part in it.'

I sigh. 'Thanks, Trevor.'

'No worries. Would you like to read it before you go? I can make you a cup of tea or something if you'd like.'

'No. That's kind but I think I'll head off. Thanks anyway.'

'You're welcome.'

I don't want to sit outside the unit reading whatever George has written, so in the end I drive into Tenterden and find a coffee shop. Settling myself at a table with a flat white and a fortifying slice of carrot cake, I pull the envelope out of the bag, open it and start to read the contents.

Dear Thea,

If you're reading this letter, it means you came to find me. I'm sorry that I'm too much of a coward to face you, but I'm so ashamed of myself that I couldn't bear to have this conversation face to face.

What I did was wrong. I know that, and I can't express how sorry I am for losing control of myself when you were vulnerable. Our relationship is a professional one and, despite being attracted to you, I've worked hard to make sure I kept within the proper boundaries: My role is to help you with the mill and advise you in line with HIBT guidelines. What happened in the barn was unprofessional, unethical and a serious breach of the trust you have put in me, and if you wish to put a complaint in about my behaviour, I would completely understand.

'Why would I want to put in a complaint, you idiot?' I murmur out loud. 'It was me that started it, or have you forgotten that?'

In light of what's happened, I have asked Charlotte to transfer me onto other projects, as I obviously cannot continue with the mill. I wish you every success with it, and once again I'm truly, truly sorry for such an appalling breach of conduct.

Yours

George

I read the letter several times, picking out different parts each time. The fact that he felt the attraction too ought to buoy me up, but the rest of it just makes me feel sad and cross that he didn't feel he could talk to me face to face so we could have straightened this out. In many ways, I'm no further forward, but his actions have made it clear that he doesn't want to see me, so maybe I should just let him go.

I'm in a sombre mood as I walk back to the car, and I nearly miss the ping indicating that I've got a new message on my phone. Knowing for certain now that it won't be George, I almost don't bother to read it. It's Alasdair again.

Are you there? Or have you changed phone numbers as well as addresses? Are you in witness protection? Ax

At least talking to Alasdair will take my mind off the mess with George, I suppose. Once I'm in the car, I call him.

'Thea!' he answers in his typically enthusiastic voice. 'I was beginning to wonder if you'd fallen off the end of the earth.'

'Not quite,' I tell him.

'Nine months to the day. I've had a countdown set on my phone. How is it out there in the big bad world? More importantly, which bit of the big bad world are you in? I was a bit surprised to find you'd sold your house. You loved that place.'

'Whoa, slow down,' I tell him. He is cheering me up at least. 'I'm not a corporate lawyer any more; I can only handle one question at a time.'

'Sorry, it's just that I've missed you and I've been really looking forward to catching up. Let's start with where you are, if you're allowed to tell me.'

'I'm not in witness protection, so it's fine. I'm in Kent.'

'Kent? What's there?'

'A long story. Do you remember my friend Rebecca?'

'The one John Curbishley knocked up?'

'A little crude, Alasdair, but that's her. We had this mad property development idea, sold up and are the current proud owners of a watermill and ten acres of land in Kent.'

'A watermill? What the hell would you want with a watermill?'

'A question I've been asking myself a lot lately, strangely. We were going to convert it into a sumptuous family home and sell it on for a fat profit, but now it looks like we might be going to open it as a tourist attraction.'

'Sorry, none of this makes sense. Well, the words make sense, but they don't tally with the Thea I thought I knew. Are you having some kind of breakdown? An early mid-life crisis? I mean, it's one thing to give up a partnership at one of the most prestigious law firms in the country, but this is next-level extreme. Do I need to stage an intervention?'

'I'm fine, honestly.'

'It doesn't sound like it. Left to your own devices, I worry you're going to turn into one of those weirdos who gets off on standing in the corners of rooms in National Trust buildings, hissing at people not to touch stuff. Give me the postcode. I'll be there as soon as I can.'

'Really, Alasdair, there's no need.'

'There's *every* need. You patently need saving from yourself, Thea, and that's what I'm coming to do. Oh, and also because I have an expensive bottle of fizz with your name on it. You haven't mysteriously sprouted a husband and five adorable kids dressed in matching gingham frocks in the last nine months, have you?'

'Even I'm not that fast.'

'Good, because I'd be having a word with the fucker if you had. One of the finest legal minds in the land, running a sodding watermill? God help us all. Postcode, please.'

In spite of myself, I'm smiling as I give him the address of the mill. I'd forgotten how much I enjoyed talking to Alasdair. His straightforward, no-nonsense approach to life might be just what I need right now. And, given that George has staged a disappearing act just at the point things were starting to get interesting, maybe some straightforward, no-nonsense sex will help me to get some perspective and cheer me up as well. Unfortunately, just as my libido starts to wake up, I realise that might prove tricky; Mum and Phil's is out as they'll be there and

I don't want to have to explain Alasdair to them, let alone run the risk of them overhearing anything. The mill is the other obvious place, but there's no furniture or anything there. For a moment, I allow myself to contemplate spreading a blanket over some hay bales in the barn, before glancing at the outside temperature display in the car and seeing that it's five degrees and we'll freeze to death, assuming someone doesn't come along and catch us in the act first. I'm open minded about al fresco sex, but not when it comes with a side helping of pneumonia and a hint of arrest for indecent exposure. Perhaps it's for the best; I don't want Alasdair to think he can just waltz in and pick up exactly where we left off, particularly while there's the faintest chance of sorting things out with George.

Thinking of George again makes me realise that Alasdair has at least taken my mind off the whole sorry mess we're in, for now at least.

28

I can't help smiling when Alasdair pulls up outside the mill late the same afternoon. Ben and Rebecca have taken Rollo and Louis to the cinema, so I'm on my own.

'*La Porsche obligatoire*?' I ask as he climbs out of his car and we hug. 'Has someone been made partner?'

'Well, ever since one of the most promising junior partners in the company's history unexpectedly threw in the towel, they've admitted pretty much anyone, even me,' he quips. 'Although I have to say, I think I've left a few bits of the car behind on your track. Janice sends her love, by the way.'

'How is she?'

'Awesome, as ever. It's very remote out here, isn't it? I was half expecting the satnav to start warning me that "here be dragons".'

'Cut it out. We're only five miles from Ashford.'

'Ashford? I have heard speak of this place called Ashford many years ago, I believe. Is it the city of legend, where the pavements are made of gold and the fountains flow with milk and honey?'

'Hardly,' I say, laughing. 'But there is a high-speed rail link to London. Thirty-seven minutes and you're in St Pancras. How long would it take you to get to St Pancras from your flat?'

'Longer than that, I admit, but who wants to go to St Pancras anyway? It's a terrible place, and the only reason to be there is if you were catching the Eurostar to get as far away from it as possible. Are you going to show me around then?'

* * *

'You weren't joking. It's an actual bloody mill,' he says in wonder a little while later. 'What on earth were you thinking?'

'I told you. The original plan was to convert it and sell it on, but it turned out that it was salvageable, and you can't get permission to rip these things out unless they're beyond saving.'

'I feel like I've stepped back into the nineteenth century. And it actually works, does it?'

'It does.' Although it's really nice to see Alasdair, who looks as out of place as he evidently feels, in his expensive brogues, tan chinos and immaculately ironed light blue shirt, his critical appraisal is making me feel surprisingly protective about the mill.

'Ernest and I ground some flour earlier this week,' I tell him proudly.

'Who's Ernest?'

'He's the guy from the Historic Industrial Buildings Trust who's helping us.'

'You mean there are organisations for this kind of thing? I mean, I get that it might be a fantasy for someone who gets off on big cogs and whatever else is in here, but it's pretty niche, isn't it? You haven't turned Amish and eschewed all mod cons, have you? Do you even have electricity this far out?'

'Alasdair,' I say firmly. 'You're in Kent, not Outer Mongolia.'

'Hmm. And this...' He waves his arm around vaguely, with a dubious expression on his face. 'This is really what you want now?'

'Why shouldn't it be?' I ask defensively. 'I wanted a change of direction. This is a change of direction. I don't get what you're finding so difficult about it.'

'Let me tell you a story,' he says, his eyes solemn. 'Once upon a time, there was a beautiful princess called Thea. She was brave and clever, and all her courtiers admired her. There wasn't a problem in the whole land that she didn't know how to solve, and solving problems made her happy. In fact, she'd devoted her whole life to learning how to solve problems so that she could be the very best she could be. She lived in a lovely palace in Walthamstow and she worked hard doing what she loved. Then, one day, a fat ugly king called John died, and Thea decided, quite out of the blue, that she didn't want to be a princess and solve problems any more. So she went to live in a land far, far away where it was muddy and cold and nothing worked properly. And she told herself she was happy, but she wasn't, because there weren't any problems to solve, and she missed it.'

'Are you having a nice time?' I interrupt crossly.

'I was going to say how she tried to go back to her palace, but nobody believed she could be a princess because she looked like a farmer and so she ended up in a muddy field crying and her hat got eaten by a goat, but maybe I've made the point. I guess what I'm trying to illustrate is that there's a difference between a change of direction and throwing everything you've ever worked for in the bin to become some kind of semi-recluse, grinding flour in your ancient watermill and complaining to your fellow villagers about "them city folk" while you sip your warm beer with dead rats floating in it.'

'Alasdair,' I say warningly.

'OK, OK. Are you sure you don't want to come back though? I mean, you've had a nice nine-month sabbatical, but aren't you bored? You've got one of the keenest minds I've ever seen. I guess I just struggle to see how this can stimulate you. I've talked to a few of the other partners, and they'd be open to finding a way back for you. Not at partner level, obviously, but I'm sure we could swing senior associate.'

I cast my mind back to my previous life. Yes, it was mentally stimulating, but I had no friends outside work, my family barely knew me and I was basically a wage slave, imprisoned in my golden handcuffs. The thought makes me shiver.

'I don't want to come back,' I tell him politely but firmly. 'Thank you for the offer.'

As he gazes around, evidently trying to figure out what this ancient piece of machinery could possibly do to make me reject a lucrative job offer, another decision starts to crystallise in my mind, catching me unawares. It may be a clanking, obsolete museum piece, but I've grown very attached to the mill and I'm suddenly sure I don't want to let it go. Even Ernest's dull monologues about how you need to learn to listen to the mill to understand what it's trying to tell you about its health, daily checks and so on have begun to penetrate, because I've started to care about it as if it were a living thing. I'd still prefer it to be George teaching me how to use it though. I briefly allow myself to indulge a fantasy where George and I are working in the mill together. It's a warm, sunny day and he's bringing in sacks of wheat, his muscles flexing under a tight T-shirt. He's smiling at me, his gorgeous lashes blinking languidly as I run my fingers over his taut chest.

'Penny for them?' Alasdair's voice brings me crashing back to reality.

'Sorry?'

'You were miles away just then. I just wondered where you'd gone.'

'It's nothing,' I say, conscious of the flush of heat creeping up my neck.

'Of course it is,' he says, laughing. 'That's why you're suddenly blushing like a lovestruck teenager. I'd flatter myself that it's a reaction to me, but you've never reacted to me like that in all the time I've known you. Methinks I have a rival for your affections. Who is it?'

Bloody Alasdair. I'd forgotten how easily he can read me.

'Nobody,' I tell him. 'And it's been nine months, so don't assume you can just slip back into my bed because that's what we used to do.'

He just stares at me, saying nothing. I know what he's trying to do; he's letting the silence draw on until I blurt what's on my mind just to fill it. Two can play at that game.

'OK. I get it,' he says nonchalantly just when the silence is getting unbearable. 'Nothing to do with me. Sorry I asked. I hope he's worthy of you though.'

'It doesn't matter, since he's currently doing everything he can to avoid me,' I reply before clapping a hand over my mouth in horror at what I've just revealed.

'Aha!' Alasdair exclaims triumphantly. 'I knew it. What's his name?'

I sigh. 'George.'

'George,' he repeats, rolling the name round his mouth as if it were a fine wine he was tasting. 'And what does George do?'

'He works for the Historic Industrial Buildings Trust. He's been advising me on the mill, which is how we met.'

I'm braced for another sarcastic remark, but Alasdair surprises me. 'He matters to you,' he says simply.

'What makes you say that?'

'The look on your face. Why's he avoiding you?'

I study Alasdair for a moment before answering. It feels odd, almost disloyal, to talk to him about George, but then he is one of my longest-standing friends and, when I can get him to be serious, his insights are usually spot on. I think back to our last serious conversation over breakfast after John Curbishley died; he wasn't completely right that time, but he certainly helped me to put my thoughts in order.

'Not here,' I tell him. 'If I'm going to tell you this story, I think we should get a drink. There's a pub in the village. Why don't I lock up and we can walk up there?'

'How far is it?' he asks dubiously. 'I'm not exactly dressed for rambling.'

'It's fine,' I reassure him. 'Ten minutes max, all on tarmac.'

'OK. I'd offer to drive, but the fewer times I have to navigate your track the better, I reckon.'

* * *

'I don't get it,' Alasdair says once I've recounted the story of George and me, culminating in his sudden disappearance from the barn and his letter. 'Why's he blaming himself when it was you who initiated things?'

'I wish I knew,' I tell him, taking a sip of my wine. It's tempting to gulp it, but I've got to drive home in a bit so I need to be careful.

'So what's the plan?'

'I don't have one yet, but I need to straighten this out one way or another. Even if nothing comes of it, I can't leave things as they are.'

'I get that. Do you know where he lives?'

'Nope, and HIBT won't tell me because of GDPR. I already tried.'

'Good for them. What about electoral registers?'

'How many George Joneses do you think there are in the south-east of England?'

'You don't even have a town?'

'Why would I? I know he grew up in South London, but he could be anywhere between here and there. He could even come from further away, I suppose.'

'So all you know about his whereabouts, other than when he's been on site with you, is this traction engine in Tenterden.'

'Yup.'

'OK, we'll have to work with that then.'

'I'm sorry? Where does "we" come into this?'

'I'm going to help you,' he says simply.

'I don't need your help!' I exclaim.

'I think you do. You're making a right royal mess of this on your own, if you don't mind me saying.'

'Wow, tell it like it is, Alasdair,' I say sarcastically, taking a mouthful of wine. 'You know how I hate it when you sit on the fence.'

'Stop being prickly. Let me get you another drink and then we'll start to plot.'

I glance down at my glass and I'm surprised to find that it's empty. On the one hand, I feel a bit resentful having Alasdair meddling in my business, but he does have a point that I'm not doing such a fabulous job of sorting the George problem out by myself so far. Plus, all that stuff he said earlier about me being good at solving problems is also true of him, so maybe having someone to bounce ideas off would be a good idea. The thing with Alasdair is that, although he's a bit like a puppy in some respects and his rudeness about my current situation is annoying, I know I can trust him completely. And, if I'm honest, I'd forgotten how much I like him.

'Go on then,' I tell him. 'Just a small one.'

29

Bloody hell, I feel like I've just done ten rounds in a boxing ring. My eyes are still closed, but whatever I'm lying on is hard and seriously uncomfortable. I shift position slightly to try to relieve the pressure on my pelvis, only to have it transfer to another part of my body. I'm not in my bed at home, that's for sure, so where the hell am I?

Cautiously, I crack open one eye a fraction. The bare bulb hanging from the ceiling isn't reassuring, and neither is the curtainless window. It must be early, because it's still fairly dark outside. I can just make out the sound of someone moving around somewhere else in the building. My befuddled mind initially decides I've been kidnapped and I'm now a prisoner in some remote part of the country where nobody will ever find me, before I realise that I recognise the window frame as one of the ones I lovingly repainted in the summer; I'm in the cottage.

I sit up, surprised to discover that I'm wearing nothing except my bra and knickers. As I place my hand on my pillow, the reason for that becomes obvious; I've been resting my head on my clothes, which are in a messy pile. Alarmingly, there is another pile of clothes next to me, which I clearly recognise as Alasdair's. Wrapping the blanket around me, I make my way over to the door and flip on the light switch, immediately having to shade my eyes from the glare of the bulb.

Once I become accustomed to the brightness, the view doesn't get any better. Our mattress, if you can call it that, is just a pile of decorating blankets, with another couple of blankets on the top to form a makeshift duvet. No wonder I'm sore this morning. Whoever thought it would be a good idea to spend the night here?

As I stare at the rudimentary bed, snatches of the previous evening start to come back to me. Alasdair, full of his customary enthusiasm, his eyes sparkling as he tested out various plans and theories. At some point, a bottle of wine appeared, and then another. Did we eat? I think we must have done, because my stomach would be growling furiously this morning if we hadn't, and my hangover, although not great, would be much worse if I'd drunk as much as I suspect I did without any food to soak it up. A memory of fish and chips swims lazily into my head, along with an image of Dave and Brooke. Were they there? I guess they must have been, for part of it at least.

'Ah, you're awake,' Alasdair says, strolling nonchalantly into the room in his boxer shorts, carrying two mugs. 'I've made you a coffee. Did you sleep OK? I've had better nights myself.'

'What on earth are we doing here?' I ask him.

'Don't you remember? It was your idea, actually. We'd both had a bit of a skinful so I suggested getting a taxi and booking into a local hotel for the night, only there weren't any taxis or hotel rooms available because we're so far from civilisation. So you suggested we camp out here. I don't know about you, but my boy scout days are a long way behind me. Give me a proper bed, preferably made up with high thread count Egyptian cotton, any day of the week. Still, at least we're awake early. We need to get to Tenterden before your friend George shows up.'

'Hang on, Alasdair, slow down. Are you saying you invited me to spend the night with you, *and I accepted*?' I think about my state of undress under the blanket. 'Did we...?' I ask in horrified tones.

'No, relax.' He smiles. 'It was purely platonic. Nothing happened. I mean, we kissed a bit, but nothing more than that.'

'Oh, God.' I feel absolutely mortified. 'Did I come on to you? I'm so sorry.'

'You didn't come on to me as such. You were a few sheets to the wind, and wondering out loud about whether George had run away because you kissed weirdly – apparently Rebecca had planted that seed of doubt in your head – so you asked to kiss me to check if you were all right.'

Another vague memory surfaces. 'And was I?'

'You were fine, as you always were. You're a great kisser, Thea.'

'But that was it? You're sure there was nothing more?'

'Positive. We came back here, had a laugh trying to find enough stuff to make a bed out of, and then went to sleep. I don't think either of us were in a fit state to do any more, and even if we had been, I knew you would have regretted it this morning.'

'Phew,' I exhale with relief.

'Thanks a lot!' he says, mock-affronted.

'I don't mean it like that. It's just that you're right. I would have felt horribly guilty if we had. It would have made talking to George really difficult. "Hey, George, I think you might be the man of my dreams, which is why I shagged my bestie last night."'

'You're all good. If it's any consolation, it was clear to me from your drunken rambling that this George has got under your skin, so there was a real risk you might have called out his name in the throes of passion by mistake. I like to think I'm a fairly confident guy and a decent enough lover, but that would put a serious dent even in my ego. Emailgate was bad enough.'

'It was only the one time, and we laughed about it afterwards, if I remember correctly.'

'Yes, but even so. Anyway, you'd better drink your coffee, splash some water on your face and get dressed. We need to get going if we're going to get there before him.'

'Remind me what the plan is?'

'We're going to stake out the industrial unit where his fabled traction engine is, remember?'

'That's a terrible plan!' I exclaim. 'How drunk were we when we came up with that one?'

'What's so terrible about it?'

'He's avoiding me, remember? He's not going to be there.'

'Of course he is. We talked about this. He wasn't there yesterday because he was avoiding you. But his mate, what's his name?'

'Trevor.'

'Trevor will have told him that you came in and collected the letter. So he'll be confident that you've got the message and won't be coming back, ergo he will turn up today.'

'What if he doesn't?'

'Then you're on your own. I'm off to New York for two weeks tomorrow.'

'OK, let's assume he does turn up. Then what?'

Alasdair looks thoughtful for a moment. 'I don't think we got that far. Let's deal with that when we get there. I'll drive.'

'Why do men always assume they're going to drive?' I ask crossly. 'I'm quite capable, you know.'

'Calm down, Emmeline Pankhurst, it's nothing to do with sexism. I'm driving because he'll probably recognise your car, but he hasn't seen mine before.'

'Oh, good point,' I concede, annoyed with myself for jumping down his throat so quickly.

* * *

It's a little after eight o'clock when we pull up outside the industrial unit. Alasdair fusses about, trying various parking locations until he's satisfied that he's found one where we can observe the entrance without being conspicuous ourselves.

'Now what?' I ask him as he settles back in his seat.

'Now we wait.' He turns the radio on low and pulls a pair of sunglasses out of the glovebox, handing them to me.

'I don't need sunglasses, it's barely light,' I tell him.

'They're for disguise,' he explains. 'If George should happen to glance this way, we don't want him to recognise you.'

I feel vaguely ridiculous as I slip them on, but I have to admire Alasdair's attention to detail. The radio programme is some kind of phone-in on the subject of immigration, and the participants are gradually winding themselves up with increasingly xenophobic remarks.

'We have activity,' Alasdair murmurs happily as a silver BMW pulls up outside the unit around thirty minutes later. I think he's honestly having the time of his life.

'That's not him,' I tell him as a man gets out of the car and walks towards the door, carrying a big bunch of keys. 'That's Trevor.'

'Eagle Two is in the nest,' he states once Trevor has unlocked the door and disappeared inside. 'Hopefully, Eagle One is inbound.'

'What on earth are you talking about?'

'I've given them code names. Eagles one to four. Just thought it would make it more exciting. George is Eagle One, obviously. Look sharp; we have another arrival.'

'That's him,' I say excitedly as George climbs out of his slightly weatherbeaten Honda. He gazes around carefully before making for the door, but thankfully doesn't spot us.

'The young gazelle sniffs the early-morning air carefully,' Alasdair whispers, trying to sound like David Attenborough. 'Danger is all around in the Serengeti, and the long grass could be concealing any number of predators. If he picks up the slightest scent, he'll be off.'

Evidently satisfied that everything is as it should be, George disappears through the door into the unit.

'And Eagle One is in the nest,' Alasdair observes. 'I'll give you credit for one thing – you've got taste. He's a good-looking guy.'

'Right. Time to confront him,' I say, reaching for the door handle.

'No.' Alasdair's grip on my arm is surprisingly firm.

'Why not?'

'Because, not to put too fine a point on it, right now you look like the ghost of Christmas past and you don't smell much better. We know where he is and he's not going anywhere, is he? He'll be there for the whole day, so we're going to use the time wisely. Let's go back to yours, get showered and then I'll take you out for a slap-up breakfast so we can get rid of the last vestiges of hangover and plan what to do next. I take it you do normally live somewhere a little more furnished than your mill?'

'I'm currently staying with Mum and Phil.'

'Good. Let's go there then.'

As I give him the postcode for the satnav, the folly of what I'm about to do hits me. By now, Mum and Phil will have realised that I didn't come home last night. It's Sunday morning, so Rebecca will probably still be at Ben's, but Saffy might be there. Pitching up with a strange man is going to set their tongues wagging from here to next week unless I have a plausible explanation.

'If anyone asks, we stayed in a hotel last night,' I tell Alasdair. 'Very much separate rooms.'

'Why would we look and smell like death warmed up if we'd stayed in a hotel?' he asks. 'Also, wouldn't we have had breakfast there?'

'You're right. Shit.'

'Are you ashamed of me?' His tone is curious rather than reproachful.

'No, of course not. I'm just trying to stop my family reading more into this than there is.'

'Personally, and maybe it's because I'm still a lawyer, I find the truth is generally the easiest option. I'm an old friend, which is true. We can leave out the fuck-buddy bit if you like. I haven't been in contact because it wasn't allowed under the terms of your gardening leave, but I came down to visit you, we ended up having a bit too much to drink and sleeping it off in your cottage. What is there to read into that?'

'The way you say it, nothing. I just have no confidence in the way they'll interpret it.'

'I'll turn on the old Alasdair charm. They'll be eating out of my hand in no time, just you wait and see.'

'Don't do that.'

'Why not?'

'Because they'll see a charming, handsome male and instantly decide to marry me off to you.'

'Handsome?' He grins.

'Behave.'

He glances at me. 'You're a curious mixture these days, Thearless.'

'What does that mean?'

'When we were in London, you used to take work, your career and your life very seriously, but the one thing you never gave a damn about was what other people thought of you. That was one of the things I found most attractive about you. Now, your career appears to be more of a hobby thing, but you're desperately anxious socially.'

'No, I'm not! Wait a minute, are you saying you no longer think I'm attractive?'

'Does it matter whether I find you attractive or not?'

I'm just about to reply that of course it does when I see the trap he's laid. If I tell him his opinion matters, I'm playing into his observation that I care too much what other people think. If I say his opinion isn't important, he can throw my previous question straight back at me to suggest I'm lying. Come on, Thea, you used to be better at verbal sparring than this.

'When I woke up this morning, I noticed that I wasn't wearing a top,' I tell him after thinking for a while.

'Mmm-hmm.'

'Or my trousers.'

'That sounds right. People normally undress when they go to bed.'

'So I stripped down to my underwear. Was the light on?'

'Yes. I couldn't risk you falling over something. What's your point?'

'Enjoy the view, did you?'

I smile triumphantly as he turns puce. Never underestimate my ability to come for you from an angle you never even considered. I may be nine months out of the cut and thrust of law, but I've still got it.

30

It's even worse than I feared. After a brief stop so Alasdair could buy emergency toiletries, we arrive home to find Mum, Phil, Saffy, Rebecca and Ben all in the sitting room. Rollo and Louis are focused on a PlayStation game, but everyone else is looking at Alasdair with eyes as wide as saucers.

'This is my friend Alasdair,' I tell them, emphasising the word 'friend'. 'We used to work at Morton Lansdowne together. It's a funny story actually, we had a bit too much to drink last night and ended up camping at the mill.'

Nobody says anything; they're all just staring at him as if I've brought home an extra-terrestrial or something.

'Mum,' I continue, trying to coax someone into life. 'Is it all right if Alasdair borrows a towel and has a shower?'

'Yes, of course,' Mum replies distractedly, still staring at Alasdair.

'That's very kind of you,' he says smoothly, and I swear Mum is batting her eyelashes at him.

'Let me show you where everything is,' I tell him, ushering

him out and away from their gaze. Having furnished him with a towel, I head back down to face the inquisition.

'What the hell was that?' I say, deciding to go in on the offensive. 'Why were you all staring at him?'

'He was with you at John's memorial service,' Rebecca says softly. 'I remember thinking you seemed very close then. You're a dark horse, Thea, I'll give you that. Does that mean you've moved on from George?'

'He's just a *friend*,' I say firmly.

'A friend you spent the night with,' Mum counters.

'Nothing happened. It was platonic.'

'Shame. I think he's lovely,' she continues softly.

'He's obviously doing all right for himself if he's driving a Porsche,' Phil observes.

'I used to have one of those! You weren't so impressed then,' I exclaim crossly.

'Did you? I don't remember.'

'Everybody just stop, all right? I knew this would happen. Alasdair is a very good friend of mine, nothing more.'

'If he's such a good friend, how come we've never seen or heard of him before?' Saffy demands accusingly.

'Because he was a friend when I lived in London, and we weren't allowed to contact each other while I was officially on gardening leave. However, that's over, so he got in touch and came down to see me yesterday.'

'Does he know about George?' Rebecca asks, seemingly fixated on my non-existent love triangle.

'He does. He's taking me over there in a minute, actually.'

'Who's George?' Phil asks, looking nonplussed.

'George is the man from the trust that Thea's taken a shine to,' Rebecca explains. 'They had a bit of a kiss but then he freaked out and he's been avoiding her ever since.'

'I was having a vulnerable moment when I kissed him,' I mumble. Even though I'm a fully functioning adult, I'm not comfortable talking to my parents about this kind of thing. 'Now he's convinced himself he took advantage of me.'

To my surprise, Phil guffaws with laughter. 'What's so funny?' I ask him, annoyed.

'Two things. The first is that you were vulnerable. Apart from that brief period when you first left your job, I've never known you to be vulnerable, Thea. And the second is the notion that anyone could take advantage of you. What were you vulnerable about, anyway?'

'Something to do with the mill, which reminds me. Rebecca, Ben, can I borrow you?'

I'm grateful for the change of subject and the opportunity to get away from the inquisition as they follow me to the kitchen.

'What's up?' Ben asks once we're alone.

'I've made a decision. I'm all in for the family farm idea and you investing, Ben. I just have one condition.'

'Which is?' Rebecca asks.

'One of my biggest concerns is that three is an awkward number. Two could turn against one at any point. So, and I'll write this into the contract if you're happy, we only go ahead with something if all three of us agree on it. Each of us has the power of veto, OK?'

'I'm happy with that,' Ben says.

'Me too,' Rebecca agrees.

'Great. That's sorted then.'

'While we have you, there is one other thing, actually,' Rebecca says, putting her hand on my arm to stop me leaving the room.

'What?'

'Ben's invited Rollo and me to move in with him.'

I'm caught off guard.

'I know it seems quick,' she continues hurriedly. 'But if we're committing to the farm together, it does make sense, and you'll be able to have the cottage to yourself without us getting under your feet.'

'It doesn't have to happen straight away,' Ben says, evidently trying to reassure me. 'We just thought it would make things easier for you.'

Before I have a chance to consider any further, we're interrupted by the arrival of Alasdair, looking much better for his shower.

'I'm sure it'll be fine,' I tell them. 'Let's look at the practicalities tomorrow, yeah?'

* * *

'That was intense,' Alasdair remarks as we pull off the drive and head for the centre of town in search of breakfast. 'Your stepfather was practically asking my intentions while you were in the shower.'

'I did warn you,' I tell him with a smile. 'I don't think I've brought a boy home since I was in sixth form, so you were a bit of a novelty.'

'Mm. Anyway, I had a thought about you and George while I was in the shower. It's bad news, I'm afraid.'

His voice is serious and my heart sinks. Is he going to pull out of helping me? I know I'm perfectly capable of sorting this out on my own, especially as I know where George is, but I am enjoying having Alasdair as my wingman.

'What is it?' I ask.

'You can't marry him, sorry.'

'I think you're jumping the gun a little, but why not?'

'The consonant thing.'

'What consonant thing?'

'You always used to say that you hated your name because there weren't any hard consonants in it. George Jones is no better. How on earth are your children going to learn to speak properly if neither of their parents have any hard consonants?'

'I don't think that's a valid objection,' I tell him with a smile.

'I disagree.'

'OK, I'll play along. So there we are, at the church, and the minister asks if anyone knows of any lawful reason why George and I can't marry. Would you put your hand up and make that argument?'

'Someone's got to look out for you. Can I be your best man?'

'No. Brides don't have a best man.'

'Matron of honour then. Chief bridesmaid, whatever.'

'I think Saffy and Rebecca are probably in the queue in front of you for that one. You could be a page boy if you like?'

'Can I wear a velvet suit?'

'Do you want to?'

'I was a page boy for one of my cousins' weddings when I was little. I had to wear a red velvet suit. I hated it at the time, but I reckon I could carry it off now.'

I try to picture him in a velvet suit. 'Do you know what,' I tell him. 'I reckon you could too. But let's cross that bridge when we come to it, shall we?'

'Fair enough. Ah, this looks promising.' He points to a pub with a big sign advertising its all-day menu and pulls into the car park.

'So, what's the plan?' he asks once we're settled at a table and have placed our orders. 'Let's role play. I'm George and you can be Thea.' He raises his arm and swings it down, thumping the table before repeating the movement.

'What on earth are you doing?' I ask incredulously.

'Hammering something. I don't know. Whatever it is you do to traction engines. I'm improvising here, OK? Come on, join in.'

I sigh. 'George, we need to talk.'

He stops the hammering movement and looks at me. 'What about, Thea?'

'About what happened in the barn.'

He gives off a big theatrical sigh. 'I don't want to talk about that. I've said everything I need to in the letter.'

'But your letter was wrong, George. If anyone took advantage, it was me. I was the one that kissed you, remember?'

'You were upset. I should have maintained the boundaries.'

'Alasdair, this isn't working,' I tell him crossly.

'Why not? Is it me? Do I need to do something different?'

'No, it's just this isn't how I want it to go. It feels like I'm having to justify myself.'

'You could just march in there and snog his face off.'

'Yeah, that didn't turn out so well last time though, did it?'

'OK, look,' he tells me, fixing me under his gaze, which has suddenly turned very serious. 'I don't know George, but I do know you. If this relationship is going to have any chance of going anywhere, he's going to need to earn your respect. It's not about you justifying yourself to him; if anything, it's the other way around. You are the complete package, Thea. He needs to show you he means business. If he can't do that, you're better off walking away now, because he'll only let you down later.'

'Wow. When did you become such a relationship expert?' I ask him.

'Ha! I'm no relationship expert, but I like to flatter myself that I'm a Thea expert. The recluse act may fool some people, but I can see your Thearless heart is still beating underneath it.'

I smile at him. 'What?' he asks.

'You,' I laugh. 'I'd forgotten what a confusing set of contradictions you are.'

'What does that mean?'

'You're funny, exasperating, clever, insightful, and somehow relentlessly optimistic. You're a hugely talented lawyer who can dissect a contract and pull out the loopholes as accurately as a surgeon with a scalpel, but you also care enough about your friend to set a reminder on your phone to pitch up outside her house the day her gardening leave ends. Oh, and then you make it your personal mission to help said friend sort out her relationship issues, even though there's absolutely nothing in it for you except an extremely uncomfortable night on the floor of an unfurnished cottage.'

'That's what friends do though, isn't it?'

'It's what you do. I'm not sure everyone would. Thank you.'

He lowers his gaze to the table and mumbles, 'It's nothing, honestly.'

'Is that a hint of a blush I can see on your cheeks?' I ask, laughing again. 'Have I embarrassed you?'

'A little,' he admits.

'Goodness me. I thought you were made of stronger stuff.'

'Do you want my help or not?'

'Relax,' I tell him with a grin. 'Your secret is safe with me.'

As we pull up outside the industrial unit once more, the breakfast I consumed so happily while exchanging banter with Alasdair feels like it's turning to concrete in my stomach. Alasdair evidently senses my nervousness because he reaches across and squeezes my knee encouragingly.

'You've got this,' he tells me. 'Thearless, remember?'

'I don't feel very Thearless,' I reply.

'He's just a man. Remind me, what does Thea mean in Greek?'

'Goddess,' I tell him automatically.

'Exactly. Go in there and channel your inner goddess.'

'What are you going to do?' I ask.

'I will wait here for exactly thirty minutes. If you don't come out within that time, I'll assume all is well and go home. I take it you still have my address?'

'Of course. Why?'

'For the wedding invitation. I'll be online this afternoon, researching velvet suits.'

Instinctively, I lean across and place a kiss on his cheek.

'You're the best, has anyone ever told you that?'

'I know,' he says simply. 'Now, go and meet your fate. Good luck.'

I reach for the handle, open the door and climb out of the car. I'm trying to take his advice and channel my inner goddess as I walk across to the unit, but my legs feel shaky so it's not coming across very convincingly. More worryingly, I still have absolutely no idea what I'm going to say when I get in there.

31

They're obviously having a tea break or something, I realise as I step inside. There's no visible activity on the traction engine, but I can hear voices engaged in good-natured conversation coming from the other side of it. A sudden bark of laughter that I recognise as coming from George reaches me and I'm completely caught off guard by the way it affects me. I have spent the last week tearing myself apart over what happened in the barn and poring over his frankly cowardly letter, and he's just sitting here, laughing and chatting easily with his mates as if nothing was wrong? I don't think so. As I listen to a little more of the conversation, with George sounding like he genuinely doesn't have a care in the world, my hackles rise. As his laughter fills the space again, I start to feel a very different conversation unfolding than the one I've been trying to plan.

'Good morning, gentlemen,' I say sweetly as I round the engine and spot them. They're sitting in camp chairs round a collapsible table, on which four large mugs and a packet of chocolate digestives are resting. They all start in surprise, none more so than George, who looks both terrified and guilty, like a dog who's been caught stealing food. I'm curious to find that my normal response to his physique is completely absent. He doesn't look sexy this morning; he looks cowed, and that doesn't do anything to help my rapidly diminishing opinion of him.

'George,' I continue in the same saccharine voice. 'I wonder if I might borrow you for a minute or two.'

'Umm...' He glances round at his friends, obviously unsure what to do. Oh, come on, for goodness' sake, I think. Show some grit.

'It's OK. I won't bite. Not hard, anyway,' I tell him. 'I just think there are a couple of things we need to talk about.'

'Yeah, sure.' He gets to his feet and leads me towards the office. There's no enthusiasm in his gait though; he looks like a naughty schoolchild being sent to see the headmaster. When we get there, I close the door behind me and lean against it. He's standing in front of me, looking at the floor.

'So, umm, what did you want to talk about?' he asks eventually, still not meeting my gaze.

'Look at me,' I command him, and his eyes slowly come up to meet mine. I study him for a moment. His face is a picture of misery, and he just looks downtrodden. I'm reminded of the scene in *The Wizard of Oz*, when Dorothy and her companions finally make it to see the great wizard, only to discover that he's a very ordinary man behind a curtain. I feel a bit like that; there's suddenly no magic to George any more and I can feel the last vestiges of my attraction to him draining away, like a balloon with a slow leak.

'Did you read my letter?' he asks when the silence becomes oppressive. 'I think I covered everything in there.'

'I did,' I tell him coolly. 'I just have one question.'

'Of course. Ask anything you want.'

'I kissed you. You kissed me back. Tell me if I'm wrong, but you seemed into it.'

He stares at me. 'Is that the question?'

'No. The question is this. If I'm right and you were into it, why did you immediately run away?'

'I explained that. It was unethical, unprofessional. I took advantage.'

'Yeah. The problem with that is that it contains an unpleasant assumption on your part.'

'Which is?'

'That I had no agency or free will in the situation.'

'You were vulnerable.'

'For fuck's sake, George. I was upset, yes, but that doesn't mean I didn't know what I was doing. Give me some bloody credit, will you?'

'I'm sorry.'

'Mm. Anyway, so, rather than staying and talking it out, like an adult should do, you chose to run away. Not very mature, is it?'

'I was confused and ashamed.'

'Again, I'm not hearing me in this. How do you think I felt when you just upped and left like that?'

My voice is calm, but my mind is now working at a thousand miles an hour and a lot of things I never saw before are beginning to slot into place, not least Saffy and Rebecca's assertions that George would never be enough for me. Compared to, for example, Alasdair, George is worryingly two-dimensional and spineless. Yes, he's beautiful, but it seems his beauty is only skin deep. I'm reminded a little of those jigsaws that were all the rage a few years ago, where the image on the box was only a clue to the actual picture. The pieces are fitting together in my head, but the image they're starting to reveal is totally different to the one I expected. I'm starting to realise that I may have got this completely the wrong way around.

'I don't know. I wasn't thinking rationally, I guess,' he says feebly. I'm rapidly losing interest in this conversation, but I'm aware that it was me that dragged him in here; the least I can do is let him say his piece.

'So it would seem,' I say, trying not so sound as withering as I feel. 'However, you must have regained enough self-awareness by yesterday to figure out that this was the only place I'd know where to find you. Opportunity number two for you to behave like an adult, but instead you hid behind a letter.'

'I'm not very good at confrontation.'

'Who's to say it needed to be confrontational?'

'It feels pretty confrontational.'

'That's because I'm annoyed, George. Yet again, you denied me my say. How do you think it felt for me, having agonised over what you might have been feeling and what was going through your head, to hear you laughing and joking with your mates just now as if you didn't have a care in the world?'

'I'm sorry. I do care about you. I've made a mess of this, I can see.'

I sigh. 'You have,' I tell him. 'But maybe it's for the best. Look, I don't want to fight with you. You've made your position clear and I'm fine with that.'

'I know I've made a hash of things, Thea,' he says, suddenly earnest. 'But I do like you. I was into it when we kissed. I am attracted to you.'

'Sorry,' I tell him kindly but firmly. 'Nice try, but that ship has sailed.'

'Can we be friends, at least?'

'I don't know. I need time to think about that. Shall we rejoin your mates? Regardless of the situation between you and me,

Rebecca and I have come up with a business proposition for you all.'

* * *

I'm relieved, but not completely surprised, to find that Alasdair is still waiting when I walk out of the building, nearly an hour later.

'I thought you said thirty minutes and you were going to be out of here,' I remark as I slide into the passenger seat of his car. There are a lot of things I need to ask him, but I'm suddenly unsure how to start the conversation.

'There was a fascinating debate on the radio. I lost track of time.'

'Was there?' I ask sceptically. 'What was it about?'

'Oh, you know. The usual.'

'You would have waited all day, wouldn't you?'

He sighs. 'Probably. I just wanted to make sure you were OK.'

'Mmm-hmm. Shall we get out of here then?'

'Yes, boss. Where are we going?'

'Back to the mill, I think. My car is there, for one thing.'

'OK.' He calls up the postcode on the satnav and eases out onto the road.

'Were you ever going to tell me?' I ask him gently after a while.

'Tell you what?'

'Come on, Alasdair, this is me you're talking to.'

Another sigh, much deeper this time. 'You figured it out, then.'

'Yes.'

'I came close, once or twice, but it never seemed the right moment.'

'Why not?'

'Because I was scared it would spook you and I'd lose you forever.'

'When did it start?'

'I can't say precisely, but it wasn't long after we became friends.'

'Why the hell didn't you say anything?'

'Because it wouldn't have been what you wanted to hear.' His voice has an impassioned tone that I've never heard before. 'You were focused on your career goals, and I understood that. I was too, in a lesser kind of way. When we started sleeping together, I knew it was only a casual thing, and in some ways that hurt because I obviously would have liked it to be more, but I knew that was all you had to give, and I told myself I was lucky to have that. Having a little bit of you was always better than the prospect of having none of you, and that's what would have happened if I'd said anything. You know it's true.'

Now it's my turn to sigh. He's right; I would have been spooked and probably dropped him like a hot brick.

'You've always had my back,' I say after another long silence.

'Of course.'

'What kind of person sets an alarm to remind them when they can contact someone else?' I laugh.

'I do. Although I didn't really need it. I knew the date off by heart.'

'But here's what I don't understand. You would have let me go. If I'd come out of that building with George, you would just have driven away.'

'Yes.'

'Why?'

'Because that would have been what you'd chosen. There's an old proverb—'

'If you love something, set it free. If it comes back, it's yours. If not, it was never meant to be,' I interrupt.

'Exactly, although you're not a thing.'

'Risky strategy.'

'Yes, but it had to be your choice. It still does.'

There's another long pause, both of us seemingly lost in our own thoughts.

'Are you OK?' he asks eventually.

'I don't know.'

'It doesn't have to change anything—'

'Of course it does!' I exclaim. 'How can it not? You expect me to carry on as normal, knowing what I know now?'

An uncomfortable silence descends again.

'Look,' Alasdair says eventually. 'I get that this is a shock for you, but I'm not a problem you need to solve. I'm a big boy; I can look after myself.'

'What happens if friends is all I can offer?'

'Then friends is what I'll take. My offer stands. You're obviously not going to marry George, based on this morning's events, but if you find someone else, I still want to be your page boy. Promise me that?'

I smile. 'I promise you that.'

32

'Did you straighten things out with George?' Rebecca asks as I walk into the sitting room that afternoon. Alasdair has gone back to London to get ready for his trip, and the events of the morning, plus a lack of sleep, have combined to make me feel dazed and sluggish. I have no idea how to begin to unpack what I've learned today. George is easy, but what the hell am I going to do about Alasdair?

'Yes,' I tell her wearily.

'You don't sound very pleased,' Saffy observes. 'I know you don't have a lot of experience in this area, but it's normal for people in the early stages of a relationship to be a bit more enthusiastic.'

'I'm not in the early stages of a relationship. George and I aren't together.'

'Oh.'

'Look, it turns out you were both right. He wouldn't have been enough for me and, frankly, I'm not sure what I saw in him. Happy now?'

'I don't think it's about making us happy,' Rebecca says carefully. 'Is it what you want?'

I plonk myself dejectedly down in one of the armchairs. 'Yes.'

'So what opened your eyes?' Saffy asks.

'I think I just realised that we weren't compatible,' I say after thinking for a moment. 'He may be easy on the eye, but the watermill is literally the only thing we have in common, and that's not really enough to build a relationship on.' I close my eyes, pleased with my answer. If I can keep them off the scent of Alasdair and his revelations, I might just escape a full-on interrogation.

'And what about Alasdair?' Saffy asks.

Shit. So much for that then. 'What about him?' I ask as nonchalantly as I can.

'Where does he fit into all of this?'

'He doesn't. He's gone back to London.'

'Shame,' Rebecca says. 'I liked him.'

'You certainly kept him well hidden,' Saffy observes.

'He's just a friend,' I explain, trying to adopt the fierce tone I know will shut down further debate, but somehow unable to muster it.

'Can I make an observation?' Saffy asks me after a long silence.

'Can I stop you?'

'Probably not. Here's the thing. You are my sister, and I love you more than you'll ever know. You're also one of the brightest people I've ever met. But, when it comes to your love life, you are a total, unmitigated fucking disaster. Even Rebecca is more switched on than you. She may have been shagging a married man who turned out to be a monster, but at least she found Ben.'

'Hey, leave me out of this,' Rebecca interjects. 'Even if I do agree with you, Saffy.'

'I mean it,' Saffy continues, evidently warming to her theme. 'For someone supposedly so intelligent, you are literally as thick as pigshit where love is concerned.'

'Don't hold back, will you?' I tell her. 'Go on, tell me what you really think.'

'Oh, I will. Don't you worry about that. Let's start with the easy question, shall we? What, in the name of all that's holy, were you doing mooning around after a cardboard cutout like George, when you had Alasdair in the wings all along?'

'I'm sorry? Which bit of "he's just a friend" did you not hear?'

'Oh, I heard it, I just don't believe it. I saw the way you looked at each other, the way you spoke to each other. There's an easy intimacy there that goes way deeper than friendship. Plus, he's patently nuts about you.'

'What makes you say that?' She's alarmingly close to the truth, but there's just enough lawyer left in me to know that you don't crumble and reveal your hand just because someone has fired a single arrow in the right direction. It might just be a lucky fluke and the next one will go miles off target.

'He was on your doorstep the first day he was allowed to contact you, and he's had your back from the moment he arrived. That's more than friendship. I don't know what went on last night, and I don't need to know, but if I'd accidentally spent the night with someone of the opposite sex who was purely a friend, I'd be a bit awkward about it the next morning, especially around my family. But not you. You and he were like an old married couple. Not quite finishing each other's sentences, but even Phil remarked that you seemed very close.'

Not a lucky fluke then. I sigh. 'Fine. He told me this morning that he's in love with me.'

'But that's brilliant!' Saffy exclaims. 'He's perfect for you.'

'I can't.'

'Why not?'

'Because... Because lots of things, OK? He's a friend, for starters.'

'Tim is my best friend. He's also my husband. So what?'

'Plus he's a lawyer.'

'You used to be one of those.'

'Exactly. Remember how I used to be? We'd never see each other. He belongs to my old life, the life I left behind.'

'I'm not sure it's that binary. What does it matter if he comes from your lawyer days? He loves you, and I think you probably feel more deeply for him than you admit to yourself. That's a solid foundation to build on. The rest is just...' She peters out and waves her hand expressively.

'What?' I ask.

'Admin,' Rebecca offers, evidently deciding to join in after all. 'Yes, he might be away a lot, but that's just life admin. You call each other when he's away and you prioritise each other when he's here. Saffy's right. Don't throw away a shot at happiness because of something as trivial as his work schedule. In fact, that makes you a really good match for him because, although it's not your life any more, you do at least understand it.'

'You two aren't going to let this go, are you?'

'No.' Saffy's tone is determined. 'How did you leave things with him?'

'He's going to New York for two weeks with work. We're going to talk when he gets back.'

'Good. That gives us two weeks to make you see sense.'

* * *

The closer the train gets to London, the more nervous I feel. Saffy and Rebecca have been relentless over the last two weeks and, after countless hours picking over it, we've agreed that I should try to see Alasdair face to face rather than talking to him on the phone. The problem is, of course, that I don't know where he's going to be. I did contemplate trying to intercept him at the airport, and I even briefly entertained a fantasy where I ran into his arms like a scene from *Love Actually*, before I realised that I had no idea which flight he'd be on or even which airport it would come into. So I've decided to head for the Morton Lansdowne offices. I've planned a cock-and-bull story for the receptionist that will hopefully allow me to find out if he's in the building. If he is, I'll simply hang around until he appears. If he isn't, then I'll head for his flat. The Morton Lansdowne offices are a much more conducive place for waiting than the street where he lives and, if I'm lucky, I might even be able to wangle a free cup of coffee or two.

My heart is in my mouth as I approach the building that was my home for so many years. Despite it being the weekend, the place is as busy as ever and a constant stream of people are coming and going through the rotating doors. I can't decide what I'm more nervous about; seeing someone who might recognise me or seeing Alasdair, so it takes me a moment to summon my courage and step inside. The low murmur of voices in the lobby, accompanied by the regular ping of the elevators, is both familiar and unsettling. 'You don't belong here any more,' they seem to be saying, and I can feel my nerve failing me. I'm standing like a rabbit frozen in the headlights, trying to decide whether to press ahead or flee, when a familiar voice calls my name.

'Thea! It is you,' Janice says warmly, striding over and giving me a hug before holding me at arm's length and openly appraising me. 'You look well. Your new life patently suits you.'

'Thanks, Janice,' I tell her. 'How are you?'

'Oh, same old, same old,' she tells me with a smile. 'Junior partners keep me busy. You know how it is. What brings you here?' She lowers her voice. 'You haven't come to ask for your job back, have you?'

'No,' I reassure her. 'I was hoping to catch Alasdair, actually.'

'Really?' Her face lights up. 'Come to your senses at last, have you?'

'I'm sorry?'

'Oh, come on. This is me you're talking to. Do you seriously think I didn't spot the connection between you at John Curbishley's funeral? Or that Alasdair seemed to have increasing numbers of ants in his pants the closer he got to the end of your contact embargo? I take it he did contact you?'

'He did,' I admit.

'Thought so. And he's been jittery for the last two weeks, so it was clear something was up. Frankly, it wasn't difficult to work out that the something was you.'

'Does anything ever get past you?' I ask her in amazement.

'I try very hard not to let it,' she tells me with a smile. 'I wouldn't be very good at my job if I did. Now, what's the plan?'

'I don't really have one. I was going to wait here for him to come down and intercept him.'

She laughs. 'That's a terrible plan! You really want to have a heart to heart with half of London eavesdropping? Come with me.' She marches over to reception and, before I know it, I'm sporting a visitor pass and riding up to the sixth floor in the lift with her.

'What if one of the senior partners sees me?' I ask nervously.

'Unlikely. Now, Alasdair's in with Helen Armitage until twelve, but I'll secrete you in his office. I'll have to stay with you until he arrives, of course. Can't have you rifling through his drawers.'

'Haven't you got other things to do besides babysit me? I don't want to hold you up.'

'I've always got plenty of things to do, but I can do some of them while I'm looking after you, and the others can wait. Have you thought about your wedding dress?'

'I think that's a bit premature, Janice!'

'OK, well, speak to me before you do, that's all. I've given commissions to a number of prominent designers over the years, so they owe me favours. Ah, here we are.'

The sixth floor hasn't changed a bit since I was last here, but I'm surprised to note that Alasdair has taken over my old office.

'He asked for it specifically,' Janice confides. 'Told the seniors some ridiculous story about feng shui and the trajectory of the sun. I don't think they believed him for a minute, but they gave it to him anyway. Coffee?'

'Yes, please.'

* * *

It's over an hour later that Alasdair finally arrives. He doesn't spot me straight away, so I have a few moments to watch him as he chats to Janice and, more importantly, observe my reaction to seeing him again. I've thought about little else other than him over the last two weeks and I was worried that reality might prove something of a let-down, but I can't help smiling stupidly. He's dishevelled after an overnight flight, his eyes are bleary and he's got a dark growth of stubble, but none of that detracts from the joy of seeing him in the flesh.

'Thea!' he exclaims as he walks into his office and sees me. 'What are you doing here?'

'I needed to see you,' I tell him as I notice Janice discreetly shutting the door to give us privacy.

'Are you OK?'

'I don't know yet.'

'What's up?'

'You, Alasdair,' I tell him, alarmed by the sudden wobble in my voice. 'You're up. I need to talk to you about the things you said before you went to New York.'

'Oh.' There are two chairs in front of the desk in his office. I'm sitting in one and he settles himself in the other. Our eyes meet, but neither of us speaks for a while.

'I need you to say it,' I tell him.

'Say what?'

'How you feel.'

'Why?'

'I don't know. I'm scared, and maybe it will help.'

'OK. I love you, Thea. I always have and I think I always will. Your turn.'

'What?'

'I told you how I feel. Now it's your turn. That's how this works.'

'I don't know,' I say quietly. His expression barely changes, but I know it's not what he was hoping to hear. 'This is all new for me,' I explain quickly. 'But I want to love you. You deserve love, and I want to be the one to give it to you. I just don't know if I can be enough for you.'

He leans forward and takes both my hands in his. 'You're already enough, Thea. You've always been enough.'

We sit there, immobile, for what feels like hours.

'What happens now?' I ask eventually.

'What do you want to happen?'

'I'm not coming back to London. You know that, right? My life is in Kent now.'

'I know.'

'And there's your job to consider. I know what it's like, remember.'

'Yes.'

'So? Come on. Tell me how this works. You're never normally short of an opinion.'

'I don't know. I guess we figure it out as we go along. That's what most people do, I believe.'

There's another long pause before the next question pushes its way to the front of my head.

'Would you really have come to my wedding dressed in a velvet suit if I'd asked you?'

'Yes. It would have been incredibly painful to watch you marry someone else, but I would have done it. That's what you do when you love someone.'

'I'm not sure I would have done it, if our roles were reversed.'

'You're a shit friend,' he says with a smile.

'Yeah, I probably am,' I agree. 'I'm sorry.'

'You don't have anything to be sorry for, at least, not where I'm concerned.'

'I disagree. I feel like I used you; I never spotted how you felt; I never had an alarm on my phone counting down the days. I was about to start seeing someone else, for God's sake!'

There's another long silence before Alasdair speaks.

'Why don't you tell me what's going on in that incredible mind of yours?' he says gently.

'At the moment, I'm terrified, excited and worried.'

'All at once? Sounds exhausting. What are you worried about?'

'How we move forward. If we move forward. I'm committed in Kent, you're never going to be around and you made it very clear when you came down that you hate the countryside.'

'Ah, I might have a confession about that.'

'Go on.'

'I don't hate the countryside at all. I admit I was grumpy when I first arrived, but that was mainly because it was so clear that you'd moved on and built this whole life that I wasn't a part of. I had this fantasy where you'd missed me like I've missed you, and it pissed me off that you hadn't. I think, if I'm really honest, I was a little bit jealous. Sorry.'

'Really?'

'So I'm not perfect. Sue me.'

'OK, you don't hate the country. I'm still never going to see you though, am I.'

'Do you want to see me?'

'Of course I do! But I'm scared, because I can't do what you did. I can't just have the bits of you that are left over. I want all of you, and I know I can't have it.'

'Says who?' he asks, smiling at last. 'Let me ask you this. Are you serious? Do you really want this?'

'I do.'

His smile broadens into a beam that lights up the whole room. 'Martin Osborne is really going to hate you.'

'Why?'

'Because I'm going to have to tell him on Monday that Morton Lansdowne is losing another partner.'

33

EIGHTEEN MONTHS LATER

'Does anyone know the phrase "rule of thumb"?' I ask, looking out at the sea of eager young faces in front of me. I get a few blank looks, but most of them nod.

'Does anyone know where it comes from?'

Nobody raises their hand. I wasn't expecting them to, but one thing I've learned since starting this is always to be prepared for anything when you're working with children.

'It's actually a milling term,' I tell them, moving over to the chute the ground flour is gently sliding down before falling into the sack below. 'The only way a miller could tell if he or she was milling the flour correctly was to take some and rub it between their thumb and forefinger, like this. That's the rule of thumb. Who wants to try?'

Several hands shoot up, and I give them each a little bit of flour to rub. It always makes a mess, but what's the fun in visiting a mill if you don't end up covered in flour?

'So, before we finish, has anyone got any questions? No? OK, I've got one to ask you then. Who can remember the names of the three main controls in a mill, and what they do?'

A little girl at the front sticks her hand up so hard I'm concerned she's going to do herself a mischief. 'Yes?' I ask her.

'The slooz gate,' she says.

'That's right. The sluice gate is one of the controls. What does it do?'

'It makes the wheel go faster and slower.'

'Exactly. It controls the speed of the mill. Who would like to tell me another one?'

The little girl's hand shoots up again, but I pick a boy near the back this time.

'Go on,' I encourage him.

'The tent screw.'

'Tentering screw, close. What does it do?'

'Controls the stones.'

'That's right. It controls the distance between the stones, so we can adjust how finely they mill the grains. Can anyone remember the last one?'

No hands go up, not even the little girl.

'The crook string,' I remind them. 'Anyone remember what it does?'

'Controls the flow of wheat?' a boy in the middle of the group offers.

'Well done,' I tell him warmly.

'What an interesting visit, don't you agree, children?' the teacher says brightly. 'Shall we give a round of applause to say thank you to Thea for showing us around her mill?'

I smile as the children clap. 'Thank you,' I tell them, 'for being such good listeners and asking so many interesting questions. If you see my colleague Rebecca in the gift shop on your way out, she has a little bag of flour for each of you to take away to remember your day here.'

They're my last class of the day so, once they've trooped out with their teachers, I begin the process of shutting down the mill. Primary school children are always a joy to have in here, because the concept of something that isn't computerised or powered by electricity is so totally alien to them that they usually find it fascinating. By secondary school, the magic tends to have worn off, and I've learned to tailor my presentation accordingly. Once the mill has stopped and I've tidied everything up, I load the bags of flour I've milled today onto the trolley to drag them over to our weighing and packing area. Although we run it primarily as a tourist attraction, we do end up milling a lot of flour here. We sell some of it in our gift shop in olde worlde brown paper bags for suitably stratospheric prices, but the majority of it goes to the trade, including our café partners.

It was Alasdair's idea to get an external company to run the café as a separate business and, after a few false starts with companies who expressed an interest only to let us down in one way or another, we came across one called The Mad Hatter. I say we came across them, but we were actually handed them on a plate by one of our other customers, the bakery down the road in Appledore, who already had a relationship with them. It's a nice setup, actually. They use our flour in their pastry products, so visitors can see the flour being made and then taste the finished products in the café. The wheat is organic and I buy it from a local farm, so it ticks all the sustainability boxes.

It's a beautiful summer's day, and I glance across at the pond as I drag the trolley behind me. We've had a bumper set of ducklings this year, and it makes me smile to see them bobbing along behind their mothers in the water. Further away, I can see a family making a complete hash of rowing one of the hire boats. There are two children holding one oar each and an exasperated-looking father evidently trying to direct them, while their mother sits in the front of the boat staring serenely at the view. It's at moments like this that I pinch myself, unable to believe that this is my life now.

Once I've weighed the flour out into the right quantities for tomorrow's deliveries, I head back to the cottage, where I'm surprised to find Alasdair sitting at the table with his laptop open in front of him.

'I thought you were in London today?' I say as I bend down to kiss him. He's wearing the sandalwood aftershave that I like, and I breathe it in deeply.

'I was, but the meeting finished early. Besides, I couldn't miss the test run.'

'Oh, yes. What time is it?'

'Six o'clock.'

'I've got time for a shower then. How did the meeting go?'

'Well. They signed.'

'Of course they did. Finest legal mind in the south of England, they'd be mad not to hire you.'

'Second finest. I hear there's this peculiar hermit woman who lives in the middle of nowhere in Kent. Legend has it she was the youngest female partner at one of the most prestigious law firms in the land, before she chucked it all in to fiddle with her flour mill.'

'Alasdair?'

'Yes?'

'Piss off.'

He laughs good-naturedly. This is a well-worn exchange. Ever since he started his own legal consultancy after leaving Morton Lansdowne, he's been begging me to come on board, but I just don't have any enthusiasm for that stuff any more, as I've told him every time we've had this conversation.

'So, how was your day?' he asks as I put the kettle on. 'Mill anything interesting?'

'Yeah, actually. This smart-arsed lawyer turned up, trying to drag me back into legal practice.'

'No!' Alasdair feigns shock.

'Don't worry. He won't be bothering anyone else. I fed his flesh to the pigs and ground his bones to a powder. It's like I've always said. Today's smart arse is tomorrow's scones.'

'Sounds like a particularly unpleasant folk tale,' he says with a theatrical shudder. 'Remind me never to cross you. Thinking of which, I had another run-in with psycho Colin this afternoon. What is his problem with me?'

'He doesn't like smart-arsed lawyers either,' I say with a grin. 'He's a bird of exquisite taste.'

'He's going to taste bloody exquisite as a Sunday roast if he doesn't knock it off.'

'You just need to stand up to him, show him you're the bigger man,' I soothe. 'He probably sees you as a threat. Good-looking guy like you is bound to turn the heads of all his chicks. Thinking of which, we had a complaint about him today.'

'Really? Who did he attack?'

'Nobody. There was a group from Rollo and Louis's school first thing and the head teacher, Mrs Steadman, came with them.'

'Is she the one that thought you and Rebecca were a couple?'

'That's her. Anyway, Colin was having one of his frisky mornings, and she complained that it wasn't suitable for young children to see that sort of thing.'

He laughs. 'What did you tell her?'

'I explained, very patiently I thought, that Colin doesn't have the same sensitivities as us when it comes to love and sex, and he wasn't trying to offend her or the children. Ultimately, this is a farm and farm animals are going to do farm animal things. That is, after all, the point of seeing them.'

'Did she get it?'

'I don't think so. I'm not going to lose sleep over it. Rebecca can deal with her.'

Although most of the animals on the farm are a great success, we do have a couple of slightly problematic ones, and Colin the Cockerel is definitely one. Ben was adamant that, although our chickens are all Rhode Island Reds, which are generally good natured and prolific egg layers (another thing we sell in the shop, along with the honey from our bees), we needed a Welsummer cockerel, because they're the proper storybook ones. I don't know whether it's his breed, his sex, or whether it's just him, but Colin is aggressive to the point that we've had to put up signs warning people not to approach him. For the most part, this works fine, but he does seem to have a particular grudge against Alasdair, and against the farm dog, Lola.

Lola is our other oddity. She's a Border collie we acquired from a sheep farmer, again recommended by the bakery in Appledore. She was the runt of her litter, so they were selling her off at a reduced price and Alasdair fell immediately in love with her. She is the sweetest thing, and even now she's lying on her mat gazing at him adoringly, but she's completely terrified of livestock in general, and Colin in particular – a fact he exploits ruthlessly.

'Right, enough,' Alasdair states firmly, shutting his laptop as I hand him a steaming mug of tea. 'Are you showering then?'

'Yes. You know what it's like. I think I have flour in places where flour has no business being.'

'Hm.'

'What?'

'Tricky stuff to get off, flour. You might need help.'

I laugh. 'Might I? Are you offering, then?'

'This is a job for a professional,' he says, rising from the table and loosening his tie. 'I'm going to have to go over every nook and cranny in forensic detail. It's hard work, but someone's got to do it.'

'You poor thing,' I say, laughing as he wraps his arms around me from behind and starts kissing my neck.

'It's just one of the many sacrifices I have to make for the woman of my dreams,' he murmurs as his kisses caress my shoulder. His hands snake under my top, and neither of us says anything for a while after that.

'You're just in time,' Rebecca tells me as we join the small group waiting outside the barn at the top of the farm. Rollo and Ben are here, of course, as well as Saffy, Tim, Louis, Mum and Phil, Dave, Brooke, Ernest and a few others that I don't know but assume must be friends and family of the traction engine crew, as we've named them. Typically, the restoration has taken much longer than any of them anticipated, and Trevor has told me gratefully on more than one occasion that they probably would have had to have abandoned it if they were still paying the exorbitant rent on the unit in Tenterden.

'I think it's nearly there,' Rollo says excitedly, bobbing up and down on his heels.

The door is wide open, and I can see George, Trevor and the other two bustling round the traction engine, checking things and calling out to each other. It's producing an impressive amount of steam and, after a few more checks, Trevor climbs up onto the platform at the back, moves a lever and the flywheel slowly starts to turn. We applaud wildly as it edges out of the barn into the evening air, under its own power for the first time. The sunlight glints off its pristine burgundy paintwork, and we all jump as the whistle sounds. It's loud enough to be heard in Ashford, I reckon, and I can hear braying and bleating from down the hill as some of the animals voice their displeasure. Above it all rises the shriek of Colin crowing. I suspect the traction engine has just made it onto his sworn enemies list.

'Good luck with that one, buddy,' I murmur as I lean back against Alasdair's solid frame and survey the view from up here. His arms are wrapped around me securely as I cast my eyes over the farm, with our cottage and the mill right at the centre of it. A thought comes to me and I start to laugh gently.

'What?' Alasdair asks.

'I've just realised something. Since I made the decision to leave Morton Lansdowne, nothing, and I mean absolutely nothing, has turned out the way I planned.'

'Is that a problem?'

I turn round in his arms and lean up to kiss him.

'Not at all,' I tell him. 'In fact, it's all turned out much better than I could ever have hoped.'

ACKNOWLEDGEMENTS

Thank you so much for reading this book, and I hope you enjoyed Thea's story.

I need to say a huge thank you to Jeremy, who patiently explained the world of corporate law to me. Hopefully, I've got it pretty much right. Thanks are also due to my sister Frances, who came with me on an unsuccessful trip to visit the watermill at the Weald and Downland museum. Thank goodness for the internet, which gave me the information I was missing. Thank you also to Mandy for your alpha reading.

Massive thanks as always to my ever-patient editor, Rachel. Your wise input always improves the story and I'm grateful for it. Thank you also to Cecily for copy editing, and Jennifer for proof reading. Of course, getting the story as good as it can be is just the beginning, and I want to say thank you also to Amanda, Nia, Jenna and the rest of the amazing Boldwood team for the incredible work you do to connect my books with readers. You really are the best publisher to work with.

Final thank yous, as always, go to my family, who could not be more supportive and give me time to write. Thanks also to Bertie the Labradoodle, my patient companion on plotting walks.

ABOUT THE AUTHOR

Phoebe MacLeod is the author of several popular romantic comedies including the top ten bestseller, *The Fixer Upper*. She lives in Kent with her partner, grown up children and disobedient dog.

Sign up to Phoebe MacLeod's mailing list here for news, competitions and updates on future books.

Follow Phoebe on social media here:

facebook.com/PhoebeMacleodAuthor
x.com/macleod_phoebe
instagram.com/phoebemacleod21

ALSO BY PHOEBE MACLEOD

Someone Else's Honeymoon

Not The Man I Thought He Was

Fred and Breakfast

Let's Not Be Friends

An (Un)Romantic Comedy

Love at First Site

Never Ever Getting Back Together

The Fixer Upper

My Not So Perfect Summer

Too Busy for Love

The Do-Over

Printed in Great Britain
by Amazon

52905794R00165